AUTUMN

A FEARLESS NOVEL

OF FEAR

GLEDÉ BROWNE KABONGO

To: Carrol
Thanks for the
support. Wish you
were here.
Glede Browne Kabongo

ALSO BY GLEDE BROWNE KABONGO

Game of Fear
Mark of Deceit (a short story)
Swan Deception
Conspiracy of Silence

AUTUMN OF FEAR

Copyright © 2018 Gledé Browne Kabongo

To learn more about Gledé and her work, visit
www.gledekabongo.com

Cover Design by Yocla Designs

ISBN: 978-0-692-08261-4

CHAPTER 1

AFTER

P AIN EXPLODES THROUGHOUT my body like Fourth of July fireworks. I groan, but no one comes to help me. I move my arms. Blinding, savage agony. When I try opening my eyes, my lids won't budge, as if they've been sealed shut by an industrial sized staple gun. Where am I? Why am I in such hideous pain?

I hear a woman's voice, soft and sympathetic, almost a whisper. "Poor thing. She'll never be the same. What that monster did to her is unspeakable. How does anyone come back from that?"

Wait. What happened? Why won't I be the same?

I move my legs slowly. They work fine. I should try speaking. Maybe they didn't hear my groans before.

"Hello?" My voice cracks. I'm tired. So tired.

Footsteps approach. "Abbie, can you hear me? Are you awake?"

It's the woman's voice again. The one who predicted I would never be the same.

Then a guy says, "Cooper, can you open your eyes?"

1

Hot tears drizzle down my cheeks. It's Ty. He's here. Everything will be fine.

"Ty, what's going on? Where am I?" With each word, I expend massive amounts of energy. I stop to catch my breath.

"You're in the hospital." His warm, comforting hands clasp mine.

"Why?" I croak.

A brief silence passes.

"Abbie, I'm Nurse Russo. We're going to take good care of you. Don't try to get up, hon. Can you open your eyes for me?"

My eyelids are heavy, and all I want to do is to go back to sleep. But I won't give in to the temptation. I blink a couple of times, and when I'm able to focus, I see Ty sitting next to the bed in a chair. His shirt is a rumpled mess. The sparkle in his usually mischievous hazel eyes has vanished, replaced with barely disguised anguish. He tries to muster a smile but it falls flat. *Am I dying?*

"How do you feel?" he asks.

"Like I just got run over by an oil tanker a hundred times."

I take in my surroundings. A typical hospital room with machines beeping, an IV bag, and heart rate monitor. A flat screen TV is perched on the wall. A finger pulse oximeter is clipped to my index finger, but even scarier, an IV needle is shoved into the flesh at the back of my hand and held down by white tape.

Ty squeezes my hand. "Nurse Russo is right, Cooper. We're going to take good care of you. I don't want you to worry about anything."

"Listen to your friend," the nurse chimes in. To my left, she fumbles with a blood pressure cuff. She looks to be in her thirties. A full, pretty face, auburn hair pulled back in a high ponytail, and blue scrubs.

She tells me she's about to take my blood pressure on the other arm and moves to the right side of the bed. My left arm throbs—a mounting pressure that demands my attention. I glance down. Most of the arm is wrapped in bandages.

"Was I in an accident? Ty, did you bring me to the hospital?"

He looks away from me.

"We'll get everything sorted out, sweetie," Nurse Russo says as she wraps the blood pressure cuff around my arm and squeezes the bulb. After she notes the results, she takes my temperature and then announces she's going to get the doctor.

After she leaves, I touch my face. It's swollen, and like the rest of me, aches terribly. My head is pounding, but I need Ty to explain why I'm here. Sleep tugs at me, inviting me to give in to blissful rest where I won't feel the pain, where there aren't important questions no one wants to answer.

"Why won't you tell me what happened, Ty? I was in some kind of accident, wasn't I? Was it a car crash? I don't remember it at all."

Ty's hands grip the sides of his chair, as if he's afraid he'll fall off. Before he can respond, the door opens and in walks a tall, slim man with thinning hair, and a short beard.

3

Nurse Russo follows closely behind.

Abbie, I'm Dr. Gray. You gave us quite a scare, young lady."

Ty stands up. "Do you want me to leave, Cooper? This is the first time the doctor's had a chance to talk to you."

"No, please don't go. I need you to stay with me."

Ty has a special gift for consoling me whenever things go wrong in my life. I have a feeling I'm going to need his calming presence in the next few moments. However this turns out, I need my best friend by my side to help me cope.

Dr. Gray pulls up a chair next to the bed, across from Ty.

"How bad was the accident?" I ask. "Did anyone die? Was it my fault? Please tell me no one was hurt."

I blink back tears and then focus on Dr. Gray, who has on a poker face. Dr. Linwood had the same look when he told us Dad had stage two colon cancer.

"Abbie," Dr. Gray begins, "Nurse Russo tells me you don't remember how you got here or where you were before you arrived in the Emergency Room. Your injuries are extensive, and we're trying to piece things together."

"So it was an accident then."

Dr. Gray noisily clears his throat. "Not quite."

"I don't understand."

Ty takes my hand in his and squeezes again. When I look at his face, I see devastation and heartbreak, as if whatever they're about to tell me is so horrible, that they can't even comprehend it themselves.

"Tell me," I insist. "What kind of injuries?"

Dr. Gray takes a deep breath, removes his glasses, blows on them and returns them to his face. "From what we've been able to gather, you were badly beaten and thrown out of a moving vehicle."

A vicious chill hits me at the core of my being, a paralyzing shock that knocks the wind out of me. *I can't breathe.* Why is the room spinning? The iciness settles into my stomach, heavy and merciless, as if it wants to crush the very life out of me. *I can't breathe. They made a mistake. It was a car accident.*

I suck in air in shorts bursts. My emotions run wild, screaming a million questions. I'm a good person. I'm nice to everyone. Who would do something so horrible to me and why?

CHAPTER 2

AFTER

I LOOK AT their faces, from one to the other. There's something they haven't told me yet, something even worse than my wounds. Dr. Gray begins to describe my injuries in detail.

"From what we can determine, you sustained severe blows to the head and face, and a sprained arm. The arm injury could be from the impact of being thrown out of the vehicle, when you hit the asphalt. You were unconscious when you were found a few hundred yards from the ER entrance."

I screw my eyes shut. For a moment, everyone in the room disappears behind a dreamlike fog, leaving me to wrestle with this seemingly impossible puzzle. Was I in the wrong place at the wrong time, a random crime victim? Why can't I recall what happened?

I will my mind to conjure up a memory, a name or place, a face, smell or sound. Nothing. Not even a shadow, real or imagined. There's an empty space in my brain where those details should have been stored for retrieval when I needed them.

"Abbie, there's more," Dr. Gray says. Something in his voice tells me that I had better brace myself. Ty won't meet my eyes.

"What do you mean there's more? How much more?"

"As I said earlier, you were unconscious when you were admitted. Naturally, we had to run blood tests and conduct a thorough examination to determine the cause. You sustained multiple bruises and scrapes from the impact, in addition to the severe sprain in your arm."

Dr. Gray looks down at his notes, but not because he needs to be reminded what to say next. He's gearing up to tell me that other horrible thing.

"Your attacker also drugged and sexually assaulted you. The toxicology results will reveal exactly what drug was in your system. It's the reason you may not remember the assault."

Everyone in the room is silent with solemn expressions. My brain seizes. I can't comprehend what I just heard. I lie here, not moving, not thinking, and not feeling. After a minute or two, I hear a pathetic whimper, a gut-wrenching snivel from some poor, unfortunate creature that needs to be put out of its misery. That creature is me. Ty wraps his arms around me, wipes my tears and whispers comforting words. I bury my head in his chest, and hot, bitter tears soak through his shirt.

I don't know how long we stay like this, but when I pull my head up, the room is empty. My guess is Nurse Russo and Dr. Gray wanted to give us some privacy. They should be back soon. As Ty fluffs my pillow and helps me get comfortable, a hundred unpleasant questions bounce around in my head: How do I break the news to my parents—and do I even want to? Will the police catch the monster who did this? Will I ever feel safe again, or am I condemned to, for the rest of my life, look over my shoulder?

"How did you find out I was here?" I ask Ty.

"The last call on your phone log was from me. Your phone was powered off and the screen cracked in multiple places. Maybe the attacker shut it off so you couldn't be tracked, but the phone still worked. Thank God the hospital called, Cooper. I've never been so scared in my life. When I couldn't find you at the party, I thought I would lose my mind.

"By the time it was over, it was coming up on one in the morning and I still hadn't heard from you. I went into full-fledged panic. I knew I couldn't report you missing because the police would wait until twenty-four hours had passed to file a missing person's report. I only had to wait for a couple of hours, though. That's when the hospital called."

I turn over what he said in my mind. I remember a party at a house in Bethany, but the details are vague. I squeeze my eyes, trying to get my memory to cooperate, to understand the missing hours between when Ty last saw me and when he arrived at the hospital. Total blank.

"You don't remember, do you?"

"No. I only recall being at a house. It was a party to celebrate our win in the big game." I squeeze my eyes again, hoping my memory will throw me a crumb or two. "I talked to a bunch of people. You were there with Kristina. I hung out with Spencer. I don't remember anything after that."

"That's good. At least you remember being there. That

can be useful. Spencer helped me look for you, but we couldn't find you anywhere. I should let him know I found you."

"Please don't give him any details. Make up a story or something. He's a nice guy, and I had fun with him, but you're the only person I trust to see me like this. I don't want to see or talk to anyone else."

"You don't have to explain it to me. I get it." He looks away and pinches the bridge of his nose, then scoots off the bed, heading toward the sink. After he splashes water on his face and dries off with paper towel, he returns to the chair next to the bed.

"I'm going to take good care of you, Cooper, and we'll find the monster who did this."

I don't answer right away. Instead, I take short, deep breaths to pull myself back from the brink—the brink of an abyss that wants to suck me into its black hole of perpetual hurt and torment.

"It's hard to explain where the physical wounds end and the emotional ones begin. It's as if they form this massive ocean of confusion and chaos that wants to drown me."

"Let me get the doctor and nurse back in here," he says and takes off.

A few minutes later, my head is throbbing and the ache in my arm has increased ten-fold.

"How bad is it?" Nurse Russo asks, as she enters the room. "On a scale of one to ten."

"A hundred," I say between pants.

Ty pulls up in the chair again and holds my hand. He says nothing.

Nurse Russo appears at my left side. "We'll adjust the

medication in the IV so you can be comfortable. And Dr. Gray will be back to see you shortly."

After a ton of questions about my medical history and a battery of additional tests, Ty and I are once again alone.

"You're going to be okay, Cooper. I promise. You already have your own room at my place. We're going to get through this together. You're not alone."

Moisture gathers in his eyes as he delivers the little peptalk. He has always known the right things to say and do, ever since we met as young teenagers. But nothing in our relationship prepared us for this.

"What about you, Ty? You have your own stuff to worry about. You're in the middle of your remaining medical school applications. I know you still have a couple of interviews left, plus your regular class and lab schedule."

"Don't worry about me. I'll make it work somehow. I just want you to be all right."

The medication is kicking in. My eyes open and shut as exhaustion sweeps over me, and the promise of rest beckons. I would give anything to go back to being a carefree college student, to before I ended up in a hospital with gaps in my memory. I want to go back to the time my body was whole instead of violated, a time where brokenness didn't circle my consciousness like a vulture. Does my attacker recall the moment I fell unconscious or the moment he threw me out of a moving car? I'd give anything to find out the truth, to learn who did this and why.

CHAPTER 3

BEFORE

IT'S THE THIRD note in as many weeks, accompanied by a rare, exotic rose. Like the previous messages, this one is anonymous and typewritten, each word carefully chosen and arranged in a symphony of charm and sensuality. I place the note next to me on the bed and bite my bottom lip. I pick up the lush, deep-yellow Caraluna rose. He called it the *gold standard* in his note. The heavy fragrance permeates the air. I sniff the flower again, inhaling its intoxicating scent.

"I don't know if I should be creeped out or flattered," I say to my friend Zahra. She's perched at the edge of the bed in my dorm room, polishing her toenails a hideous shade of orange that makes my eyes hurt.

She looks up from her task. "Stop thinking the worst and go with it. It's sweet and romantic that he sends you these amazing and obviously expensive roses. He may have gone through a lot of trouble to find them. Some could have been imported. What was the last one he sent?"

"The Kaiserin Vikotoria Auguste tea rose, white with a yellow center."

11

"He has excellent taste, that's for sure. I'm so jealous."

"But why did he target me?"

Zahra sighs loudly, places the cap back on the nail polish, and tosses it into her purse. "There you go again, using words like *target*, making it sound like some big conspiracy. Why don't you read the note aloud this time? See if you spot the conspiracy. Maybe you missed it last time." Her tone drips with sarcasm.

I give her a dirty look, and she sticks her tongue out at me. I pick up the note and read:

My Sweetest Abbie,

I hope you approve of my latest choice. It reminds me of you, the gold standard, beyond compare and unrivaled in beauty, grace, mind and spirit. I spotted you walking across campus the other day. As always, you walked with purpose. I desperately wanted to say hi, ask if I could walk you to wherever you were going, but I didn't have the guts. I was afraid I would embarrass myself in your presence. So I watched in silence, dreaming of the day I will finally get up the courage to introduce myself. I've been close to you a few times but you were too busy to notice me. I don't blame you. I tend to fade into the background anyway. For now, seeing your gorgeous face makes my day. By the way, I like the new hairdo—the chic, chin length bob brings out your eyes–big, bright and magnetic. Next time I see you, I hope I will be a little braver, and one step closer to revealing my identity. Until then, I will be dreaming of you.

Your Humble Admirer

"I feel sorry for him, Abbie. He's shy and afraid you'll reject him. That's why he sends the roses with the notes."

"He wasn't shy about finding out where I live and how to get these notes to me without anyone knowing." My suspicion grows by the minute. "My roommate says she hasn't seen anything out of the ordinary, and no one on this floor saw anything either."

"The guy's in love," Zahra teases. "People do strange things when they're in love. I bet he pays someone to slip the notes under the door."

I scoff and roll my eyes at her. "Who sends anonymous letters these days to girls they like? Do you get anonymous love notes?"

"No, but that's because no one pays attention to me, and the guys that I do like don't feel the same way. I haven't had a date since I got here."

"You should stop behaving as if you're invisible. You haven't had a date because you're not confident and give off that vibe like there's something wrong with you. Guys notice these things."

"What's your excuse?" She sits up straight and folds her arms. "You turn down every guy who asks you out under the pretext of your course load and working for your mother. You even turned down that hot prince who chased you like a lovesick puppy."

We have this argument constantly, about why neither one of us is dating anyone. I have my reasons. I may have been interested in one or two, but the truth is, they aren't *him*.

"Did you forget I'm on an academic merit scholarship? It would be embarrassing to lose it because I let my grades tank. Secondly, making guest appearances on my mother's TV show takes a lot of preparation and work. And that prince you mentioned actually pulled the 'do you know who I am?' line on me, like that made up for the fact that he's an insufferable pig every day of the week. Hot or not, I wouldn't date him if he were the last guy on the planet."

I finish my rant with a self-satisfied smirk.

"So sad." Zahra shakes her head. "I still think these letters are harmless. It's merely a guy crushing on you and he's a little intimidated. Maybe he saw you tell that prince to take a flying leap and that scared him." She starts cracking up like it's the funniest thing she's ever heard.

I glare at her until she stops laughing and then clears her throat. Is she right, that this is a harmless crush or is trouble brewing?

CHAPTER 4

—◦—

BEFORE

I 'VE BEEN WATCHING her for the past two weeks, since the fall semester began. I hang out several rows back from her usual spot in the noisy dining hall but close enough to catch a glimpse the minute she walks in. I know her routine cold: fresh fruit and yogurt for breakfast most days, and when she wants to mix it up, she slathers maple syrup all over her pancakes, dips her finger in the syrup, and licks it when she thinks nobody is looking.

I like observing her without her knowing—the way she bounces when she walks. Or the way she writes in the palm of her hand instead of a notebook or laptop when she's with her study group and something has her stumped. I'm not some creepy stalker or anything like that. She's important to me, although she doesn't know it yet. I want to get close to her, learn everything there is to know without her finding out. Not yet anyway. Timing is everything.

I make sure my hoodie covers my face. I place my non-descript black backpack on the floor and wait. I have her schedule memorized. She's a biology major (molecular, cellular and developmental). She spends a lot of time at the Sterling Library with her study groups (she has three), and hangs out with that fat friend of hers. What's her name? Zahara? Zahra? Something exotic sounding, but that's not important right now.

Abbie Cooper is a different breed, I'm finding out. A puzzle I look forward to solving. One minute she's glamorous, sophisticated, and untouchable, and you think she's a snob for sure. You know, one of those girls you're scared to talk to because they might laugh in your face. The next minute, she's a regular, down-to-earth chick. Plus, I find her understated sensuality extremely sexy. Most hot women I've met know they're hot and want everybody to know it. Not Abbie. She keeps it close to the vest, and you have to pay real close attention to notice.

I've done my homework. I watched footage of her on her mother's show for the Cooking Network, *Shelby's Kitchen*. Episode after episode, for hours, to learn her body language, voice and gestures. She's taller than the average girl, around five-foot-eight if I had to guess. Her skin sparkles like chocolate diamonds under the studio lights. For the summer episodes, she wears her hair in tiny single braids. I hate those episodes. The braids make her look like she's in middle school, peddling Girl Scout cookies.

Her Facebook and Instagram posts are private, but I still gathered profile information. She's often photographed with one of her closest friends, Callie Furi, daughter of the movie director Nicholas Furi, and with her mother when they do press for *Shelby's Kitchen*.

The dining hall is packed and noisy, exactly the way I

like it. Long lines form at the waffle and omelet stands. Those who were smart enough to come early chow down at their tables. I managed to grab some corn flakes cereal, a hard-boiled egg, a glass of orange juice, and seasonal fruit. She should walk in by the time I'm halfway through eating.

And right on schedule, she does, with her fat friend in tow. Her statuesque figure is draped in an oversized top, infinity scarf and skinny jeans. I put my head down as she passes near my table, giggling about something her friend said. It's always like this. So close and yet she's oblivious.

CHAPTER 5

BEFORE

T HE LIVING ROOM space now doubles as a dance floor. Half-drunk co-eds are shouting and holding up beer bottles and red plastic cups as they sway to the thumping hip-hop beat. It's Thursday night, and another epic frat party is in full swing.

As I leave to grab a drink from the kitchen, someone tugs at my arm. I turn around quickly, a few choice words on the tip of my tongue for the unfortunate person who grabbed me, but the words never leave my lips.

He sports a navy, gingham sport shirt with rolled sleeves and dark jeans—a combination that highlights his fit, slender frame. He winks at me in that friendly yet flirty way of his, the flecks of green in his hazel eyes gleaming under the dim lights.

"I've been looking for you all night. I knew you were here but I got worried when I couldn't find you."

"I'm perfectly fine, Ty." I take a few steps back so he gets a good look. "Besides, I thought you were all wrapped up with Kristina."

I want to hate Kristina Haywood for completely irratio-nal reasons but have failed miserably. She never has a mean word to say about anyone, spent last summer building wells in a remote village in Bangladesh, and wants to save the world when she graduates. She's a double major in global affairs and economics. The fact that she's drop dead gorgeous and enamored with Ty doesn't rub me the wrong way at all.

He ignores my sarcasm. "I promised your dad I would look out for you."

"I'm a big girl. I can handle myself."

He blinks, and then rests a hand on my shoulder. "Are you okay, Cooper? Is something bothering you?" He yells over the thumping music.

I say nothing. He inches closer to me, and lifts my chin so we're eye to eye. "Something is definitely wrong. There's tension coming off you."

"Why don't you go back to whatever you were doing with Kristina. I'm going to get some fruit punch and mingle a little."

"I'll feel better if I get you that drink myself. I want to make sure it's not spiked. Be right back."

He disappears through the crowd of people. Checking on a drink to make sure there's nothing wrong with it is exactly the kind of thing he would do. He never forgets my birthday or Christmas and always picks out the perfect gift and knows exactly what to say in the accompanying cards. My parents love him. He's the only Y chromosome in my age group that my father trusts around me. Dad is seriously paranoid about me living away from home. New Haven, Connecticut is only a couple of hours away from my hometown of Castleview, Massachusetts, but it wouldn't surprise me if my dad asks Ty for a weekly report.

I close my eyes and sway to the beat of the music coming from the sound system, a slower tempo than the thumping hip-hop and techno beats from earlier.

"You know if you want to dance, just ask. I would be happy to oblige the most gorgeous girl at this party."

My eyes flutter open. I'm used to guys using tired pickup lines, especially at parties. It's a rite of passage I suppose. But the one standing before me is anything but a typical college guy trying to chat up a girl. At five feet eight inches barefoot, I still have to look up to get a clear view of his face. He wears a toothy grin and boy-next-door charm like a second skin.

"I don't dance with strange men," I say flippantly. "But I will give you points for being polite with that clichéd pickup line."

"I'm only telling the truth." He smiles again, revealing the cutest dimples. Mario Lopez-deep dimples.

"I'm Spencer." He extends a hand. "Spencer Rossdale."

His grip is firm and confident, large hands with long fingers and neatly trimmed fingernails. "Abbie Cooper."

His mouth opens in surprise. "So you're *the* Abbie Cooper. I saw you talking to Ty Rambally. He and I were teammates on the crew team. He's mentioned you a few times."

"Ty and I go way back. We've been friends since freshman year of high school."

"Friends?"

"Yes. *Friends.*"

I don't know why I feel the need to emphasize that Ty

and I are *just* friends.

"Whatever the two of you were discussing earlier looked intense," Spencer says.

Ty returns with a red plastic cup in hand, squashing any response from me. Handing me the cup he says, "Spencer, you've already met Cooper. Saves me from doing the introductions."

"You call her by her last name?" Spencer throws an amused glance at Ty.

"Everyone else calls her Abbie. She'll always be Cooper to me."

I take a sip of the punch and then chug down the whole thing.

Spencer slaps Ty on the shoulder. "I don't blame you for being protective. Abbie seems like a pretty special girl."

"She is," Ty agrees.

I stiffen when I observe Kristina Hayward making her way toward us. When she catches up, she places a possessive arm around Ty's waist. She's quite striking with her waist-length raven hair, and model-like cheekbones.

"I thought you ditched me." She drops a kiss on his cheek.

"I'm a gentleman. I would never do that to you."

"You better not."

"He's right, Kristina. Ty is a gentleman and would never leave you hanging."

"Thanks for the reassurance, Abbie. It's good to hear that from a friend."

There's something about the way she said *friend* that I don't like. As if I'm an old pair of shoes—comfortable and dependable. Not hip and stylish new shoes, worthy of attention.

"So Abbie, how about that dance we talked about?" Spencer says.

I mentally thank him for having the instinct to save me from the awkward encounter. He takes my hand and leads me to the packed dance floor. I don't know if it's the soaring, invigorating beat of "The Greatest" by Sia or the company, but I find myself shouting the chorus at the top of my lungs and breaking out dance moves I didn't even know I had. Maybe I let my guard down because Ty knows Spencer, so my comfort level is, well, comfortable. When Spencer draws in closer to me, barely a breath separating us, I go with the flow without breaking my rhythm.

Slightly out of breath, we sit opposite each other in two leather armchairs near the fireplace. The dance floor crowd has thinned out and the DJ is spinning slower tunes, signaling that the party is winding down.

"You have impressive dance moves," he says, grinning.

"Not really."

"Don't be modest. Your movements are precise and controlled with reckless abandon thrown in."

I raise a brow, forcing him to explain himself.

"I don't mean anything disrespectful," he says quickly. "You surprised me, that's all."

"We just met. How could I surprise you?"

"Well, you strike me as intense. When I first saw you, you were leaning against the wall, checking out the action. You had this look on your face like you were above it all."

"Are you saying I'm snooty?" My hand flies to my chest in mock offense.

"Whoa," he says, holding up his hands. "I'm not judging

here." Then he says softly, "It was a nice surprise, on the dance floor I mean."

I chuckle. "Some people think I'm a robot, did you know that? They think all I do is study, and I'm weird because I'm a college student who doesn't drink, smoke or . . ."

"Or what?" He leans in closer, his laser beam blue eyes bursting with curiosity.

"Nothing. You're so nosy."

"I am. About you."

"Why are you curious about me, Spencer Rossdale?"

"You intrigue me."

"That's not very original."

"I tell it like it is."

"Why do I intrigue you?"

I think back to the letters. Could Spencer be Mr. Anonymous? I dismiss the idea. I don't observe any of the traits of my secret admirer in Spencer. He's confident, not shy, and the kind of guy you notice: athletic, tall, ridiculously good-looking, and charm to burn.

Spencer stares at me, puzzled. "Is that a serious question?"

"It is. You're out of here in a few months. Why are you hitting on a sophomore? A sophomore who, by your own words, struck you as intense and untouchable. Not exactly an easy target, if you get my drift."

He shoots back, "Well, this sophomore is high on herself. Who says I was hitting on you?"

If ego smashing were a sport, he would be the reigning champion, although the playful grin tugging at the corners of his mouth tells me he's only half-kidding.

"So you go around telling random women they intrigue you for no reason? You should re-evaluate how you spend your time, dude."

He throws back his head and laughs. "You've proven my point. Most girls would have been offended, called me a jerk, and stomped out of here."

Before I can respond, a pretty, half-drunk brunette with a nose ring and caked on mascara approaches us, her eyes focused on Spencer.

"Hey Spencer, are you coming by later?"

Spencer stays silent for a few beats as he shifts in his chair multiple times.

Well this is awkward. Is he a player? It wouldn't surprise me.

"I think she's waiting for an answer," I whisper.

The girl teeters on skyscraper heels. If she doesn't sit down soon, she might face plant right in front of us.

"I'm kind of busy, Karen," he says, his voice terse.

Her face reddens. "Oh. I see. Well, call me tomorrow then." She adjusts her blouse and stomps off, almost twisting her ankle.

After Karen leaves, a painful silence follows. I admit to feeling a little something, that spark of attraction when he introduced himself. How could I not? But if he's a player, I had better steer clear. I don't need the drama or distraction.

"It's getting late," I announce, in case there's anyone around who didn't know that. "I should get going."

At that moment, Spencer's cell phone buzzes. He pulls it from his jacket pocket, looks at the number, and then frowns. He excuses himself to take the call. When he returns, he's obviously agitated.

24

"Is everything okay?" I ask, still seated.

"Yes. It was my sister annoying me on purpose." He sits and lasers in on me. "Now, we were having the most stimulating conversation before we were interrupted. Where were we?"

"It's okay to be upset. You don't have to pretend that you're not."

"I'm not upset," he says softly. "When I saw the call from my sister, I thought something serious had happened. She almost never calls me and as you said, it's late. I took the call thinking the worst, only to find out it was about something trivial she could have texted me about."

"Siblings are like that sometimes. It's their job to be infuriating."

We talk for a while longer and then I pick up my purse and stand. "Need to get some sleep, marathon study session ahead tomorrow and into the weekend. Professor Baker's molecular biology class is the bane of my existence."

"I'm sure you'll have no problem acing that class," he says.

"How would you know?"

"Ty says you're a whiz. He talks about you constantly. About how smart you are. He admires you."

"He runs circles around me when it comes to academics. It's always been that way for him, even in high school."

"Funny how you both ended up at the same university."

"Yeah. Funny how it almost didn't happen."

"Why not?" His inquisitive eyes hold mine with eager anticipation, like a dog about to receive his favorite treat. But I'm not about to confide in a total stranger the events that almost destroyed my chances of ever getting into college, let alone the Ivy League.

"You know how competitive Yale is. I wasn't sure I would get in."

After I grab my coat off a coat rack in the foyer, Spencer asks, "May I walk you back to your dorm? You shouldn't be walking alone this late at night."

"That's nice of you, but I came with my friend Zahra, whom I haven't seen since we arrived. She'll be here soon. Ty is walking with us, too. He has to include this party in his weekly report to my father."

His eyes go wide. "Are you serious?"

"Maybe. Ty thinks it's his job to protect me on campus, and my dad is his most enthusiastic cheerleader."

"Then in that case, I bid you goodnight." He reaches for my hand, raises it to his lips, and lands a soft kiss on the back of it. "Sweet dreams, Abbie."

Sweet dreams. I'll be dreaming of you. Those lines from the last letter I received pop into my head. But if our conversation tonight is any indication, Spencer Rossdale says exactly what's on his mind. He couldn't be the Humble Admirer who has been anonymously showering me with romantic gifts and letters.

CHAPTER 6

BEFORE

STUDY GROUP IS wrapping up. We occupy a dimly lit corner on the eighth floor of the university's largest library, which houses millions of volumes on over a dozen floors in a Gothic-style building that looks more like a European cathedral than a library.

When Beth Compton suggested we create a formal study group for our probability and statistics class, it made sense. Most of us in the group—Beth, myself, Noah Fenton and Justin Tate—are either pre-med or math majors. I'm glad the session will soon be over. I haven't contributed much, too distracted by thoughts of the letters and why I have a hard time chalking them up to a simple crush. As if that weren't bad enough, I feel like someone is watching me or following me. I can't prove it, but it's there, like a dull ache that won't go away no matter how many painkillers you take. What if the letters and roses are much more than a guy with a crush?

Justin peers over at me like I'm some peculiar creature he just discovered for the first time. "Are you okay, Abbie?"

Justin is painfully shy, a highly intelligent and capable

kid who was raised by a single mother in a rough section of Cleveland but managed to make it to the Ivy League on a partial scholarship. He's what I call geek chic—red-framed glasses that are too large for his narrow face, khakis and navy blue vans.

"What?" I ask. Everyone around the table stares at me. "Did I miss something?"

"Um, you were supposed to share your notes from the last class. We've asked you like three times and you just zoned out," Beth says.

"I'm sorry, guys." I click through the files on my laptop. "I have the notes somewhere." Everyone is quiet. They must really think I'm losing it. Each week, one person in the group is assigned to take notes. This week is my turn.

"It's okay, Abbie," Justin says. "Everyone has those moments. It's about time you did."

He smiles at me, the sweetest, most innocent yet beguiling smile. I can't help but smile back as a thanks for coming to my defense. It was strange, though. He's never done anything like that before, content to be the quiet one in the group. I see Justin every so often around campus, but I don't pay much attention.

My mind begins to work overtime again, like pieces of a jigsaw puzzle straining to fit together. Could it be? I shake off the speculation. *You can't go around suspecting every guy who is nice to you of sending you anonymous love notes. Get a grip.*

"Thanks Justin. It was sweet of you to defend me."

"Can we hurry this up?" Noah Fenton asks. "I have a paper I need to finish, due tomorrow."

"Stop acting like you're the only one with an intense

schedule," Beth snaps. "We're all on the struggle bus, and it's only the beginning of the semester."

Noah hangs his head and mutters, "Sorry."

"Abbie's not struggling," Justin says. "She aced her first tests."

I look at him curiously.

"How would you know?" Noah asks, his earlier embar-rassment forgotten.

Yeah, I'd like to know, too.

"I overheard her pre-med advisor talking to Professor Flynn."

All eyes now turn in my direction. "You should take over the study group, Abbie," Beth says. "I'm barely getting by with a B. That is not going to get me into a top medical school. We all know how competitive it is."

"Beth, you're doing a great job. I don't see any reason to change."

I look around the table and everyone nods in agreement.

"Great. Now that we have that settled, I'm going to the printer to pick up the notes."

After two hours of intense exchange and testing each other's knowledge, the conversation turns to discussion of The Big Game, one of the biggest football rivalries in college history, and the epic parties that follow.

"I think we should meet once more before the big test coming up," I say, as everyone prepares to leave.

"Can't," Noah says. "I have another paper due around that time. Can't afford a bad grade in that class either."

"Okay. If anyone wants to meet before, text me."

"I'll study with you. I don't mind at all," Justin says. Everyone gawks at him in disbelief.

Why the sudden interest in getting me alone, Justin?

"That's thoughtful of you, Justin. Don't feel obligated to study with me, though."

"I don't," he says, his tone firm. He picks up his books, not bothering to place them in his backpack, and then walks out of the library.

BY THE TIME I exit the library, it's still light out. A warm September breeze rustles the trees, whose leaves are in the beginning stages of turning colors for the fall. I sling my bag over my shoulder and begin the near ten-minute walk to the dining hall for dinner. It's one of the ways I get my exercise. I loathe going to the gym.

"Hey, wait up," someone says. The voice is male. I turn around instinctively, but I can't quite make out the figure. He could have been calling out to one of the cluster of students scattered around. I keep walking.

"Hey, Abbie!" That stops me in my tracks. The voice sounds friendly and called me by name. Spencer Rossdale catches up to me, his face beaming.

"Hi, Spencer." I continue walking, and he falls in step with me.

"You're really in a hurry. I saw you leaving the library. I had to run to catch up with you once I made it outside."

He didn't sound out of breath to me, but then again he is—or was—a Division One Athlete.

"I'm trying to grab dinner before the dining hall closes."

"Which Residential College?"

Each of the fourteen Residential Colleges, more commonly known as dormitories, has its own dining hall, although students have access to all fourteen. I tell Spencer where I reside.

"Can I walk with you?"

"Sure." A leisurely stroll was not on my agenda, but I don't want to be rude.

"How is your sister?" I ask.

He hesitates as if confused by the question.

"You said your sister called to annoy you when we were at the party the other night."

"Oh, yeah. She's okay. I told her not to scare me like that again. Do you have any siblings?" he asks quickly.

"A brother. Two actually—Lee is my half brother. He's older."

I tuck a lock of loose hair behind my ear. "So where did you grow up?"

"Here and there. The East Coast mostly. Bethesda."

"Really? I was born in Bethesda."

"No kidding. Which neighborhood?"

"Crestview. I don't remember much about it. My mom was a Post-doctoral Fellow at the NIH when I when I was born. We left when I was four."

"Your mom worked for the NIH? That's cool."

"Yep. Dr. Shelby Cooper was an employee of the BBCB, Division of Biomedical Technology, Bioinformatics and Computational Biology."

"Is that why you want to go into medicine, because of your mother's background?"

"Partially. I've wanted to be a neurosurgeon since I was twelve years old."

"Whoa. That's a lot of pressure on a little girl."

"I know what I want and do whatever it takes to get it. You've never wanted anything that badly?"

"Yes," he says softly. "You."

The statement hits me with the force of a wrecking ball. I stop in my tracks and so does Spencer. I gaze at him. "What did you say?"

"I didn't stutter." His voice is calm and unflustered.

Okay, I admit there was flirting going on the night we met at the party. But how did we end up here? How do you go from flirting to *I want you* in a matter of days? Is that how it works? I seriously need to keep up with dating rituals. I'm in the dark here.

"I don't think that's a good idea, Spencer."

"Why not?" he challenges.

"You're on your way out and I don't do casual hookups. It's that simple."

He backs up a step. "I'm sorry if I came on too strong. I make it a policy to say what's on my mind so there's no misunderstanding. If I like a girl, I tell her. She can take it or leave it."

"A little full of ourselves, are we?"

He chuckles. "Maybe. But your reasons don't hold up."

I frown. "What does that mean?"

"The fact that I'm a senior shouldn't matter. As for casual hookups, there's nothing casual about you."

"What is this, then?"

"I've already told you. I like you. It's that simple," he says, echoing my earlier statement.

No beating round the bush for him. I appreciate his straightforward, no bull attitude. It's not as if he's the first guy to hit on me, but why so insistent? Could it be as simple as he says, or is there more? He's poked my curious bone. I accused him of being nosy when we first met, but I'm twice as bad.

"Okay, Spencer. Put your cards on the table. All of them."

"All of them?" he asks with a mischievous grin. "That wouldn't be fair now, would it?"

"It's the only way I'll play."

"You drive a hard bargain, lady."

"Take it or leave it."

"Okay. I've been asking around since the night we met. You're not dating anyone. Ty confirmed it."

"You asked Ty about me?" That surprises me. Ty never said anything to me about it. Perhaps he forgot.

"I would be an idiot not to. He knows you well."

"You're not going to quit, are you?"

"Why should I?" The challenge is clear on his face. "I wouldn't do this if I didn't think you felt something too. Tell me I'm wrong."

He's not. However, I won't admit that I'm attracted to him. That's why I don't mind his boldness. If it were some other guy, I would have told him to get lost a while ago.

"I admit nothing."

"That's an admittance in itself. What are you afraid of?"

"Don't try to psychoanalyze me."

"I'm not. I just think it's strange that a girl like you won't date anyone. Unless guys are not your speed. If that's the case, I'll step off and never bother you again."

"You know perfectly well I'm straight. Otherwise, you

wouldn't have bothered to approach me the other night or ask Ty if I was involved."

"What is it then?" He swallows several times.

"It's not the end of the world if I don't go out with you, Spencer. I'm sure you'll survive."

"Maybe I won't," he says. He draws in closer and peers down at me. "You do things to me, Abbie Cooper. I'm not ashamed to admit it."

The audacious part of my personality takes over. "What kinds of things?" If he's going to make crazy claims, then he has to explain himself. I don't budge, matching his intense gaze with one of my own.

"You make me restless. I maintain a tight rein over my thoughts, actions and emotions. That hasn't happened since I met you."

"Wow. You give that much power to a girl you just met?"

"You see my dilemma then. So, what are you going to do about it?"

I'm starving and the dining hall closes in thirty minutes. I can't solve this tonight.

"I'll think about it."

"It's better than no. That's progress. When would be a good time to check back in with you, to see if you've made a decision?"

I giggle, and shake my head. He smiles sweetly, like a kid who got permission to have ice cream before dinner.

"Meet me for breakfast in my dining hall two days from now at 7:15 a.m. sharp."

"It's a date," he says.

"No it isn't. It's an appointment. Big difference."

CHAPTER 7

BEFORE

THE NEXT DAY, Wednesday, number four arrives. My classes for the day ended at 1:30 p.m. I gaze out the window of my dorm room as the rain pelts the windowpane. Students with their hoodies up sprint to their destinations, trying to avoid getting soaked. There's a knock at the door.

Zahra stands in the doorway in a rain-splattered raincoat, umbrella in hand and oversized purse hanging from her shoulders. "I came as soon as I got your text."

I sent the text mere minutes ago. She obviously ran all the way here. She enters the room.

Zahra sits on the tiny, floral sofa and I join her with an envelope in hand, one larger and thicker than the previous ones.

"Go ahead, open it," she says, as she takes off her raincoat.

I remove the ribbon and open the gold gift box. Resting on the delicate white tissue paper inside is a deep pink rose. Large petals and a heavy perfume scent make this the most intriguing one yet. I pass the box to Zahra.

"Wow! The boy has skills. And that smell." She takes a whiff of the rose and closes her eyes. "I could inhale it all day."

I reach for the box again, expecting another note. He's consistent if nothing else.

Sweetest Abbie,

Do you like it? This one is called the 'Ecstasy' Rose. Its name, intense color, and fragrance make up the perfect metaphor that represents how I feel about you. Did you have a good time at the party the other night? I saw you dancing with someone else but I wasn't jealous at all because he's not worthy of you. I think you already know that. Don't be alarmed. Soon, all will be revealed.

Your Humble Admirer

Zahra and I stare at each other. I let the note fall from my fingers and it lands at our feet. I leave the sofa and return to the window.

"Why would he tell me he was at the party and saw me dancing with Spencer Rossdale? Wouldn't that prove he's stalking me? Why isn't he afraid I will report this to campus police?"

"There's nothing threatening in any of the notes, only some poor soul expressing his devotion for a girl he has crush on," Zahra says. "What would you tell campus police? You get love notes and roses from a secret admirer?"

I fiddle with my scarf, twisting the edges around my finger. "The funny thing is, he could be in one of my classes and I wouldn't know."

"Who says it has to be a student? It could be a professor. Maybe that's why he hides behind letters. He could be fired if anyone finds out he's making moves on a student."

I move away from the window and plop back next to Zahra on the sofa. "That's a stretch. Besides, professors don't hang around off-campus parties."

"People do crazy things in the name of love."

"Speaking from experience?"

"I plead the fifth." She holds up her palm.

"Don't make me call Dahlia to find out your deep, dark secret," I threaten with a grin.

Zahra and I met at a freshman mixer and hit it off right away. Something about her made me comfortable, as if we'd known each other for years. Then one day, she invited me to her dorm room and when I saw the photo on her wall, I almost keeled over. It was a picture of a family reunion, but the girl next to Zahra in the front row looked like her identical twin: same wild, dark brown curly hair, cynical expression, and lips that looked like they were sculpted by Michelangelo. The only difference was the girl next to Zahra was tall and stick thin, Zahra was shorter and has been struggling to go from a size fourteen to ten ever since I've known her.

The girl in the photo turned out to be Zahra's cousin, Dahlia Sessions. Dahlia and I attended St. Matthews Academy, an elite boarding school in my hometown of Castleview. If it weren't for Dahlia and her then-boyfriend Lance Carter, I wouldn't have made it to college.

During senior year, I had received a series of anonymous notes threatening to expose my secret—the horrible mistake I made that could have gotten me expelled from my high school. The person behind the threats promised to contact admissions at all the colleges to which I had applied if I didn't agree to her blackmail scheme. Because of Lance Carter's tech savvy, I found out who was behind the threats and why.

"Go ahead," Zahra says with confidence. "She'll give you a hundred lectures about how you can't seem to stay out of trouble. Lectures with major attitude."

"Fine. I won't call Dahlia."

"What if Humble Admirer isn't random and you know him?" she asks.

"What do you mean?"

"Ty showed up at the party with Kristina. You told me yourself that you and Spencer were already chatting by the time Ty came around and did a formal introduction. Mr. Anonymous admitted he was at the party, but how would he know that Spencer wasn't worthy of you?"

"Unless he knows Spencer."

"Exactly."

"That doesn't make sense, Zahra."

"It makes perfect sense. Ty is testing the waters."

"Then why show up with Kristina?"

"He's way too smart to be obvious."

I walk to the window again and watch the raindrops multiply. The note said Spencer wasn't worthy. What does Ty know that I don't?

My gaze returns to Zahra. "If Ty had reservations about Spencer, he would tell me, not put it in a note. Plus, this is so not his style."

"The clock is ticking and he wants to protect himself from possible rejection. By hiding behind this persona, this anonymous guy, he has nothing to lose and everything to gain."

"Seems far-fetched to me. I agree that Ty has always been a details guy, especially when it comes to my likes, dislikes, moods and such. The writer of the letters hit all the right notes, so there are similarities there, but I still have my doubts. On top of everything else, Spencer is making a move, hardcore."

I fill her in on my discussion the day before with Spencer. When I finish, she looks at me incredulously. "What are you going to tell him?"

"I don't know. I haven't had much time to think about it."

"Do you like him?"

"I'd like to get to know him, yes. My sassiness doesn't bother him. He gives as good as he gets. I like that. And he's very pleasant to look at."

Zahra gives me a look as if I should be committed to a mental ward. "I sense a but coming on. What's wrong with this one, Abbie? You always have a reason why you won't just go for it."

Maybe it's time to let go. Admit that what I've been holding on to for so long is a fantasy. My chest aches. I walk back to the sofa, my feet heavy, and flop down next to Zahra.

"All this speculation is making me crazy. There's only one way to find out if Ty is behind the letters. I can move on once I have the answer."

"What are you going to do?"

"I'll begin with the subtle approach. Drop a couple of hints and see how he reacts."

"Are you sure that will work? If he went to all this trouble, it won't be easy to trap him."

"I have to start somewhere."

CHAPTER 8

BEFORE

M Y PHONE ALARM didn't go off, and when I open my eyes and glance at the screen, it's already 7:00 a.m. on Thursday morning. Crap! I told Spencer to meet me in the dining hall at 7:15 a.m. sharp. There's no way I can shower, get ready and be there in fifteen minutes. I grab my toothbrush and paste, a towel and soap, and make a mad dash for the bathroom. It's not that I care so much if I'm a few minutes late, but it's the principle. I made a big deal about the time.

By the time I get dressed, grab my materials for classes, and arrive at the dining hall, I'm thirty minutes late. I scan the space for Spencer, stretching to see above the tables and chairs and the crowd of students heading back and forth from the breakfast stands. I spot him at a table near the back and make my way over.

"I'm so sorry." I plop down in a seat and place my bag at my feet. "It's a lame excuse but my alarm didn't go off, I swear. By the time I got myself together . . ."

"Abbie, it's okay," he says, calm and casual. "Stuff happens."

"Really? You're not annoyed?"

"There's nothing for me to be annoyed about. You made it. That's all that matters."

"Thanks for being understanding. I feel terrible. I don't like to be late for things."

He changes the subject. "You must be starving. What can I get you for breakfast?"

"You don't have to do that," I say, standing up. "I'll get something quick."

"You need to learn to relax. It's not a big deal. Do you want some fruit or yogurt, eggs?"

"It all sounds good."

"I'll be right back."

The royal treatment. Who wouldn't like that? And he wasn't even annoyed that I'm so late. Am I wrong about him? I have been known to overthink things. But still . . .

He returns balancing a tray on each hand like an expert waiter. I take one of the trays from him. He has a seat and chugs down his glass of milk. I nervously poke at my eggs, manage to get a forkful into my mouth, and chew slowly.

It feels like we're conducting a business negotiation and whoever speaks first has to make concessions that benefit the other party. Since I called this meeting, I guess I'm going to be the loser. For now.

"I've thought about our discussion. There's no reason we can't be adults about this. Once we establish the ground rules and agree on them, sure, we can hang out."

"Hang out?" He says it like I just cursed him. Then he gives me a lopsided grin. "Tell me what you mean by 'hang out'."

I rip the cover off my yogurt, pick up my spoon, and stir.

My eyes never leave his face. When I'm satisfied that the fruit on the bottom has thoroughly blended in, I lick the extra yogurt off the spoon.

"Yeah, hang out. You know, we can go places together, the movies, the museum, a coffee house, stuff like that."

"Good. So we're dating."

"Whoa, dude. Let's not get crazy. Nobody said anything about dating."

"What you just described is what people do when they're dating." Amusement crackles in his eyes.

"I do all those things with my brother Lee when I'm home. It doesn't mean I'm dating him."

We look at each other and can't hold back anymore. We burst out laughing at the same time. Once the laughter subsides, he says, "I knew you were funny. I could tell, even if you come off as serious most of the time."

"You caught me on a good day."

"I think that's what you want people to see. But I believe there's another side of you."

"What side would that be, since you've known me all of five minutes?"

He leans forward and so do I. "It goes deeper than funny. Beneath the intense, in control, all work and no play exterior beats the heart of a closet bad girl who's dying to come out and play."

"Oh yeah? Prove it."

"You're on."

CHAPTER 9

AFTER

THE PAIN IS back with a vengeance, and I want nothing more than to be pumped full of drugs and fall into a deep sleep. Maybe when I wake up, everything will be normal again. But I know that won't happen. My pain is beyond physical. Before I was discharged from the hospital, I gave my consent to have the rape kit tested for evidence. The fact that they examined me while I was unconscious has me oscillating between gratitude that I wasn't awake for it, and emotional distress that my body was invaded again so soon after the initial trauma. Even though it was for a good reason.

My cheek hurts where the blow caused swelling and makes my face feel puffy. An unrelenting ring of pain circles my neck because he tried to choke me, and the almost broken arm throbs in its cast. The scrapes and bruises on my arms and legs ache too. Even with Ty holding on to my good arm so I don't collapse, putting one foot in front of the other takes a herculean effort.

"I got you, Cooper," he says. "Nice and easy."

I barely register his comment. My eyes are focused on

the sofa with its warm sheets, blankets and pillows. When we reach it, he holds on to me as I slowly lower myself into the warm comfort of the sofa. The TV remote control and a gorgeous bouquet of sweet smelling flowers in a vase rest on an end table to the right of the couch, where I would have use of my good hand.

He sits next to me, his face grim. "You're in pain. I'll pick up your medications in a bit, but I wanted to get you home first so you can relax. I'll order lunch from that Italian restaurant around the corner."

"Good. I don't need to worry about dying from your horrible cooking."

"That hurts, Cooper." He clutches his chest, pretending to be offended. Then he gets unnaturally quiet. The nervous twitching of his hands in his lap is not a good sign.

"We have to tell your parents. I will respect your wishes, whatever you want to do, but something this big, I don't think you should keep it from them."

I gently touch his arm. "Ty, I know you mean well, but I can't tell my parents about this. Not now. Maybe some time in the future, but now is not the best time."

"Why not?"

I take a deep breath. "It would devastate them, especially my dad. His cancer is in remission, and I don't know what this news could do to him. The stress and anxiety could cause him to relapse. I can't risk it."

"Are you sure? Your dad can handle anything. This situation has personal and legal implications."

I would love nothing more than to spill my guts to my parents and bask in their love and support. As painful as it is not to share this with them, I have to think of the long-term. If my father relapsed, I would never forgive myself. Having him around for a long time is more important than my current problems.

"Yes, I'm sure. It has to be this way for now."

"Okay. I ask because I had to lie to your mother while we were in the hospital. She called me yesterday, anxious because you wouldn't return her calls. I didn't want to freak her out, so I told her you were at the library studying for a major test, and you would call. Until you're feeling better, we'll have to pretend everything is okay and make excuses as to why you can't go home for the weekend."

I bite my lips. I haven't had time to process what has happened to me, let alone the ramifications—including what I would say to the people in my circle. But Ty has already thought of that, and I feel nothing but guilt because I'm disrupting his life. He promised to take care of me as I come to grips with the attack. Ty always keeps his word. He confided that he might have blown the Harvard interview earlier today, all because he was worried about me. Harvard is his first choice for medical school. I pray that he gets in. We didn't get to practice beforehand as planned because someone decided to brutalize me for sick, twisted reasons that only he can rationalize.

"What were you thinking just now?" he asks.

My voice cracks. "What if I never remember what happened?"

"You have to be hopeful that you will. Your memory of that night could come back."

As the words leave his lips, a scary thought strikes me.

What if I don't want to remember? Reliving the horror, looking into the face of the monster?

"Even if I do remember, it's my word against his unless evidence comes back from the rape kit. Slim chance of that happening. Do you really think somebody who did what he did to me would leave evidence behind? I bet he's done this before. Drugging women could be part of his MO. He took my clothes and my shoes. And the jacket."

Ty's head jerks up. "What jacket?"

"I was wearing Spencer's jacket. I got cold while we were outside, in the back yard at the party. He draped his jacket around me."

"You're right. I don't recall him wearing a jacket when we were looking for you."

"Did he accept what you told him in your text, that I left the party because I was embarrassed about kissing him?"

"I think so. He said he would ping you later. What are you going to tell him?"

"I don't want to see or talk to anyone right now, so we need to get our story straight."

"Which is what?"

"I caught a bad strain of the flu and the doctor has ordered me to stay in bed until I get over it, and the raging fever."

"Sounds like a good explanation. We'll run with it."

His phone chirps. He removes it from his pocket, looks at the number and declines the call. He puts the phone back in his pocket.

"Please don't put your life on hold because of me. You can't slow down because some psycho attacked me."

"We're as close as two friends can be. My friend needs

me. That takes priority in my book."

I turn away from him. Tears sting my eyes. I wipe them away with my uninjured hand.

"I feel like a burden, Ty. That's what I mean. I'm physically unable to care for myself right now. I have to think about pressing criminal charges if they ever find this guy. I've got to find the strength to psych myself up for the battle, the scrutiny, and fear that I won't be believed. The shame. There are those who will say I was some spoiled college brat who partied too much and got herself in trouble. You know how this goes, with the victim blaming and all that.

"You told me yourself you got the sense that's what the medical staff was thinking when you first arrived at the hospital. He poured alcohol down my throat. He knew exactly what he was doing. That's the impression he wanted to give. It could have killed me, the combination of the alcohol and the drugs."

I can barely breathe. I sink back into the couch. My throat aches and my head is throbbing. Exhaustion takes over.

"You need to rest, Cooper. We'll talk about all of this later. Right now, call your mother so she doesn't worry. Then sleep. I'll head to the pharmacy to get the medication and come right back."

He must have seen the pathetic pleading in my eyes. *Don't leave me.*

"Don't worry. You're safe here. The security in this building is top-notch. There are cameras everywhere. You're the only person who ever had a key to this apartment, and nobody can come up without security ringing first."

"I know."

"Also, don't forget you need a new phone."

"We can go to the store later once I rest up," I say, yawning.

Ty gently flips out the leg rest of the sofa and pulls the blankets all the way up to my chin.

"I'll be back soon."

"Okay."

CHAPTER 10

BEFORE

"MAY I HELP you?" The old man in the black suit asks. He glances at his watch. "It's almost six. We'll be closing the store soon."

He looks more like an undertaker than a clerk in an upscale boutique in downtown New Haven. His tone says I don't belong there and he wants me gone. I will leave when I'm good and ready, after I've selected the perfect gift and not a second before.

"I don't need help, but I will be sure to let you know if I do." I glare at him to let him know it's best he leaves me alone. He takes the hint and occupies himself straightening out silk ties on a display. The dark-haired girl who was scoping out purses when I first entered the store glances in my direction and smiles. I don't smile back.

I scan the boutique for inspiration. What would make a great gift for Abbie Cooper, the girl who has everything? I've set the bar high with the roses. My next gift can't be a letdown or she will become suspicious. Keeping up this game is costing me a fortune, but I'm the kind of guy who likes to look at the big picture. What's a few hundred bucks now compared to what I'll gain when the big payoff comes?

My eyes race past the expensive perfumes, purses, watches and the case that houses jewelry. Gold earrings? Nah. A colorful display of scarves catches my eye and I walk over to get a better look. I run my fingers through the material: beautiful, floral silk, rich in texture and appearance. Perfect.

I head to the register, satisfied with my choice. I plop down the cash on the counter as the clerk rings up the order. He slides his glasses down his nose and then looks at me.

"Do you have a problem with cash?"

He briefly hesitates. "Not at all."

I pull up my hood and leave the store. I have just enough time to meet up with my contact, who will make sure that Abbie Cooper receives the latest token of my affection. Then I need to get the heck out of town before trouble comes looking for me.

CHAPTER 11

BEFORE

T HIS WAS LEFT for you outside the door," my roommate Julie says. "I hope it's okay that I brought it in."

She must have read the trepidation on my face. "Are you okay?"

"I'm fine." I take the small, square package from her and toss it on the bed.

"Aren't you going to open it?"

"I will. I'm in no hurry. There's no return address, so I don't really know who it's from."

"Oh. That's strange. Sorry for picking it up. I thought it might be something you were expecting."

"Don't worry about it. I'll know who sent it once I open it," I reassure her.

"Okay. Well, I'm off to Econ," she says, picking her bag off the floor. "See you later."

After Julie leaves, I pick up the box wrapped in brown paper and shake it. No sound. No object moving back and forth. The box is light, around six inches in length. I open the desk drawer and grab a pair of scissors from the pile of school supplies. I cut through the taped edges on either side to reveal a plain white gift box. I remove the top and part the delicate tissue. A gorgeous scarf with a vibrant orange and red pattern stares back at me.

I remove the scarf from the box and let it drape lightly against my arm. It's silk. Expensive silk. I turn it over in search of the label. My brow twitches when I see the designer: Hermès. I search for a note in the box. He did not disappoint.

Sweetest Abbie,

I couldn't help myself. Please accept this small token of my affection.

Your Humble Admirer

Who is this guy? Why is he sending me expensive gifts? There are only two people I know who wouldn't think twice about gifting me a four hundred dollar scarf, and one of them is thousands of miles away in Texas. The other is much closer.

IT'S EARLY AFTERNOON, and I meet up with Justin in one of the coveted Group Study Rooms at the Sterling Library. The room is set up with small, individual blackboards peppered along the walls, and a large, rectangular table with chairs at the center.

When I enter, he's standing at the blackboard but immediately makes a beeline for me. One would think I was visiting royalty the way he fawns all over me.

"Hi, Abbie. Thanks for coming. I wasn't sure you could make it, but it's great that you did. Are you thirsty? I know we're not supposed to bring drinks into the library." He pats his bag. "But I figured were going to be here a while, so why not, right? We're not hurting anybody."

He's nervous. That's a lot of words coming from him in one breath. What happened to quiet, shy Justin?

I drop my bag on one of the chairs. "Slow down, Justin. I can only stay an hour, maybe a little longer, but it's not going to be one of those marathon sessions we do as a group."

His pained expression tugs at my heartstrings as he lowers his head.

"Don't worry. There will be other opportunities to study together. This probability and statistics class is not easy, so I could use the extra study time."

He looks up at me as if his faith in humanity has been restored. I smile at him and tell him we should get started. He outlines on the chalkboard an analysis of variance model problem that has been particularly tricky for us. He methodically walks through the problem.

He ambles toward the table and chairs and picks up his bag. He takes out two bottles of water and hands me one. My instinct is to say no, but I don't want to hurt his feelings so I take it and thank him. When he unscrews the cap and takes a large sip of his, I feel obligated to do the same. We both place the bottles on the table afterward.

"So are you going to do any more episodes of your mom's cooking show this year?" he asks, totally out of left field.

"Um. . . I don't know. It depends on how the semester goes. If I can't squeeze it in then, I won't do it."

"You can do it, no problem. You're like superwoman. Except you're much more beautiful, smarter, and can do anything. No superpowers needed."

"That's sweet of you to say, but I'm not as cool as you think."

Perhaps referencing my mother's show for the Cooking Network is his way of trying to establish a personal connection with me. All our interactions thus far have been academically focused.

"I would never say you're cool," he says.

"Oh. Okay."

"What I mean is, I would never use such trivial vocabulary to describe you," he explains, with a superior air.

An awkward lapse in conversation follows. I grab the bottle of water on the table and take a long swig.

"I must be thirstier than I thought," I say, breaking the silence.

"You don't like to be complimented?" He removes his glasses.

"Boy, you're really talkative today. Full of surprises."

"Does it make you uncomfortable?"

"Me? No," I say, and wave my hand in a dismissive gesture. "Don't be ridiculous."

He smiles and returns his glasses to his face. "That's why I dig you, Abbie. You don't take yourself so seriously, even though you're the shiznit."

I stare at him like some enigmatic creature who just revealed himself. During our group study sessions, he barely speaks to me. Now he's asking me about my mother's show and comparing me to comic book super heroes. This qualifies as one of the strangest days of my life. Am I giving off some weird pheromones that cause the men I encounter to behave strangely?

"I had no idea you thought so highly of me, Justin. Thank you, I'm flattered, but I'm no different than any other girl on this campus."

"I disagree. Strongly." He utters the words with an authority I never thought him capable of.

"Why?" I ask.

"You see people."

"I don't understand."

"You're nice to everyone, but it goes beyond that. You see people. You look beyond socio-economic status or superficial labels."

"So you're complimenting me for not being a snob? And how would you know that about me?"

"I hear things," he says. "I heard you turned down an invitation to join the rich girls club."

"The what?"

"That sorority. You know the one I mean. Good thing you got out early in the recruitment process." He jams his glasses further up his nose bridge. "My personal view is that fraternities and sororities are elitist and exclusionary, a waste of time for regular folks. The rich gravitate toward each other anyway, so what's the point?"

"Things aren't always so black and white."

"When you grow up the way I did, they are."

The conversation has taken an unexpected turn, and I'm now curious to learn more about Justin and how he grew up, what circumstances shaped his world view, and how he sees his place in the world, especially here at Yale. Studying takes a back burner. He pulls up a chair, his hands clasped and resting on the desk.

"My parents divorced when I was young. My mother stayed home to raise us, myself and my brother and sister, while Dad worked as a general manager at a car dealership."

"That doesn't sound so bad."

"Nothing lasts forever, right? When I was ten, Dad lost his job. Our family never recovered. Dad wasn't nice to us once he started drinking. Mom got the brunt of it. He used to beat on her."

"Justin, I'm so sorry. That must have been hard for a kid to witness."

He shrugs with indifference, as if his experience is the most normal thing in the world. Then he continues, "Mom finally left him and they divorced. Haven't seen or heard from my dad since. Mom did her best. She moved us into a new neighborhood where she could afford the rent. She worked three jobs, you know."

"Wow. That must have been hard." What can I say? Even to my own ears, my responses sound like clichéd platitudes.

Justin goes on to explain that their new neighborhood was rough, but his mother was determined that her children wouldn't become urban statistics. Somehow, she managed to keep them together even if she spent most of her waking hours working. Justin practically raised his younger siblings.

"Your mother sounds like a warrior," I say. "Kudos to her."

"I owe her everything," he says. "She pushed and she never let me get caught up in all the bad stuff that surrounded us. Although money was always tight, she made a home for us. We didn't feel like we were worse off than anybody else. Then I come here and see how the other half lives."

His earlier comments make sense to me now, the intersection

of his two worlds. "Do you feel guilty about attending an Ivy League university? You shouldn't. You've earned it. Your mother sacrificed so you could be here. Nobody handed you anything for free."

He chugs down the last of the water from his bottle. "I know people in my neighborhood who never made it out, guys who were more talented than me. So why me and not them?"

"Your mother fought. Maybe she fought harder than the other moms. I don't know, Justin. Who really understands how the universe works? You're here for a purpose. Enjoy the ride instead of questioning everything. Do it for yourself. Do it for your mom, and those guys who didn't make it."

Silence passes between us. Justin has an intense look of contemplation on his face. Then he says, "Thanks for listening, Abbie. You're easy to talk to. I can tell you anything and you'll understand."

"Getting people to bare their souls is a special talent of mine," I joke. "Just ask my brother, Lee."

"I was wrong. You do have superpowers. Although you will disagree with me."

"Fine, Justin," I say chuckling. "I'll be your superhero with superpowers if you want me to."

"And don't forget you're the shiznit."

I'll accept that only because you insist."

"Glad we had this talk," he says.

"So how come you're so quiet in study group then?"

"Because I'm thinking the whole time," he says, pointing to his head.

"You're a special case, Justin Tate."

"Glad you think so, Abbie Cooper."

CHAPTER 12

BEFORE

ZAHRA AND I meet outside the Sterling Library after my study session with Justin. I remove the Hermès scarf from my bag and hand it to her.

"Too cute. Where did you buy it?"

"I didn't. My Humble Admirer sent it."

"Oh."

"I have to put a stop to this. Find out what's really going on."

"How?"

"Let's start with Ty. I'm going to search his apartment for clues. If I come up empty, I will keep looking until I uncover the truth."

"What?" Zahra's yell catches the attention of a couple of students passing by.

"I mean are you crazy?" she asks in a lower voice.

"I can't stand it any longer. Four notes in the past few weeks. Now this gift. He knows which building I reside in. No one has a clue how the gifts are delivered outside my door. I have to find out if it's Ty or if I should really be worried."

"I don't think you should search his place, Abbie. Ty

trusts you to respect the boundaries of your relationship. When he gave you the keys to his apartment, I don't think he meant for you to spy on him."

"I know it might be a bad idea, and ordinarily I would never dream of betraying his trust. But I don't like this uncertainty hanging over my head. I would rather find out it's Ty and ease my worries. I don't have a choice. If it's not Ty, it could be trouble. Haven't you seen the movies? He starts as Mr. Nice Guy, charming and sweet. Then halfway through the movie, he's a full-on psycho and some poor girl is running for her life."

On the other hand, it could be Justin, which means what? That it's really just a guy with a crush?

Zahra sighs loudly. "You could be right. I still don't like this idea, but it's the best one we got so far. Do me a favor. Don't get caught."

"That's why we're taking your car and you're going to be my lookout."

Zahra screws up her face in protest. "Seriously? I want no part of this deal, your plan to destroy your relationship with Ty. He's the only hot guy I know who treats me with respect."

"Come on. Don't be chicken." I poke her in the ribs.

Zahra grumbles under her breath and shoots me a dirty look.

"We'll pull into the parking garage. You stay, I'll go up and take a quick look. I'll be back before you can finish that pack of Oreo cookies you've been hiding in your bag. You better save me some."

"Why do I let you talk me into these things? Fine."

Zahra and I take the brief car trip from campus parking to the Metro Crown, a luxury apartment complex with great sprawling views of New Haven and easy access to dining, entertainment and culture. It's within walking distance of campus, but we need to make a quick getaway, so driving makes sense.

We pull into the underground parking garage and I stick the passkey into the slot. The gate opens and I slide into the nearest parking spot I can find near the elevator.

"I'll only be a minute," I say, as I leave. "If Ty comes home, he won't recognize your car right away. You know his car right?" It's a—"

"Matador Red Lexus GS Hybrid 450 H F Sport."

I look at Zahra like she's a freak of some kind. I don't even want to know why she knows his car so well, down to the shade of red.

"What? It's a nice looking car, hard to forget."

I take the elevator to the eighth floor. I step into the carpeted hallway, which is thankfully empty. I retrieve the spare key from my jacket pocket and open the door slowly.

I step into the apartment and call out. "Ty, are you home? It's me, Abbie."

Silence. I had to be sure. He could have decided to come home early. I call his name two more times but no response. Once I'm convinced the apartment is empty, I pace the living room for a few seconds, contemplating the best place to start looking.

I start with the bookshelf in the living room, pulling books out of their spots, and thumb through them. I place them back exactly as I found them. I'm mostly looking for books about love or romance, perhaps a book of poetry or *Love Letters of Great Men.* I have my mother to thank for this. She decided the *Sex and the City* movie would be a great choice for one of our recent mother-daughter bonding movie nights.

Nothing. Not that I expected to find something. I do a quick run through of the kitchen. Ty must have left in a hurry. There's spilled milk and a half eaten bowl of cereal on the otherwise pristine granite counter top. Ty keeps his private life private, so I won't find any declarations of undying love lying around. I know he has a spare computer in his bedroom with a flat screen monitor.

I climb up the stairs that lead to the bedrooms. I gently knock on his bedroom door, just in case. Eerie silence is my only companion.

His bedroom is spacious and bright with hardwood floors, white walls, and two large windows with a view of trees and another apartment building across the way. His bed is neat and made up. A few items of clothing spill out of the overflowing laundry basket in the corner near the large walk-in closet. The computer, perched on the small desk near the window, beckons me. But first, I scan the top of the dresser then quickly open the drawers in case anything significant is hidden there. I feel awful ransacking his stuff.

Panic overtakes me. This isn't right. I have to get out of here. I shut the drawer and stand still for a moment, assessing the room. Besides the computer, where could I look? Under the mattress? I dismiss the thought. The closet? Yeah, that sounds more reasonable. I open the double doors of the walk-in closet. Like his room, the closet is neat and organized: jackets, slacks dress shirts all have their place. I look up at the shelf and lift a few T-shirts and other items to see if anything is hidden underneath. I come up empty.

I turn my attention to the computer. I press the power button and wait for the machine to boot up. I nervously tap my fingers against the desk. The screen comes to life and I quickly type in the password Ty gave me just in case I ever needed to use this particular computer. An avalanche of guilt and shame slam into me. Zahra was right. When Ty gave me the keys to his apartment, it wasn't to invade his privacy.

I can't do this. I shut off the computer. When I get up to leave, the bedroom door is wide open. Ty leans against the wall, arms crossed tightly against his chest, with a look in his eye that sends shivers up and down my spine. Anger I can handle. Betrayal I understand, but what I see in his eyes is something that terrifies me. He now sees me as less than. His trust and respect have been diminished. That's worse than losing his friendship.

My legs feel weak, but I won't fall apart in front of him or throw myself on his mercy. If our friendship is going to be over, I don't want his last memory of me to be that of a sniveling Judas.

"What are you doing, Cooper?" His voice is barely audible, but I can't help but catch the bitter undertone.

I have no excuse. No justification that will suffice, so I remain quiet.

"I asked a you a question." He walks further into the room. "What's going on?"

"I was looking for something, but it isn't here," I stammer.

"Tell me what it is, maybe I can help you find it."

It's not really an offer of help. I've only ever seen that look on his face once before—when an over enthusiastic and drunken freshman wouldn't take no for an answer and started pawing me. It took three guys to pull Ty off him, and the freshman's face swelled to the size of a large grapefruit.

I fumble for an answer but none comes. "I'm sorry" is all I can come up with.

"Come on, Cooper. You can do better than that. I'm sure you can explain why you came to my apartment and ended up in my bedroom. I don't mind, but I don't think your visit is social. What are you looking for on my computer?"

My cell phone chimes in the pocket of my coat. I let it ring.

"I want an answer this decade," he says, the volume of his voice rising.

"I don't have one." I stare down at the floor.

"You weren't expecting me to come home at this hour of the day." He glances at the digital clock on the nightstand.

I look up. "No, I wasn't."

"So whatever you're looking for, you didn't want me to know about it."

I hang my head slightly, ashamed and embarrassed.

"I expected better from you, Cooper. Of all the stunts girls have pulled on me, I never thought my best friend would do this to me. I gave you free and open access to my home because we trust each other implicitly. I see now it was a mistake."

My phone chirps again. I don't dare reach for it. The tension in the room is thick.

"So that's it?" he asks.

"I got something in the mail and I thought you sent it."

He blinks in confusion, or maybe it's skepticism. I can't tell because I won't look him directly in the eye.

"If I had something for you, I would give it to you, not mail it."

"Well, it wasn't exactly mailed, it just arrived outside my dorm room."

"Oh, I see. So what was it?"

He thinks I'm lying.

"A note. It was unsigned."

"So you received an anonymous letter in your dorm and you thought I sent it. Come on, Cooper. Really?"

"It's true."

He extends his hand and I know what he's asking for. I reach for the key in my other pocket. I place it in his outstretched palm. I move past him without a backward glance.

"Bye, Cooper," he says.

"I'VE BEEN TEXTING you like crazy, but you wouldn't answer," Zahra says once I enter the car and shut the door. "What happened?"

"Just drive," I tell her.

"Ty busted you, didn't he?"

"I don't want to talk about it."

"You have to. What happened?" She reverses out of the garage.

"He found me in his bedroom turning off the computer."

"Oh, Abbie, I'm sorry. We knew there was a risk. I don't understand, I didn't see his car at all. I was just texting you to find out how things were going."

"He probably parked in front of the building, on the street. I didn't think of that."

"What did he say?"

"He asked me what I was doing there, and I had no answer." I explain the conversation to Zahra, and how I tried to tell him the truth at the last minute, but it was too late. He didn't believe me. The trust was already lost, and to put a period on it, he asked for the keys back.

"I really messed up. Ty will never look at me the same way again. That's the most painful part of this whole debacle."

"I know," she says, merging into traffic. "He just needs a little time to cool down. You and Ty will never be done with each other."

"You didn't see the way he looked at me. I'd rather not be his friend at all than have a shell of what we used to."

"You underestimate the strength of your friendship," she counters. "Ty adores you, Abbie. I can't see him kicking you out of his life forever."

"What's the point of being friends if he doesn't trust me? I know this makes me sound selfish and entitled, but I liked that he doted on me, that he cherished our friendship. I won't have that privilege anymore." I lean back in the front passenger seat and pout.

"I don't blame you for feeling that way, but you know what's even worse?"

"What could possibly be worse?"

"Now that you and Ty are on the outs, he's going to spend all his free time with Kristina Haywood."

"Ugh! You're such a good friend, Zahra. Thanks for bringing that up so I can spend the rest of the week seething with hatred for Kristina, and wallowing in self-pity and guilt."

"You forgot to add self-loathing," she points out. "You did betray the trust of someone you've been tight with since high school. Someone who treated you like *the* Queen in his life. Just saying."

As much as I don't want to admit it, she's right. She has this way of making the truth hurt extra, twisting the knife a little deeper.

"I know that." I slump into the seat in a defeated heap as we pull into the parking lot. My traitorous heart climbs up to the back of my throat and lodges itself there so I can't speak, not that I want to.

I may have lost my best friend for good because of stupid notes by some random person who's playing cat and mouse games with me. I just *had* to try and find out who was behind it. This game costs too much. I can't afford any more losses.

CHAPTER 13

BEFORE

I T WAS TIME Spencer threw her a bone. She left five messages in two days. The messages were always the same: Why hasn't he called? She misses him, she worries, on and on. He knew he should care that she worried, that it was cruel to not return her calls for long stretches of time, but she was a liar. A woman whose lies he couldn't forgive. Silence was his way of punishing her. He would call her back eventually, have a sixty-second conversation, forty-five if he could help it—enough to remind her the sky wasn't falling and he was a grown man, not a child.

Diana Rossdale, his sweet, beautiful, but deceitful mother had caused a huge mess he now had to clean up. Her betrayal had created complications for him, but in time, with careful planning and patience, it would all work out. When he was done, they would no longer be able to pretend that he didn't exist. Losing was not an option.

He shook off the agitating thoughts. Someone had caught his attention as he rounded the corner of the Literature & English section of the library. The guy's back was to him, but he was certain it was Justin Tate. He had a sketchbook and was drawing furiously, with deep concentration, although Spencer couldn't see his face. He had to be careful how he approached. Several students wandered around, some searching for books, others studying or writing papers on their laptops.

He casually walked over to where Justin was seated and peeked over his shoulder. Justin was so focused on his task that he didn't even sense the presence behind him. Spencer glimpsed a sketch of a girl in a black leather jacket, short black leather skirt, and black, knee-high leather boots. Next to her were the words *Black Diamond*. She carried some kind of sword, labeled *Sword of Truth*.

"What's her super power?" Spencer asked.

Justin jerked and quickly closed his sketchbook. Spencer pulled out a chair and sat. "You're not going to tell me? She's a superhero right, one that you just created?"

"It's none of your business."

"Don't be paranoid, Justin. I was just admiring your work, that's all."

"Well it's private, not for anyone to see," he snapped.

"Not even Abbie? It *is* her in the sketch, right? Black Diamond? That's a cool name for a female superhero."

Justin lowered his gaze and shifted about in his seat.

"Does Abbie know you're obsessed with her?"

Justin looked at him with an intense gaze, jaw clenched. "Abbie is my friend and study partner. I respect her. But a frat boy like you wouldn't understand that. To have a friendship with a smart, attractive woman without trying to figure out how you can get into her bed. I saw you all over her at that party last week. It was disgusting."

Spencer wanted to punch the sanctimonious jerk in the mouth, but he restrained himself. As angry as the comments had made him, this self-righteous douchebag was valuable. He'd made Spencer a lot of money. Justin was a member of the Aces Club, an elite, secretive group of math geeks who used their skills to gamble and win big—everything from blackjack to poker to sports betting and craps. The group was led by Lucy Knox, a Mathematics Ph.D. candidate who cleaned up in Vegas more than once.

"Don't be a hater, bruh. Abbie Cooper is way out of your league. Stick to card counting and betting. I'm sure you'll eventually find a nice girl, but don't waste your time fantasizing about Abbie. It ain't happening."

"You know what ain't happening?" Defiance radiated off Justin. "You and Abbie. She'll see right through whatever game you got going. And she's nice to everybody. So don't misread the signals. *Bruh.*"

Spencer felt his teeth grind together. He opened and closed his fists multiple times. Justin had just made an enemy of him. He would keep an eye on him, and if Justin continued to get out of line, Spencer would have to take care of him by revealing his secret to the right people.

"See that you stay focused during the next big game," Spencer said with as much disdain as he could muster. "And for the record, I don't think Abbie is interested in slumming it. I mean, you're from two completely different worlds that just don't mesh. She's nice to everyone. Don't misread the signals, bruh."

Justin gave him the middle finger as he got up from his seat to leave. Spencer returned the gesture with a wide, devious grin.

CHAPTER 14

BEFORE

A WEEK GOES by and nothing. No text messages, emails or phone calls. Ty has been avoiding me, and it hurts. We've had disagreements before, but he always reached out within a day or two, even if it was to beg me to come over to make one of my famous home-cooked meals.

"You're just going to accept defeat?" Zahra sits on the floor of her dorm room polishing her toenails again, a hideous green this time. I'm perched at the edge of the bed twirling her stuffed animal.

"It's been a week. I think he's said everything there is to say, unlike my Humble Admirer."

"What do you mean?"

I reach for the bag I dumped on her desk when I first arrived. I pull out a white gift box and hand it to Zahra. "See for yourself."

She removes the top box and stares at what's inside. "Is he for real?"

I roll my eyes. She pulls the gift all the way out of the box—a beautiful portrait doll wearing a white, off-the-shoulder ball gown, her hair in an elegant up-do.

"Wow! That's unbelievable. She's a perfect replica of you. This guy just took it another level."

"Read the note."

She reaches into the box again and pulls out the note. Typewritten, and in the same font as the others.

My Sweetest Abbie,

You may think this latest token of my affection and esteem is too much, but I say it's not. Nothing can ever capture your true beauty and essence but I wanted you to have this memento. Do you remember that night when you wore this stunning evening gown, the New Year's Eve Ball at Bedford Hills? I'm sure all the other girls paled in comparison. Soon, I will reveal myself. I only hope you won't be disappointed.

Your Humble Admirer

Zahra returns the note to the box and frowns. "What is he talking about?"

I explain to her that in my senior year of high school, I dated Christian Wheeler, and that I spent New Year's Eve with his family at their annual Black Tie Charity Ball.

Zahra gapes at me, her eyes wide with shock. "When you say you dated Alan Wheeler's son, you're not talking about the Chairman and CEO of Levitron-Blair, the company that owns all those cable channels, TV networks and movie theatres, and radio stations, are you? Because you never mentioned that to me. That's the kind of stuff a

71

friend would tell a friend. So I can only assume you mean a different Alan Wheeler."

I thump my forehead with my knuckles. "It just never came up. It's not something I talk about much."

Zahra throws a venomous glare in my direction. She leaves the sofa, heads to the desk, and boots up her laptop. She taps on a few keys and then scrolls. She stops, stares at the screen, and then looks back at me.

"What?" I join her at the desk. She Googled Christian, and several photos came up.

"I so hate you right now. How could you not tell me that you dated this beautiful boy? Look at him."

I roll my eyes and head back to the sofa. "Now that you've sufficiently yelled at me, can we please get back to the issue at hand?"

"Do you keep in touch with him?" she asks, ignoring my request.

"Yes, and his mother too. Now can we talk about the fact that a complete stranger, who's getting creepier by the minute, had a doll made of me wearing the gown I wore that night, a gown that's still hanging in my closet at home."

Zahra threads one of her curls through her fingers, straightening it out the way she does when thinking. After the curl springs back to its natural state, she says, "What if Christian *is* the Humble Admirer? What if he's not over you and wants another shot, but he's too scared to tell you to your face? You never said why the two of you broke up."

The question is one that has never occurred to me. Over the past two years, since we left St. Matthews, Christian and I have kept in touch and even met up on a few occasions.

We've joked about his love life. I never sensed that he was interested in rekindling our relationship, which I would have told him was a bad idea anyway. It would be silly, considering the reason we broke up in the first place.

"I don't think so, Zahra. When Christian and I were together, we were straightforward and honest with each other. He wouldn't have hesitated to say he wanted me back if that was the case. Besides, he saw what I went through senior year of high school, with that stalker who was sending me anonymous and threatening notes. He wouldn't use the MO of anonymity. He just wouldn't do that to me.

"Plus, he's at the University of Texas, Austin. We ended our romance because we're realists. We knew it wouldn't last with us attending college in different parts of the country, so why bother pretending it would? Remaining friends works for us."

"So where does that leave things? Are you thinking this secret admirer attended the ball too?"

"Either he was present at the New Year's Eve Ball the same time I was or he was at the mansion at a later date and saw the painting."

"What painting?"

"Christian painted a portrait of me from the night of the ball. He said it was just for him and he would never show it to anyone. I begged to see it, and he brought it with him later that summer when he came to visit me. He took it back with him."

"If Mr. Anonymous was at the party that night, why wait all this time to start communicating with you?"

"I don't know. If this guy, whoever he is, was there that

night, something nefarious is definitely going on."

Zahra scoots off the sofa and stands in the middle of the room. She then moves to her desk drawer and pulls out a pack of Oreo cookies.

"You want one?"

"Yeah, five."

She hands me the pack and I scarf down five cookies in minutes.

"You know what you have to do, right?" she says. "You have to find out from Christian if he showed the painting to anyone else. If he didn't, then we know the guy attended the ball and that's how he knows what you looked like. If Christian did show the painting to other people, then you have a good shot at narrowing down the suspects."

"I can't imagine Christian showing the painting to anyone. He's private about his art. He showed me his work before he showed his own mother. I had to convince him to share it with her."

"Think about it." Zahra licks the cream off a cookie. "What if he showed it to one of his guy friends and the guy developed a crush on you?"

"That would mean the friend goes to Yale and asked Christian a ton of questions about me. As far as I know, Christian doesn't have shady friends. I mean, what would be the point of waiting two years after he saw the painting if as you say, he developed a crush?"

"Unless he didn't see the painting two years ago," Zahra says, her eyes lighting up. "What if he saw it last year or over the summer? The fall semester just started. That's when the notes and the roses started to appear."

"So all I would need to do is confirm with Christian whether or not the painting is still private."

"And if he says he's shown it to others, then you have nothing to worry about. You said Christian doesn't have psycho friends, so maybe this guy sends anonymous notes because he knows you and Christian dated and didn't want to scare you off the idea of him."

"So he's hoping that sending me the letters and roses will show me he's a really sweet guy and I should give him a chance when he does eventually reveal himself?"

"Exactly," Zahra says, snapping her fingers.

I focus my attention on the wall above the desk, the photo of Zahra and Dahlia at a family reunion. Something about this situation doesn't add up. It's difficult to put into words.

"He's watching me, Zahra. The fact that he mentioned it in the notes and tells me not to worry, that he will 'reveal himself' doesn't make me any less disturbed."

Zahra sighs. "I know. You really are worried, aren't you?"

"I am. My instincts tell me something is off and I need to pay attention."

"Christian could help clear up this whole thing."

I look her square in the eye. "And what if he can't?"

CHAPTER 15

BEFORE

IT'S EARLY EVENING, and after I pack for the weekend trip home, I dump a bag of groceries into my car and take the brief drive to Ty's apartment. I pull into the parking garage, kill the engine, and place my head on the steering wheel. I can do this, I tell myself. I messed up and I have to set things right. I'll go in there, apologize with maturity and sincerity, cook a delicious meal as a peace offering, and then leave. I'm supposed to meet up with Spencer afterward, anyway.

I arrive at the apartment, prop the grocery bag under one arm, and knock on the door with my free hand. The handle turns and the door opens. I freeze. I feel the bag slipping, but I'm powerless to stop it from hitting the ground and spilling the contents.

Right there in front of me stands Kristina Hayward wearing *his* shirt. Her long, dark hair is a mess, her eyes bright and shiny like a new penny.

"Um," I begin, and then stop. Neither one of us knows what to say, so I bend down to pick up the spilled groceries.

Kristina does the same, and we do this in strained silence.

"Hey Kristina, have you seen . . ."

We both look up from our task, as if programmed to react to his voice and presence. He's right behind Kristina. A white towel is casually draped around his waist, his bronzed torso dripping with beads of water. My eyes laser in on a tattoo that starts at his shoulder blade and extends to the top of his arm—a tattoo of a man and a topless woman wrapped in a passionate embrace. I didn't know he had that tattoo. I want to move, run away, save myself from this embarrassing moment, but my feet won't budge.

I force my brain to form words. The fog starts to lift slowly. "I'm sorry, I should have called first. I just came by to say I'm sorry, really, really sorry."

I forget about the groceries and bolt out of there. I don't stop running until I get to my car in the garage and shut the door. A sudden burning in my chest is gaining traction. I try to catch my breath. A headache pushes to the front of my skull.

A loud knock on the driver side window startles me. It's Ty. He must have been right on my heels when I ran like I was being chased by a pack of wild dogs who wanted to maul me to death. He's wearing only a t-shirt and jeans, his wet hair still dripping.

I wind down the window with the push of a button. "Yes," I say, my voice calm and steady.

"I didn't know you were coming."

"Obviously."

"Why don't you come back to the apartment?"

"I don't think so."

He disappears and then reappears at the passenger side door. He gestures for me to open the door. I hesitate. He's persistent.

I unlock the door and he climbs in. I look straight ahead, mostly into the concrete walls of the garage.

"Look at me, Cooper," he commands.

I won't.

"Come on. Don't leave me hanging."

I finally look at him. "Why are you here, in the car with me? Shouldn't you be with Kristina?"

He ignores my question. "What's going on with you? Why have you been acting strange lately? I'm worried."

"Don't be. You have enough to fret about."

"Are you mad about Kristina? Is that why you left in a hurry?"

The question catches me off guard, although I'm not sure why it did. When I saw him with Kristina at the frat party, I thought they were just hanging out for the evening. But seeing her at his place, I can't describe what it did to my insides. Ty isn't the fooling around or the rack up the conquest type. If a girl is at his apartment, wearing his shirt, she means something to him. Makes me want to throw a tantrum that would make a toddler proud.

I swallow hard. "Ty, what you do and with whom is none of my business. I came by to apologize because what I did the other day was wrong."

"Then why did you do it? You're not acting like yourself. Something is wrong, Cooper, and I'm not leaving this car until you tell me what it is."

"You don't have to babysit me. I can take care of myself."

"I know that. But it doesn't mean I should stop caring. You know I will never stop, right?"

"I thought you had written me off for violating your privacy."

"I admit I was angry, but I also know you weren't behaving normally. Whatever is troubling you must be huge for you to do what you did. What I don't understand is why you won't tell me. We tell each other everything, Cooper."

"Really? You didn't tell me you and Kristina were serious."

Why do you keep bringing Kristina into the conversation? Stop.

"Anyway, it doesn't matter," I say quickly. "You don't have to share every detail of your life with me. You're allowed to keep certain things private. I'm happy for you."

"You mean that?" He eyes me with a curious glance. "Because Kristina is a great girl. And she thinks you're cool."

I don't have a comeback. Kristina is obviously important to him, and he's asking me to get with the program. "Sure, Ty. Kristina is a great girl."

He holds my hand and squeezes. "What's wrong, Cooper? I can't help you if I don't know what the problem is."

Don't cry like a big baby. Keep calm and level-headed.

"It's like I told you the other day. Anonymous packages have been arriving at my dorm room. At first, I thought they were harmless, but now I'm not so sure." I give him the run-down on my Humble Admirer, the gifts, the roses and the notes, and why the last gift has me uneasy.

"I had no idea all of this was going on. Why didn't you tell me sooner?" His tone is accusing.

79

"It's not your job to rescue me every time something goes wrong in my life. You have to get over this hero complex."

He frowns. "What has gotten into you? I've never heard you talk this way before. We're friends. Whatever concerns you concerns me. That's how it works. You don't get to pick and choose when we're friends and when we're not, when our friendship is convenient and when it isn't."

"I knew I shouldn't have said anything." I look out the window, anything to avoid looking at him, but he's having none of it.

He reaches over and turns my face toward him. "Don't be like that."

I let out an exasperated sigh. "Like what?"

"Defensive and bratty."

"If that's the way you feel, then get out of my car. You should go back to Kristina so you don't have to deal with my attitude."

"That's the third time you've brought up Kristina since I've been here. Are you jealous of her for some reason?"

Well, yeah. She gets to touch you and kiss you and feel you . . .

I bite the inside of my cheek, and then glare at him. "What is wrong with you? Why would you ask me such a ridiculous question? I don't know anything about Kristina except that the two of you have been spending time together. She doesn't register on my radar in the least. I have serious problems I need to address, and you're asking me if I'm jealous of your girlfriend?"

I sound like a shrew, and his eyes widen in surprise. I didn't mean to yell at him. The situation must be stressing me out more than I care to acknowledge. I'm about to break out into sobs and I struggle to hold back the tears. The last thing I need is to fall apart right now. I'm such a big baby. I promised myself I wouldn't do this, and now . . .

"I'm sorry. I didn't mean to upset you." He reaches over and pulls me toward him. "Come here," he says, his voice gentle and soothing.

Because I'm a big sap, I go willingly into his embrace. I greedily inhale the scent of him. He must have showered with the Bleu De Chanel bath soap he's so fond of lately—a sensual, aromatic fragrance that combines cedar and citrus. I mentally slap myself. Cut it out. He was just *with* another woman, for goodness sake. That unpleasant thought jolts me out of my pathetic meltdown. I swipe my nose and straighten up.

"Let me see your phone," he says.

"Why?"

"Just do it, Cooper."

I hand him the phone without further protest. After a couple of taps, I ask, "What are you doing?"

"I'm opening your Companion App so I can add Eric and Hak as companions. That way, if you can't reach me for whatever reason and you feel unsafe on campus, you can message them."

I say nothing. It would be useless to protest because he would ignore me. At least he doesn't hate me after what I did, so I should shut up and let him do what he always does.

"I'm getting you a Taser, and it wouldn't be a bad idea to take self-defense classes." He hands me the phone.

I neither agree nor disagree. His friends Erik and Hak treat me like their little sister. I wonder if this will set off any

81

alarm bells with them as it has with Ty? I don't want to cause any unnecessary worry, since I have no clue if my admirer poses a serious threat or not. I suppose it's better to be cautious.

"Don't you think you're going overboard?"

"Not in the least. We can't take chances. As you said, this guy is watching you. He could be dangerous. I don't care how innocent the notes sound. Hiding behind anonymity and some vague promise to reveal himself doesn't inspire confidence."

"You're right." Until I can get answers from Christian, I have to operate under the assumption that danger is a possibility.

"And from now on, you check in with me at least twice a day. Even if it's just to say you're okay or nothing strange occurred that day. Don't fight me on this." With one hand on my knee, he looks at me, his eye contact strong and determined.

"I wasn't going to object."

"Even if you did, I wouldn't back off."

We chat for a few more minutes, and Ty makes me promise to let him know right away if I receive any more notes and gifts, or if anything out of the ordinary occurs. I notice the clock on the dashboard. I'm supposed to meet up with Spencer at the Pub Pizzeria. I'm late.

CHAPTER 16

AFTER

"I KNOW IT'S awkward Cooper, but it's necessary," Ty says. "I promise I won't look."

"How are you going to see what you're doing?"

"I'm going to be a doctor one day. I'm well-versed in human anatomy."

"That's not funny."

"I'm not laughing."

Ty and I are in the bathroom, having a serious discussion about how he's supposed to help me with my bath without looking. I already feel like a jerk. He ran me a warm bath, scented the space with my favorite fragrance, jasmine oil, and even brought in his phone to play soothing music. I still haven't regained full use of my injured arm. It's only been twenty-four hours since my release from the hospital, but I'm impatient. I expect my arm to magically heal because I need to get back to my life. No such luck. Physical therapy is going to be painful.

I slouch against the sink in a long t-shirt, looking at Ty with trepidation. When I was cleaned up at the hospital, it was only sort of a bath, and there was always a nurse on hand to assist me.

"I'll leave once you're comfortably in the tub. I'll be right outside the door if you need more help. Just yell. But let's get you into the tub first."

"Fine," I say, resigned to my fate.

He slips his arms around me for support as I place one foot and then the other into the tub. The water is warm and inviting, as if it's been waiting patiently for me to get in. He lowers me with such care, one would think I was an infant. I sit with my legs outstretched. Now he has to remove the t-shirt. I hope the frothy bubbles will cover my breasts.

Ty fumbles in the water for a good angle to grab the t-shirt and pull it over my head without looking.

"Lift your right arm," he instructs me. "I'll pull it out of the armhole of the t-shirt. Once you do that, it makes it easier to pull over your head and down past the cast."

I do as I'm told, and after the t-shirt is successfully removed, I sink deeper into the tub.

"Thank you for being a gentleman," I tease.

"I don't know if you'll feel that way by the time this is over." "What do you mean?" I ask sharply.

"I have to wash your hair. And your face, arms and neck. Your legs too."

"Oh." I haven't thought that far. "Well get on with it. It will save us both awkwardness the faster it's done."

His eyes lock with mine, shining with playful mischief and something else. "I like to take my time," he says.

Without taking his eyes off me, he strokes my arm with a washcloth.

"Let me know if this is too hard."

"It's just the right amount of pressure."

"Good."

A stretch of awkward silence fills the space as he moves the small towel up and down my arm. I tremble involuntarily.

"Is the water getting cold?" he asks.

"No, it's fine." He knows perfectly well the water isn't getting cold.

"Cooper, I wanted to talk to you about something. Maybe you've already thought of it, but I wanted to bring it up anyway."

"What is it?"

"You should see someone. A therapist, I mean."

I swallow hard and bite the corners of my thumb. My nail biting has been a nervous habit I've had since high school. I know I'm supposed to see a therapist to work through the trauma, but I'm not ready to bare my soul. I'm still coming to terms with the event, with the memory loss, struggling to decide if I want to expose myself to scrutiny.

I sigh. "I guess it's part of the process, but I can't worry about that right now."

"I'm really concerned."

"About what?"

"What happened to you isn't normal. Yet, you haven't freaked out or gone bonkers. That scares me."

"I thought we agreed we weren't going to allow this event to change me. That's what he wants, if the so-called Humble Admirer is behind the assault. I can't wrap my brain around the kind of twisted, diabolical mind it takes to do something like this. How do you pretend—so convincingly to pursue someone with sweet, caring words and thoughtful gifts, and then just like that, turn into this depraved animal? It doesn't make sense."

"He's obviously a psychopath who may have done this before. He stayed well hidden in the shadows. Nobody knew how he was getting those gifts and notes to you. He had to have known you would attend the post-game party to put his sick plan into motion. But Cooper, as horrific as this is, you can't hold everything in. It's not healthy."

I look him square in the eye. "I want revenge in the worst way, and it's all I think about when I'm alone. I want him found and I want him to suffer. I want him to feel what it's like to be violated and at the mercy of someone with no conscience. I keep those thoughts to myself because I know they can be destructive if I dwell on them too long. But it's one of the few things that keep me from falling apart. Do you understand?"

"Cooper," he says softly, "it's okay to fall apart. Sometimes that needs to happen so we can get back up again."

"No! I won't fall apart. I won't be his victim a second time. I'm not going to see a shrink, and I'm not going to curl up into a ball and die."

CHAPTER 17

BEFORE

I REACH FOR the heavy black door handle of the Pub, known for its excellent pizza, fun ambience and a dance floor in the back somewhere. I can't stand my own company right now and look forward to chatting with Spencer to get my mind off my troubles. The place is packed, a mixture of locals, the Yale crowd and employees of nearby biotech firms. I find Spencer at a booth, looking down at his phone. I slide in the opposite seat and apologize. Seems I'm developing a habit of keeping him waiting.

"I was just about to text you," he says. "I thought you had changed your mind about meeting me."

"No. I got held up."

"You okay?" His face brims with concern.

"Yes."

My phone buzzes, and I reach for it in my purse. Ordinarily I wouldn't pick up, but ever since Dad went into remission, I get nervous something could go wrong at any time and the family might need to reach me. So I pick up my phone whenever it rings, as long as it's within reach.

I apologize to Spencer again. It's a text message from Lee.

Lee: All ready for tomorrow? I can pick you up a little earlier if you'd like.

Me: What time?

Lee: Around 10:00 am.

Me: Sounds perfect!

Lee: See you then.

"I'm so sorry, Spencer. That was my brother, Lee. He's picking me up tomorrow and moved up the time." I owe him an explanation for my rudeness. I would be irritated if he pulled that stunt on me without an explanation.

"Not a problem, Abbie. You're busy. I get it. You're close with Lee, aren't you?"

I can't help but smile. "Yes, Lee and I have a special bond."

"Tell me about him," he says, his face attentive. "He's your half brother, you said the other day."

"Yes. My mother had him when she was young. He and I became close when I was in high school, at St. Matthews Academy. He was one of the guidance counselors there. Back then, I didn't know he was my brother."

"How come?"

"Because he was adopted. As I said, my mother had him when she was very young and couldn't take care of him. We became close—Anyway, I couldn't have asked for a better big brother."

"What were you about to say?"

Be careful. Don't reveal too much about your family,

especially since you don't know that much about Spencer.

"Nothing. Just that Lee and I have a special bond."

"What's he like?"

"Intense. He's a straight arrow who needs to lighten up. In spite of that, he has a big heart, although he tries to hide it."

"Your family is so fascinating."

"We're just like any other family. What about yours?"

"Nothing much to tell. My sister Brynn is a freshman at the University of Maryland, so our mother is an empty nester."

"What about your father?"

Spencer looks uneasy, or maybe I imagined it. "My parents are divorced. I don't see my father much."

"Sorry to hear that, Spencer."

"Don't be. It's for the best."

"You don't like your father?"

"I don't know my father," he replies, bitterly. "He left when I was six. Before that, he worked a lot and was never around. I have very few memories of him."

"I see. Unfortunately that's a common story, although I'm sure that hurt you."

"It did but I've learned to adapt."

He's obviously uncomfortable talking about his father. I thought I saw a flicker of what I could only interpret as hatred in his eyes. But it disappeared quickly, so I'm not sure I saw it at all.

"My parents worked a lot too. But they made time for us, my brother Miles and me."

"Is that why you're so driven, because of your parents?"

"That's a big part of it. They gave us a comfortable life, but they also insisted on hard work and discipline."

He swallows repeatedly. "That's what I like about you, Abbie. You're grounded and don't take your privilege for granted. You have every reason to play that card but you don't. It's refreshing."

"Don't be too quick to compliment me. I have my moments. You should see me in hair and makeup for my mother's show. If the makeup is too caked on or wardrobe gives me something that's too short or revealing, I turn into a total diva and refuse to go on the air until they fix it. True story," I conclude with a giggle.

He laughs out loud and says he doesn't believe I have a diva bone in my body. We order food and return to the booth—a Greek salad and fries for me, and a Bacon Cheeseburger and onion rings for him.

"Why were you upset earlier?"

"What do you mean?" I dip a fry in some ketchup and pop it in my mouth.

"When you walked in here, you were upset. I could see it in your face, the way your body tensed."

"So you're an expert on my body, now?" I'm only half-teasing.

"I hope to be," he says, his voice low, lips parted.

"Spencer, you're being naughty." I fold my arms across my chest and let out an exaggerated sigh. "We already talked about that. It was part of the rules, remember?"

"I don't like rules. Besides, we have a bet going, one I intend to win."

"What bet is that?"

"To prove that you're secretly a bad girl."

"You might be right about that."

"What happened?"

"It's the reason I was upset earlier. I did something I shouldn't have. I knew it was wrong, but did it anyway. The worst part is, I did it to someone who means a lot to me. How is that for your bad girl?"

"Care to talk about it? I'm a good listener."

I'm not about to reveal to Spencer the circumstances that led to me betraying Ty's trust. In fact, I don't even know why I brought it up in the first place.

"I betrayed his trust. I tried to fix it. I think he forgave me, so it'll be okay but it's still upsetting."

I flash back to the image of Kristina wearing Ty's shirt. She looked too comfortable in his space, like she belonged there. Ty is a grown man and can have whomever he wants over his apartment. I'm not his babysitter—yet I didn't like the image. Maybe if it was anyone else but Kristina. She's too good to be true with her perfect looks, perfect body, and save the world complex.

I can see why Ty likes her, beyond her looks. They're both highly intelligent, goal-oriented people who also share an Indian heritage in common, Ty because of his dad Bobby and Kristina because of her mother. In spite of those qualities, something about her bugs me. I still feel that she can't be trusted.

I shake off the thoughts and notice Spencer watching me intently. "Was this friend Ty?"

I nod.

"It doesn't surprise me that he forgave you."

"Don't let me off that easy." I cram salad into my mouth. Spencer has barely touched his food. "It was a bit embarrassing. I went over to apologize and Kristina was there. Talk about awkward."

"Kristina, the girl he came to the party with the night we met?"

"That's the one."

"Does it surprise you that they're hooking up?"

I cock my head to one side and give his question some thought. Ty isn't the hooking up type unless he changed on me, which I doubt. So the answer would be yes, I was surprised to find her at his apartment with that stupid post-coital glow on her face and that smirk she tried to disguise.

"No, I wasn't surprised. I was prepared to cook a quick meal as a peace offering and get out of there. I didn't know he would have company. But I dropped by without warning him I was coming over."

"Well there you go. You wanted to surprise him with a peace offering and you got surprised instead. You shouldn't beat yourself up. Ty wouldn't want you to either."

"Why are you being so sweet?"

"Because you're sweet," he says bluntly.

My Sweetest Abbie. The salutation from all the notes sent by my so-called Humble Admirer pops into my head. Could it be Spencer? I dismiss the thought yet again. Spencer and I had already met when the last notes and gifts arrived—the Hermès scarf and the porcelain doll in my likeness. If it were him, there'd be no logical reason to keep up the charade.

"Are you flirting with me, Spencer?" I tilt my head to one side.

He traps me with his firm gaze. "No. If I were flirting with you, I would do this."

He reaches over and runs his index finger over my arm, slowly, his touch light as a feather.

Before I can react, I hear, "Hi, Abbie."

I look up, startled. Spencer pulls back and rests his hands in his lap. Justin Tate has appeared out of thin air, standing inches from our booth. His bright, friendly smile is focused on me.

"Oh hi, Justin," I say. "How are you?"

"Fine, now that I've seen you."

Spencer visibly stiffens, but Justin has yet to acknowledge Spencer's presence. How strange. Do they know each other, and if so, is there bad blood between them?

"You see me all the time, Justin."

"It's never enough."

Spencer interjects, "Thanks for stopping by—Justin, is it? As you can see, Abbie and I are on a date, so we would appreciate it if you kept it moving."

That was harsh. And I can speak for myself, Spencer.

Justin glares at Spencer but won't budge. Then he says to me, "I'll see you next Tuesday, Abbie."

"Next Tuesday?" I ask stupidly.

"We have a big probability and statistics exam coming up. Our study group is meeting. Don't tell me you forgot?"

"Forgot? Um, no, I didn't forget."

"Great. I'll see you then. Looking forward to it."

And just as quickly as he appeared, he disappears into the masses.

The evening has taken a strange turn. Why the hostility between the two? I decide the direct approach would be best.

"Do you and Justin know each other?" I ask Spencer.

"No," he says, his voice flat.

"Are you sure? I caught this weird vibe between the two of you."

"Not from my end. He was interrupting us and I just wanted him to leave. Sorry if that's harsh. My time with you is precious, and I don't want anyone or anything interrupting it."

"Precious?"

"You're busy. I know you go out of your way to make time to see me and I appreciate it."

"Everybody is busy these days. I'm not unique in that regard."

"Didn't you see the way Justin was looking at you?"

"What way?"

He chuckles. "You don't know much about guys do you?"

"Only a little."

"That guy is crushing on you. He was not happy to see us together."

Spencer says this with conviction. I think back to my last conversation with Justin and how he opened up to me about his childhood and his family situation. Perhaps Spencer is right.

"Maybe he does," I concede. "He's harmless, though."

"He's going to ask you out," Spencer says.

"He won't."

"I bet he does," Spencer insists.

I paste a smile on my face. The emotional undercurrents I observed go beyond male testosterone. You don't flat out ignore someone you just met, even if the guy is hanging out with a girl you like. A cold and unenthusiastic "nice to meet you" is the way most people would handle that situation. But that didn't happen here. Both Spencer and Justin lied to me.

CHAPTER 18

BEFORE

THE UBER DRIVER pulls up behind a long line of cabs and luxury cars near the entrance of my midtown Manhattan destination—The Ritz-Carlton Central Park. I thank him and exit the car. The doorman opens the door, and I step into the lobby.

When Christian texted me last night to say he was in New York and wanted us to meet up, I took it as a sign. I ditched the idea of heading home for the weekend. He insisted that he come to Connecticut, but I wanted to get away from campus. What better place to escape to than New York City?

I walk into the dimly lit lobby of the hotel with uniformed staff behind the reception desk checking guests in and out, and bellhops with luggage carts accompanying guests to the elevators. Christian is treating me to lunch, and we agreed to meet in the hotel's Auden Bistro & Bar.

I spot him right away at a corner table with a view of Central Park—his bushy, wheat blond hair covers his eyes as he looks down at his phone. I make my way through the crowded area of wait staff and guests being seated.

"What's so fascinating on that phone?" I ask.

He dumps the phone on the table, comes around, and pulls me into a big enthusiastic hug that lifts me off the ground. His Spanish-blue eyes glitter like jewels as we both sit.

"You look great as always. Still haven't changed at all."

"Neither have you." He's added a few pounds of muscle to his lean frame, but it suits him.

"I'm glad you could make it."

"Your timing was perfect. I needed to get away. How are Mr. Wheeler and Katherine?"

"Dad is Dad. Still the dealmaker and wants everyone to know that Levitron-Blair is firmly under his command. Mom took on a part-time consulting gig for some think tank in DC."

"We have so much catching up to do." I prefer to ease into the conversation about the real reason I'm here.

"You first. I can see you're doing just fine," he says, with an appreciative gaze.

"Really, Christian?" I scold.

"What? Just because we aren't dating anymore doesn't mean I can't admire the view."

"You will never change. I feel sorry for the girls of UT Austin."

"They have nothing to worry about. You've spoiled me. I'm much more discerning since we dated."

"Is that so?" I tap a finger against the tabletop.

"Yes. A guy can change, can't he? Just last week, a freshman hottie made me an irresistible offer, but I politely declined. You should be proud of me."

I give him a quiet round of applause and we both crack up.

"I miss you, Abbie," he says seriously. "I miss how funny you are, and that I can tell you anything and you won't judge me. I miss how you could tell me off one minute and be vulnerable the next."

"We're still friends, aren't we?"

"You know what I mean."

"We happened a long time ago."

"It's only been two years," he counters.

"A lifetime ago for us. We were kids, trying to figure out who were, and we still are."

"You always knew who you were. Even in high school. That's one of the things that attracted me to you."

"I thought you were drawn to me because of my 'considerable assets.' At least, that's what you told me when you first started showing up at my locker."

He grins in embarrassment. "Yes, I did say that. And you straightened me out right away."

"I couldn't let you get away with it, could I?"

Against the backdrop of clanking silverware and the chatter of lunch patrons, we continue catching up. A waiter comes by to take our order. We forgo appetizers and go straight for the meal: grilled NY strip with a Caesar salad for me, and salmon for Christian.

"I have a serious question for you," I say after the waiter takes off to place the orders.

"Go ahead."

I take a deep breath and tuck a loose lock of hair behind my ears. "It's about that painting you made of me."

"What about it?"

"Did you show it to anyone?"

He blows out a short breath. "What happened?"

I bring him up to speed on the situation and how the last note made specific reference to the New Year's Eve Ball. I also mention the doll and my suspicion that the sender either attended the ball or saw the painting and had the doll created from that image.

He chugs down his water and places the empty glass on the table.

"And you have no idea who this guy is?"

"None whatsoever."

"Do you think he's dangerous?"

"I don't know for sure. So far, he seems harmless, sweet almost. From everything he says, he hasn't worked up the courage to speak to me in person. He says he will reveal himself soon, as if he was reassuring me I have nothing to be afraid of."

"But you are?"

"I wasn't until the doll arrived."

"Huh." Christian rubs his neck. "For the longest while, I kept it in my room. One day, Mom came in to talk to me and noticed it. She really liked it. It was the first time she had seen any of my work and she was so excited about it. You were the one who told me I should share my work with her, to help mend our relationship.

"Anyway," he continues, "she told me the painting was too beautiful to stay hidden away in my room. She said it should be placed somewhere more conspicuous. I had it hung on the wall above the grand staircase. I thought it made sense, since that was the image I captured in the painting, you coming down the grand staircase."

"So anyone could have seen it?"

"Right. I got tons of compliments about it, by the way. I still think it's my best work to date."

"You always know how to make a girl feel special," I say, teasing him.

"I don't have to make you feel special." He lowers his voice. "You just are."

Silence falls over our table as we each retreat into our thoughts. The waiter comes by with the meals, places them on the table, then leaves to attend to other patrons. With the painting out in the open, anyone who visited the Wheeler mansion could have seen it. The Wheelers are generally private, but they're also known for throwing lavish parties. Could Mr. Anonymous be someone who worked one of the parties as part of the catering staff or security? Is he the son of a party guest or friend of the Wheelers? There's just no way to know for sure.

"Where is the painting now?" I cut through the greens of the salad.

"I took it back to my room. It wasn't mine anymore, being out there for everyone to see. I guess I got possessive about it. Everyone who saw the painting wanted to know about you."

"And what did you say?"

"I told them the truth—that you were someone special to me."

We both dig into our meals and eat in silence for a beat. I take a sip of my water and then ask, "Do you recall anything out of the ordinary? An odd comment from someone who looked at the painting, any weird reactions to it?"

He shakes his head. "Nothing stands out. I'm sorry, but now you have me worried."

"Don't be silly. This is not your fault." I reach across the table and gently squeeze his shoulder. "It's just a guy with a crush who may be overzealous, that's all."

"I don't want some weirdo targeting you. You've been through enough."

I smile at him. "Thanks for the concern. Perhaps I'm being too cautious."

"No such thing. If your intuition tells you something is off, then it is."

"He hasn't done or said anything weird. I don't want to walk around looking over my shoulder, paranoid for no reason."

He reaches over and clasps my hands in his. "If anything happens, promise you will let me know." His blue gaze burns into me.

"I will."

I shift the conversation to Christian and the reason for the New York trip. He'll intern at Levitron-Blair's Austin location in the spring, but Alan exploits any opportunity to teach him about running the business. During this trip to the Big Apple, Alan will be negotiating an acquisition and wants Christian in the room to observe and learn. As the only child of Alan and Katherine Wheeler, it's no secret that Christian will run the multi-billion dollar empire one day.

When Alan Wheeler appears at our table, I'm surprised to see him but Christian isn't. We shake hands and he says it's good to see me. Alan is a towering presence, a strapping man in his late fifties and an older version of Christian.

"How are things at Yale?" he asks, still standing.

"Everything is going well. Thanks for asking."

"Glad to hear it. Are you keeping Christian in line? You're the only girl who ever could."

"I'm trying, Mr. Wheeler, but you know how he is."

"Don't I know it? Well, I'll let you kids get back to your meal. Abbie, say hello to your parents. Tell your father I'm waiting for a rematch on the golf course, and he can't use cancer as an excuse. I'm still going to whip his butt."

"I will, sir."

After he leaves the restaurant, I turn to Christian and say, "He's in a chipper mood."

"Maybe it's the young new girlfriend."

"Really? So cliché."

"I know. But that's the way he's always been and sadly, he may never change."

"Poor Katherine. You had better not even think about it. I'm coming to your wedding. I don't care how long it takes you to get married. The day you start messing around on your wife, I will hunt you down and beat you. I mean it, Christian."

He holds up his hands. "Whoa. I'm not my father."
"Are you sure?"

He grins at me, mischief in his eyes. "I can't predict the future, but I'm going to try not to be my dad."

"That's the closest thing to a promise I will get from you. I'll take it."

CHAPTER 19

BEFORE

LYING LITTLE WITCH! How could she do this to him? Spencer dug his fingers into the tattered vinyl seat of the taxi taking him to Penn Station. The faint whiff of cigarette smoke in the cab did nothing to calm his rage. Neither did the car horns blaring, the huddled masses, and endless traffic of New York City.

Faint, foreign music drifted from the front of the cab. He wasn't in the mood for chatting, and luckily neither was the driver, who only asked him where he was headed once he got in. He leaned back in the seat and allowed his fury to run unchecked. She had made a show of responding to a text from her brother, who was scheduled to pick her up this morning for the trip to her hometown, where she was supposed to spend the weekend. Instead, she secretly met with *him* and his dirt bag father. How he loathed them both, father and son.

He had Justin Tate to thank for uncovering her duplicity. After he had seen Abbie to her car last night, Spencer didn't go back to campus right away. He went back inside the Pub

Restaurant to take in the ambience and think. Justin hadn't left either.

Later in the evening, during their second encounter, Justin had taunted him. He explained how he had texted Abbie, hoping she would be around for the weekend so they could get a couple of extra hours of studying in before the group meet on Tuesday. That's when she revealed that she was planning to hop a train to New York on Friday to meet up with a friend. Justin implied that she was meeting up with a secret boyfriend. That had made Spencer see red.

He made an educated guess that she would take the Acela Train out of New Haven and arrive in New York within an hour. Once he spotted her in the crowd leaving the station to hitch a ride, he hopped in a cab and asked the driver to follow her Uber ride.

When her ride stopped outside the Ritz-Carlton Hotel, he had no choice but to follow at a safe distance, making sure his hat was pulled low and the glasses he donned for the occasion looked natural. He spoke very little and sat several tables away from them in the restaurant but close enough to observe them. Too bad he couldn't hear what they were discussing.

His stomach churned when he observed Wheeler constantly ogling her. The way he kept finding reasons to touch her. The worst part was, she didn't seem to mind. In fact, it looked like she enjoyed the attention. He wondered if they were really over.

When Spencer had tried to kiss her goodnight after he dropped her off to her car last night, she'd sidestepped him like a pro. Less than twenty-four hours later, she had no problem allowing Wheeler to slobber all over her. Spencer was so caught up in the memory of this soul crushing and humiliating experience, he hadn't realized the cab had pulled up near the train station. He paid the driver, exited the cab, and made an important call.

"WHO KNOWS, SHE might not come back until tomorrow or Sunday," he said.

Spencer shot a murderous gaze at Zach. They'd known each other as long as he could remember, and always had each other's backs. That did not include being reminded that Abbie might hook up with Wheeler. He was still fuming about what happened at the restaurant earlier. Zach had agreed to meet Spencer at Penn Station before he headed back to New Haven. They sat inside a Seattle Coffee shop on the concourse level. On a Friday afternoon, the bustling crowds were thick with commuters who lived in New Jersey and Connecticut, and out of town business people scrambling to get out of the city and head home. The announcements of arriving and departing trains to various cities along the eastern corridor added to the volume and busyness of the station.

Spencer took a sip of his coffee as the scent of fresh popcorn popping from the stand next door wafted into the space.

"Don't be a douchebag," he said to Zach. "She's not the hooking up type."

"And you believe her? Zach said incredulously. "The girl who said she was heading home for the weekend but instead snuck in a trip to the city to meet up with her ex? Come on, man. Wake up."

"They remained friends after high school. I'm sure there was a reason she changed her plans. If she wanted the trip to be top secret, she wouldn't have mentioned it to Justin."

"Yet she didn't tell you about it," Zach said.

"Why would she? I'm not her man. She didn't make any promises to me."

Zach studied him as if he was some poor loser who needed to be hurled into reality. Then he said, "So that's how you want to play it?"

"I have to think about the bigger goal and not allow emotions to get in the way. This is a long game. I can't afford to lose my head this early on, no matter what she throws at me."

"I see," Zach said, clutching the paper coffee container. "And I'm sure it's not as easy with her."

"No, it's not. She's tougher than I thought, but I'll see the plan through."

Silence fell between them. Zach took several gulps of his coffee. A few customers entered the shop and Spencer felt claustrophobic in the tiny space. As much as he rationalized the situation, was Zach right? Had he allowed Abbie Cooper to play him for a fool?

He had filled in Zach on progress thus far, and from the get go, Zach had maintained a healthy dose of skepticism. But Spencer would do well to keep his focus and not lose his head. She was the centerpiece of their revenge scheme, and he couldn't afford to isolate her.

"Maybe it's not a bad thing she met with them," Spencer

said. "Now we know their connection is still strong, proof that we're on the right path. She's important to them. Alan Wheeler went out of his way to see her."

"You're right," Zach said absently.

"Of course I'm right."

Zach nodded, and then steepled his fingers together. "Okay, but I think you need to up your game. Based on what you've told me so far, she's shut down every attempt to get close to her. What are you going to do about it? For this to work, she has to be completely under your spell in every way."

"I'm working on that," Spencer said.

CHAPTER 20

BEFORE

O UR TUESDAY EVENING study group is breaking up in the library. We've been going at it since 7:00 p.m., and it's now 10:00 p.m. Beth and Noah scramble out of the study room, leaving Justin and me behind. I grab my belongings and head for the door. The library is quiet, although there are a few die-hards with their noses in textbooks or staring at their laptop screens.

"How was the New York trip?" Justin asks as I press the elevator down button.

"It was nice catching up with my friend. I'm glad I went. Why do you ask?"

"No reason." He steps into the elevator after me. "It's good to get away sometimes."

"For sure. Don't you?"

"Where would I go?" he asks as the door closes. "Most of my friends are back in Cleveland or dead."

I hit the button for the first floor, and we descend in silence. The elevator dings and the door opens. As we head toward the large double doors to exit the library, I say,

"That's rough, Justin. But you can go exploring. There's so much to see and do. New York is only a hop, skip and jump away, and if you're up for it, you can head north to Boston or Providence."

"What kind of loser goes to places like that by himself?"

I stop, my hand on the door. "You shouldn't talk like that. You're definitely not a loser, and plenty of people do fun stuff alone. Trust me, life can be just as fun alone as it is with someone else."

He shakes his head slowly, as if he received some grand revelation. "Thanks, Abbie."

I push the door open. A cool breeze greets us as we step into the night. "Don't forget, you'll also make new friends here."

He doesn't answer and says instead, "Can I walk you to your dorm? It's dark and I don't think you should be walking alone on campus at night."

"But I'm not alone, Justin." I pull out my phone from the pocket of my bag. "I have the Companion App installed. No less than three people are tracking my movements as we speak. Besides, it's not completely dark. There are lampposts everywhere lighting the way, and my building is close by. It's a short walk."

"Still. I don't feel right about letting you go by yourself. I don't want anything to happen to you."

"Thanks for caring, Justin, but I promise I'll be fine. I'm going to crash once I get in. I'm tired. If it will make you feel better, I'll text you once I'm safely inside the building."

"You got yourself a deal," he says. "Goodnight, Abbie. Sweet dreams."

I stand frozen to the spot as I stare at Justin's disappearing figure. *Sweet dreams.* Those words again. I'm seriously paranoid. It's a common phrase used whenever someone refers to bedtime. Before I can twist myself into further knots, my phone rings. It's Ty.

"You okay?"

"Yes."

"I'll stay on the phone with you until you're inside the building."

Ty and I chat until I arrive. Only then does he hang up. I make my way to my room and send Justin a quick text on the way. My roommate Julie gives me a sleepy hello although her laptop is propped up against her knees as she types away at an insane speed. I dump my bag at the foot of the bed and go through my bedtime routine. After I'm done, I climb into bed and pull up the covers all the way to my chin. My phone dings. It's a text message:

Spencer: Are u up? Sorry if I texted too late.

Me: It's okay. Just fell into bed.

Spencer: Up for a movie tomorrow?

Me: Sure. My classes end early afternoon.

I stifle a yawn after I hit send.

Spencer: How was the weekend with your family? Did you hang out with Lee?

I ponder that for a moment. I didn't tell him about my change of plans, not that I was obligated to.

Me: Change of plans at the last minute. I didn't go home.

Spencer: Why not?

Me: I went to New York, met up with a friend.

Spencer: That's cool. Boy or girl? Should I be jealous of this friend?

Me: It was a boy and no, there's nothing to be jealous about. You and I are just friends, aren't we?

A series of sad faced emoticons follow.

Me: Does Spencer need a hug?

I pull up the appropriate emoticon and hit send.

Spencer: All better. Looking forward to tomorrow.

Me: Goodnight then.

Spencer: Sweet dreams, Abbie.

CHAPTER 21

BEFORE

S HE HAD INSISTED that they meet at the movie theatre, which meant that they would be heading back in separate cars. She gave him the excuse that she planned to stop by Ty's apartment after the movie because she promised to cook dinner for a group of friends. Spencer couldn't deny that it hurt, just a little.

He had already purchased the tickets for the movie they had agreed on, or rather, the one she picked—*Atomic Blonde*—an action packed spy thriller starring Charlize Theron. Not exactly conducive to making out, which he suspected was the reason she picked it.

The theatre was almost empty, only a handful of couples mixed in with some teenagers who most likely cut class. He stood near the door, blocking a couple of movie posters. He could hear the popcorn machine working overtime in the near quiet space, and the smell floating in the air. It was a small theatre that showed films after they were pulled from the major chains. They had half an hour to kill before the movie started, and he planned to make good use of it.

When she walked through the door looking like a million bucks in a pair of jeans that flattered her slender figure, and her hair styled in loose waves, Spencer quickly forgot his earlier griping.

"Hey you," she greeted him. "I have to warn you that I'll probably go through the whole tub of popcorn before the movie starts."

"No problem," he said as they walked toward the concession stand. "We can refill."

After they ordered popcorn, drinks and snacks, Spencer walked up to the usher and handed him the two tickets.

"Let's hang out here for a bit," Abbie said, surprising him.

He pulled back the tickets from the usher and followed her as she led the way to a corner peppered with futons and a vinyl wrap around sofa. She placed her drink and popcorn on the sofa and Spencer did the same.

"You don't mind, do you?" she asked. "I figured since we were going to be in a dark theatre for a couple of hours, we can sit out here and enjoy the afternoon sunshine."

"It's okay with me, Abbie. Whatever you want to do is fine."

She smiled at him, and for a moment, he forgot what he wanted to say. Then he remembered Zach's warning. He needed to up his game for the plan to work. She should be falling under his spell, not the other way around.

He looked down and noticed her shoes, open-toed pumps made of snakeskin, with a pattern of pretty colors.

"Nice shoes," he said. "Really cool."

"Thanks." She looked down at her feet.

"Where did you get those?"

"They were a gift."

"Oh. From who?"

The look on her face fell somewhere between none of your business, and why are you curious about my shoes.

"Sorry," he said with a nervous chuckle. "They're beautiful and obviously expensive. I'm sure you get great gifts all the time."

"Most guys don't notice stuff like that, so it took me by surprise that you asked."

"I notice everything about you, Abbie."

"That doesn't sound creepy at all."

He couldn't tell if she was being sarcastic or not.

"I just want you to know that I pay attention because everything about you is fantastic, even your shoes."

"They're Louboutin pumps. I got them as a present on my eighteenth birthday from my ex."

Spencer turned away for a second or two. He hoped she couldn't hear the raucous beating of his heart, as if it were about to pop right out of his chest.

"Are you okay?"

"Yes." He quickly grabbed the cup of soda next to him and took a sip. "Popcorn got lodged in the wrong spot."

"You looked like you couldn't breathe for a second. I thought I was going to have to perform CPR on you."

"I wouldn't have minded." He didn't want the moment to escape him, so he said, "Wow. I don't know too many high school guys who can afford to buy their girlfriends expensive designer shoes."

"You're right. But Christian is generous and his family is wealthy. And how do you know he was my high school boyfriend?"

Take it easy. She can't find out that you know who her ex is or the fact that you loathe him.

"What?" He shoved a lock of hair away from his eyes.

"You said you don't know too many high school guys who can afford designer shoes for their girlfriends. How do you know we were in high school together?"

"Lucky guess," he said, without hesitation.

Spencer chided himself again. He needed to be more careful. He couldn't allow his hatred of the Wheelers to spill out at the most inconvenient times. He had to maintain a tight rein over his emotions at all times, especially around Abbie.

"Christian must have spoiled you rotten," he said. "I know I would."

"Maybe we should go in. The movie will start soon."

He had pushed her too far. He could see it in her eyes. She clammed up and now the mood had soured. *Smooth, Spencer. Real smooth.* He would find a way to do damage control, he promised himself.

CHAPTER 22

AFTER

IT'S BEEN A little over a week since I was discharged from the hospital. My left hand is still in the cast, but I don't have to wear the sling. If I'm careful, I should be able to make it through the day. I managed to dress myself this morning, but my hair was another matter. I'm meeting up with Zahra. I have to tell her the truth about what's been going on with me, since I told her a whopper of a story.

We squeeze through the morning breakfast crowd in the dining hall. I protect my hand as much as possible, although it's not easy. A few people bump into me. Anxiety builds in my chest. Why am I uneasy? I've been here dozens of times. I welcomed the noisiness, and busyness, the chatter, the ambience. Now, all I want to do is run back to the apartment and slip under the covers.

"Are you okay, Abbie?" Zahra asks.

"I'm fine. I guess it's a bit strange returning to the routine."

"I can understand that. Why don't you find us a seat and I'll get the food. What do you want?"

I'm too anxious to eat, but I need to keep up my strength. I tell Zahra I'll have some fresh fruit and yogurt, and she heads off to the food stations.

I find a table with only one person sitting on the far end. That's as good as it's going to get, so I plop down at the opposite end to wait for Zahra. My phone chirps with a call from my mother. I've been avoiding her. I had better take this call.

"Hi, Mom."

"What's wrong?" she asks without preface.

"Mom, I've barely rolled out of bed. It's 7:30 in the morning and I haven't had any caffeine yet. Sorry if I'm not bouncing off the walls like a toddler on a sugar high."

I drink coffee only occasionally, but lack of caffeine is a good reason to sound like death this early in the day.

"Sorry sweetie, I don't mean to be suspicious. I worry about you. You've been avoiding me this past week. I just want reassurances that you're being a typical college kid, caught up in living her own life, and that's why you've been calling less and less. You haven't been home in weeks. And Ty has been answering your phone a lot lately. What's going on?"

I stifle a sigh and an eye roll, even if she can't see me. Though my mom and I are as close as a mother and daughter can be, right now I'm irritated. The only reason I haven't made up an excuse to get her off the phone is that I feel guilty that Ty has had to lie to her and my dad about why I didn't return their calls and text messages for days. Plus, he's had to talk them out of coming down for a visit.

"Nothing is going on, Mom, I promise. Look, I had a bad

case of the flu and it really kicked my butt. I was hanging out at Ty's place a lot, that's why he's been answering my phone. I was just too wiped out to do much, even return a simple phone call."

"And you didn't tell, me? Abbie, I would have been down there in a flash to take care of my baby."

That's exactly what I was afraid of. She would show up, take over Ty's apartment, and refuse to leave until she made sure I went to the doctor and my so-called flu had disappeared.

"Mom, I have to go. My class starts in less than thirty minutes."

"Okay, I won't keep you. Call me tonight. I want to talk about the Thanksgiving show. Bye, sweetie. Love you."

I stare open mouthed at the phone in my hand. I completely forgot that Thanksgiving is not too far away and she would want me to co-host the Thanksgiving episode of her cooking show. I'm doomed. It will be a while before the cast comes off, and I don't know if the left arm will be strong enough to do all the things required on the show: lifting pots and pans, stirring, chopping really fast with extra sharp knives, slicing, and cooking dishes that need to be flambéed or sautéed.

Zahra shows up with her hands barely holding on to two breakfast trays. I snap out of my trance and relieve her of one of the trays.

"You look like you're in a daze."

"My mother just called. She wants me to do the Thanksgiving episode of *Shelby's Kitchen*."

"Oh, dang," Zahra says, looking at my arm.

"I know."

Zahra sprinkles some brown sugar on her oatmeal and scoops a spoonful. "What did you tell your mother?"

"She wants me to call her tonight to discuss."

"What are you going to say?"

"I don't know."

I have to find a way to get out of it gracefully without arousing suspicion or hurting my mom's feelings. She loves doing the show with me. She wants me to collaborate with her on her next series of cookbooks, each one focused on a different theme: healthy eating, vegan cooking, and comfort food. She even wants to do one specifically for cancer patients. She drastically changed my dad's diet after his colon cancer diagnosis. I think that's one of the reasons he's doing so well.

I drag a spoonful of yogurt to my mouth. I barely taste it. I force myself to finish it anyway.

Zahra puts down her spoon and pushes the tray away from her, and then she asks, "What really happened the night of the party, Abbie? I don't believe that you left without saying a word and went back to your room, or that you injured your arm when you slipped in the shower and fell. And then you caught the flu? Come on. Nobody has that much bad luck."

I tap my foot under the table. "I can't tell you what happened."

Her mouth falls open and she asks, "Why not?"

"Because I don't remember."

"How can you not remember?" She tugs at her dangling earrings. "Abbie, what's going on?"

I expel a puff of air and delve into the story. When I'm finished, Zahra sags into her chair. She extends her arm and clasps my hand in hers as she chokes back tears. I'm about to lose it too, so I can't look at her. Instead, I focus my attention on the hustle and bustle of the dining hall.

I SNAG AN empty seat in the back of the lecture hall mere minutes before the class begins. Along with thirty-five other students, I remove my laptop from my bag and boot up. Professor Cross begins her lecture. My head is pounding and I stop typing. This genetics class is a core course for my major. I have to pay attention, but my head feels like a marching band has taken over. I try to relax in the chair and it isn't working. I'm tempted to pack up my things and leave but I can't. This class is too important. Besides, Professor Cross was kind enough to allow me to take the last test a few days ago privately, thanks to a well crafted note from the doctor who treated me.

Somehow, I manage to make it through. I barely register any of the content. Looking at the PowerPoint slides on the large projector screen in the front of the room makes my head hurt even worse. When the professor calls the class to come down to her desk to pick up the last test before we leave, I stay put in my seat, afraid if I try to walk down the aisle with other students, I may face plant.

When the two last students pick up their tests, I make what seems like the longest journey of my life to the front of the room. I can feel Professor Cross staring at me, but I avoid eye contact. In her late fifties, with blue-gray hair she never dyes, and a round, pleasant face, she's always been tough but fair. I pick up the last test and begin to walk away.

"What happened, Abigail?" she asks.

I freeze. I slowly turn around to face her. "What do you mean, professor?"

"Have a look at your test."

I do as she says. Written with a big, bright red marker is the number 70, accompanied by a handwritten question, *What happened, Abigail?*

My chest aches. The room spins around me. I force my eyes to meet the professor's.

"Why don't you have a seat?" she says, gesturing to the first row.

I move with the speed of a sloth and eventually plop down in one of the seats. She comes over. My lips tremble as I look at the big red number 70 on the page. Everyone keeps asking me what happened. I don't know what happened.

"I don't understand." I look from the test to the professor.

"Everybody has an off day or two, but this isn't you. You've had access to the assignments while you were unable to be physically present. I'm glad you're back, but you don't get these kinds of grades in my class. That's not what you're here for."

"I'm having trouble focusing," I blurt out. I don't know where it came from. It escaped me like vomit you can't control. Then I burst out crying, right there in front of one of the toughest professors I've ever had.

CHAPTER 23

———◦———

AFTER

AS PROMISED, MOM calls me later that evening to discuss my appearance on *Shelby's Kitchen*. She insisted on FaceTiming me. To give the appearance that everything is just peachy, I'm hiding under a blanket on the couch. I place my iPad strategically on the end table next to me.

"I thought you said you were better. Why are you curled up under a blanket?" she asks, with a disapproving frown.

"I'm fine. Had a rough day, that's all."

I should have known she wouldn't be easily placated. Before she continues, my brother Miles walks by in the background. He comes in closer, and soon he's over Mom's shoulder waving and grinning. I wave back and after he disappears from view, Mom lets me have it.

"What's going on? What happened today? I knew you weren't a hundred percent."

I stop her before we go down some rabbit hole that will end up with her jumping in her car and coming over tonight, despite the fact it's almost 8:00 p.m.

"I didn't do as well as I wanted on a couple of tests. No

big deal. I'll rebound."

But it is a big deal. After my meltdown in front of Professor Cross, my day didn't improve. I received a B minus on my probability & statistics test. By the time I made it to the apartment, Professor Cross had sent me an email.

Don't let the bastard win. You didn't come here for that.

Then she concluded her note with the name and contact information for a trauma psychiatrist at St. Luke's Medical Center—a Dr. Grace Shanahan. Another meltdown followed. The headaches have hardly let up. The nightmares continue. I'm always falling, the hand gripping me around the neck. I wake up sweating and scared. I don't tell Ty about these episodes. He has enough to worry about.

"Sweetie, I'm sorry to hear that. You're right. You will bounce back. It's not that easy, is it?"

"No, it's not. I have to think about future medical school applications. Everything I do now matters."

"I understand. I have every confidence you will turn this around. Please try not to stress. And don't worry about the show. Focus on your schoolwork. I'll be fine."

"Thanks for understanding, Mom."

"Anytime. You're my brave girl, my warrior. This too shall pass."

I have to end the chat. I feel tears welling up in my eyes. I tell Mom I gave to go, that I haven't had any dinner yet. Once I close down the iPad, I pull the blanket over my head and weep.

"WHY ARE YOU crying?"

I wipe my tears, pull myself together, and remove the blanket covering my head. I didn't hear Ty come in. He sits next to me on the sofa.

"I just got off FaceTime with Mom. I couldn't hold it together afterward. She said I was her brave warrior. What a crock."

"But you are. Warriors have bad days too, and sometimes they lose a battle or two, but in the end they win the war."

He inches closer to me and pulls me into his arms. I rest my head on his chest. We stay that way for a minute or two. In spite of his efforts to comfort me, there's tension in him. His heartbeat is out of whack.

"What's wrong?"

He hesitates then says, "Nothing. I just want you to be all right."

"I flunked a couple of tests, but otherwise I'm just dandy."

He frowns at me.

"Okay, I didn't actually flunk, but I may as well have."

I discuss my recent grades.

"Warriors have bad days, too," he repeats. "Don't forget."

I stretch and then ask, "When are you going to tell me what's wrong?"

He looks at me intently. "Cooper, if I don't get into Harvard, it means I will have to attend school in another state, maybe even California. UCLA ranks high as one of the top medical schools for surgeons. Harvard is number one. If I end up at UCLA, I won't see you for months on end."

"We knew there was a possibility you could attend

123

medical school away from the East Coast when you got into UCLA and Northwestern."

"I know but I had my heart set on getting into Harvard. Since your attack, I've been thinking about it a lot. I have to stay close. Cambridge is forty-five minutes from Castleview, and two hours from Yale. No matter how busy medical school gets, at least I can see you from time to time."

Guilt is tearing up my insides. It's not fair that he thinks of me first, even when faced with one of the most important decisions of his life. He deserves so much more. So much more than the stress of trying to figure out how to stay close to me. The cost of possibly losing out on his first choice of medical school because he couldn't focus during the interview—that second chance that was supposed to erase all doubt from the admissions committee.

Also, there's the Kristina factor, always lurking around in my head no matter how much I try to suppress it. I don't know the status of their relationship, and I'm too afraid to ask. Does she plan to remain on the East Coast after graduation?

He did everything right. He studied hard. His extra-curricular activities included a stint on the university's championship crew team. During the summertime when he should have been taking a break, he was shadowing doctors and completed two medical internships, including one in Pulin, Croatia. He led a program to help inner city kids focus on education, especially on science and medicine. He donated his time and money and put his heart and soul into that program. He still gets letters and emails from some of the kids in the program. They tell him that because of him, they want to go to college and become doctors, lawyers, teachers, and politicians. They want to have an impact on their community.

"You will attend medical school wherever suits you best," I say forcefully. "If you get into Harvard, great. If not and you decide that UCLA is the place for you, I'll help you move to California. We can make it a cross-country trip. It's settled. I don't want to have this conversation again, Ty."

He gives me the thumbs up sign. "Okay, boss."

CHAPTER 24

BEFORE

I WANT EVERY last detail. Don't leave anything out this time. It's been torture waiting to meet face to face to get the goods."

Zahra is chomping at the bit to get all the details of my weekend trip to New York and date with Spencer. Our schedules finally allowed us to meet up at my dining hall. With the amount of time Zahra spends eating here, she may as well move into my building.

"Christian couldn't pinpoint anyone who could be Mr. Humble Admirer. He did have the painting on the wall near the grand staircase, but then he took it down and returned it to his room."

"So that brings us back to square one," she says, cutting into a pancake. "We're still as clueless as we were when the first rose and note appeared."

"I just wish I knew why he chose this way."

"What do you mean?"

"Anonymity and secrecy instead of openness. That's what worries me. The mention of the ball sealed my anxiety. If he

126

hadn't mentioned it, I might be less apprehensive."

Zahra takes a sip of her orange juice. I haven't touched my egg white omelet or green tea. I'm trying to make a connection in my head between all the recent events that don't add up.

"Spencer has been acting weird," I say.

Zahra looks up from her food. "Weird how?"

I explain to her the bizarre encounter last Thursday night. "There was obvious hostility between them, but when I asked Spencer if he knew Justin, he denied it. Then last night at the movies, he asked me about my shoes and practically choked on a popcorn kernel when I said they were a birthday gift from Christian."

Zahra frowns. "That's a strange reaction. You think he knows Christian?"

"I don't know. If he does, why keep it a big secret? The strange thing was, when I mentioned that my ex gifted me the shoes, he knew it was my high school boyfriend. When I asked how he knew that, he claimed it was a lucky guess."

"Did you mention Christian's last name?"

"No, I didn't."

"Maybe it's like he said. Lucky guess."

"He has been pouring it on thick, though. With the compliments, and flirting."

"Is that a bad thing?"

"I'm not sure. He just seems too good to be true, and you know how the saying goes."

"If it seems too good to be true, it *is* too good to be true," Zahra recites.

"Right. But—" I hold up my index finger. "I've also been known to overthink things."

"Let's look at what we do know." She props her elbows on the table and clasps her hands together. "We have an anonymous guy sending you notes and gifts and who mentions a ball you attended two years ago. Spencer Rossdale is all over you and pretends he doesn't know Justin Tate, and then freaks out when you mention Christian. How do they all connect?"

"Why did Spencer freak out when I mentioned Christian? That's the question that could help us link back to Mr. Anonymous who mentioned the ball and sent me that doll."

"So do Spencer and Mr. Anonymous know each other?" Zahra asks. "That could explain why he choked when you mentioned Christian. Christian did attend the ball with you."

"If they know each other, what would be the point of both of them pursuing me?"

"That is kind of freaky," Zahra admits. "And let's not forget the Justin piece of the puzzle, but I don't see Justin and Spencer moving in the same circles, especially since Spencer is a senior. So how do they know each other?"

"I only know Spencer because of Ty. Otherwise, I would have ignored him at the party." I let my mind buzz for a bit, and then it occurs to me the only thing these seemingly unrelated incidents and people have in common is me. I share that thought with Zahra.

"So we're talking three separate guys with the same agenda, to land Abbie Cooper."

"And that kind of stuff is just not normal. Think of the timing. The notes and gifts start showing up, shortly thereafter I meet Spencer, and then Justin starts showing an interest."

"What if Spencer and Mr. Humble Admirer are one in the same?" Zahra says.

I drum my fingers on the table. We keep circling back to Spencer, and each time, I've dismissed him as the culprit. Was that a mistake?

"From what I've observed, Spencer is neither shy nor insecure. He's in your face, confident, says what's on his mind. He's hot and he knows it. He goes after what he wants. That doesn't align with what we know about the Humble Admirer so far."

"You could be right."

"Unless it's a game," I add.

"How do you mean?"

"What if you're right? What if Spencer is the Humble Admirer, and he's trying to throw me off his scent?"

"You mean like a dual identity kind of thing?"

"Exactly."

"But why?"

"That's what I need to find out. Then again, I could be grasping at straws."

"Are you sure you want to cross Christian off the list as a suspect? How did he behave when you met up in New York?"

"He was fine." I frown in confusion at the question.

"No, I mean, how did he react to your presence, what was his body language like, what did he say to you, and how did he say it? I'm sure you guys didn't just talk about the painting. The conversation must have gotten personal at some point."

I reach back in my memory bank to retrieve the details

of that meeting. I didn't think much of Christian's behavior. To me he was just being Christian.

I let out a deep sigh. "He was thrilled to see me. He was flirting, no doubt. He said he missed me."

"And how did you react?"

"I did what I always do, deflect and dismiss."

Zahra taps a fingernail on the table. "He could be our guy."

"I don't see it, for reasons I already explained. He's like Spencer in that regard. He says what's on his mind. Also, let's not forget the Humble Admirer implied that he's forgettable, you know, like he fades into the background and he hoped I wouldn't be disappointed when he revealed himself. You've seen photos of Christian. Does he fit the profile of someone who's forgettable?"

"Heck, no," Zahra says forcefully. "How dare you make that comparison?"

We both giggle, then I say, "Christian took me to Bedford Hills and introduced me to his family when we were dating. He had never done that with a girl before. And as I told you, I still keep in touch with his mother, Katherine. This is not his style."

"Maybe all we can do is wait for whoever this guy is to make his next move." Zahra shrugs.

"And be a sitting duck to whatever he has planned?"

"What choice do we have? His next move could provide clues. He keeps promising he'll reveal himself. You don't say that if the person already knows who you are, as is the case with all the guys we mentioned."

"So you really think this is a stranger, someone I have no clue about?"

"It looks that way, Abbie. We've outlined every scenario, and none of it fits with the people we do know."

My phone buzzes and I pick it up from the table. It's a text from Spencer.

Spencer: Can I see you this evening?

Me: What's up?

Spencer: I was a jerk at the movies the other day.

Me: You've already apologized for that.

Spencer: Not face-to face. I still don't feel right about it.

Me: Stop beating yourself up. It's okay.

Spencer: It isn't. I was jealous.

Me: Why?

Spencer: Um . . . can I see you?

Me: Sorry, tonight won't work but may I get back to you?

Spencer: Sure.

I place the phone back on the table.

"Spencer," I say to Zahra in response to her curious stare.

"What did he want?"

"He wants to see me. Said he felt bad about the way he acted at the movies."

"I thought he already apologized for that."

"That's what I said. He claims he was jealous but wouldn't say why. I admit, I'm curious."

131

"So what's the real deal between the two of you? How far are you willing to take things?"

"To answer your first question, he's a handsome and charming distraction. I have fun when I'm with him. The answer to your second question is a bit more complicated."

"What does that mean?" Zahra asks, her eyes glowing.

"I limit his access to me. Otherwise, it would set a bad precedent. I don't want him thinking that I'm willing to take things to a place I have no desire to go. I made that clear from the beginning, although I don't know if he believes me."

"Why wouldn't he?"

"Because of what I've already told you, his behavior. Besides, he's a guy. He might see me as a challenge, and if he does, that could spell trouble."

"Why?"

I take a sip of my green tea. It's cold and tasteless. I place the cup down on the table. "Spencer is persistent, and if he believes his persistence will pay off, things could get messy. I don't know how he will react once it sinks in that I meant what I said, that nothing can happen between us."

"Okay, I get that but then why hang out with him and give him hope?"

"You think that's what I'm doing?"

"I don't know. Is it?"

Zahra is questioning my motivation, which I never thought to do before. I'm a nineteen-year old college student who spends the majority of her time with her nose in a textbook or looking at a computer screen. I don't drink or smoke or do drugs. I'm not a party animal. So, what's wrong with having a little fun? Why does Zahra's question make me uncomfortable?

"Spencer said he could handle it. I took him at his word. I've never lied to him, and I'm not stringing him along if that's what you're thinking. Let's not forget that he's graduating in a few months. Perhaps I'm the one who should be worried."

I rake my hands through my hair and continue, "I had my reservations from the beginning, but he was persuasive. Besides, I don't know what he does when I'm not around. As far as I know, he could have several girlfriends."

The night we met, that girl Karen was obviously expecting to see Spencer later that night, but he was not receptive to the idea when she mentioned it in my presence. For all I know, maybe they did meet up after he left the party.

Zahra nods in agreement. "You've really thought about this, huh?"

"I wouldn't be me if I didn't overthink it," I say with a chuckle. "If Spencer doesn't like how things are going, he can always bail."

"I like the way you roll." She gives me a high-five.

"You think that was mean, don't you?"

"Not if it's the truth. But I have a question you may not like. Is Ty the reason you won't give Spencer a chance?"

I rub my nose and leave the question hanging in the air, unanswered.

THE TWO WOMEN walk pass me, my gray hooded sweatshirt providing the anonymity I need. I keep my head down.

They didn't notice me when they walked into the dining hall earlier or when they sat at the table in front of me. It helps to be good at being invisible. I'm just another co-ed in the crowded dining space, nothing special, dressed the way thousands of college students across the country do.

I inhale the aroma of the rare rose I've been holding— the sweet smell of success to come. Every word of their conversation is recorded in my memory. Abbie Cooper is flailing around in the dark, trying to figure it all out. She won't. At least, not until I want her to. For now, I will remain anonymous and keep her wondering, off balance and frustrated. She's not the only one having fun.

I almost feel sorry for that fool Spencer, putting in all that effort into what will amount to a big pile of nothing. If I were in his shoes though, I would make her pay for stringing me along and giving me false hope. But I doubt he has the guts or cunning it will take to bring Abbie Cooper to her knees.

CHAPTER 25

BEFORE

T HE MUSIC BLARES, and the whooping and hollering adds to the festive atmosphere. People are plastered along the walls of every inch of this suburban home in Bethany, less than thirty minutes from campus. We're celebrating trouncing our opponent in The Big Game, cementing our leader status in one of the NCAA Division One's most intense rivalries.

I spot Ty, minus Kristina, elbowing his way through the thick crowd. He waves to get my attention and I wave back. We meet up in a small enclave off the foyer.

"This is some party. Glad you could come. You deserve to have some fun." He yells in my ear, trying to be heard above the music.

"I almost didn't come," I respond.

"Why not?"

"I don't know. All these parties are the same, but I figured I could show my school spirit by celebrating our victory over our football nemesis."

"Me too, even though I can't stay out all night."

I shoot him a puzzled glance, and then I say, "It's a Saturday night. Live a little."

"Monday is my big interview with Harvard. I have to get enough sleep this weekend and go over final preparation. It's the second go round with them. They're on the fence about me, and I need impress them out of their doubt."

"Wait, this coming Monday? I knew you were anxious about it, but I didn't realize it was coming up so fast. You're well prepared. I know you'll impress the admissions committee."

"Thanks Cooper. Your support means a lot to me."

Something about his words cuts me. I don't know why. It's an unexpected twinge of something. Sadness? Maybe the realization that he's moving on, and he'll be gone in a matter of months.

I force a smile. "I have a great idea. I can help you run through potential interview questions and have a look at the suit you picked out. Only if you want."

"Really, Cooper? You would do that?"

"Sure. Why not? I know you have everything under control, but it doesn't hurt to do one final run through."

"That would be great. I appreciate the offer. Why don't you come home with me and we can spend tomorrow practicing and hanging out?"

"We have plans for tomorrow," a clearly irritated voice exclaims. We both turn around to see a not-so-happy Kristina aiming a poisonous glare in Ty's direction.

I've never known Kristina to be catty, but her claws are definitely showing. She wraps a possessive arm around Ty as if to warn me to back off, Ty belongs to her. But I'm not one to do what I'm told, especially when it comes to him.

"Plans change, Kristina. You should know how important this interview is to Ty and his future. Right now, your hurt feelings don't matter one bit. There are more important things at stake."

Kristina's mouth is gaping open, her skin flushed with embarrassment. I don't give her a chance to respond. I say to Ty, "Text me when you're ready to leave. I still have some clothes over your place so I should be all set, no need to stop at my dorm on our way out." Without another word, I leave them both and head toward the living room area.

My cell phone vibrates in my purse and I pull it out.

Spencer: Are you here?

Me: Yes, what's going on?

Spencer: Save me! I'm about to die from the world's most boring conversation. She went to the bathroom. Here's your chance to be my hero.

His message is followed by a sad face emoticon.

Me: Forgot to pack my super hero costume.

Spencer: I bet it's super tight and clings to you in all the right places.

Me: I'm not telling.

Spencer: What a tease you are. Have some sympathy.

Me: I'm plenty sympathetic.

Spencer: You won't let me catch you.

Me: Why do that when the chase is so much more fun?

Spencer: I'd like to do more than chase.

Me: I know you would.

Spencer: So why won't you let me. I won't hurt you.

Me: You can't guarantee that.

Spencer: Meet me out back.

Me: Okay.

The party crowd has also spilled out to the back yard, the murmur of conversation floating on the cool, October night air. Several lights from the deck pierce the darkness, illuminating the area. I spot Spencer leaning up against a tree at the far corner of the yard and join him.

"Now that you're here, my evening just took a turn for the better," he says.

"Is this the part where I blush and say 'Really, Spencer?' in a high-pitched, girlish voice, and give you a big old smile because I'm so flattered?"

"You're so cynical," he says, grinning. "Lucky for you, I love a challenge. The tougher the better."

"Is that what I am, a challenge? And then what? Hypothetically speaking, of course."

"Life is all about experiences, Abbie. That's what makes memories and shape us as people. Sometimes, those experiences are good, sometimes they're bad and sometimes, they're life-changing."

He turns to look me square in the eye. Even in the semidarkness, I sense his intensity. "The college experience is a one shot deal. Right here, right now, this moment is all we have. You don't get to live college over and over again. In the blink of an eye, you're going to be out of here, too. When you look back on your experiences here, what are you going to remember? The classes you took, how many hours you spent studying or . . . ?"

His voice trails off and the question hangs in the air, demanding to be answered. He angles his body so that he's facing me directly. My senses tingle and my heartbeat accelerates.

"Or what?" I ask, my voice a hoarse whisper.

He inches closer to me, until not even air separates us. When he pulls me into a tight embrace, I don't object. He lowers his head and kisses me, a slow, penetrating, pleasant kiss. I relax my shoulders and go with the flow. His breathing is increasingly rapid. He trails kisses along my neck. When his hand reaches around and squeezes my butt, something goes off in my brain. *You know this isn't right. You're not ready for where it could lead. And he might not even be trustworthy.*

I wriggle free from his embrace.

"What's wrong?" Surprise registers on his face as he tries to get his breathing under control.

"I can't do this."

"I thought you liked it."

"I do. I did."

"So what's the problem?"

"We shouldn't have started anything."

"We were just kissing. You make it sound like a federal offense. We're two consenting adults."

He's pissed. I understand that. But I don't want to get in over my head. Kissing leads to other things, and I don't want to lead him on. It's better to put the brakes on before things go any further. Besides, I'm confused. I don't know what I'm afraid of exactly. But I know it doesn't feel right.

"I'm sorry, Spencer. I'm not playing games, I swear. I don't know why, but I just can't take this any further."

He frowns and then his eyes pop wide. "Are you a virgin?"

"What?" The question is not a shocking one. I just need time to gather my thoughts and formulate the right response. If I say yes, it will explain what I'm sure he thinks is odd behavior. If I say no, he'll think I'm what he accused me of: a tease. That won't go over so well.

"Does it matter?" I want to artfully dodge the question without making look like I am.

He looks at me, curiosity mixed in with tenderness. "I'm so sorry, Abbie. I just assumed . . . I just assumed a girl like you—"

"A girl like me?"

"I didn't mean it to come out that way. It's just surprising. You had a boyfriend in high school. Christian. And then I thought that maybe you and Ty at some point . . ."

I let out a nervous laugh. "You thought Ty and I hooked up?"

"It would be the logical thing. He adores you. I thought you two may have hooked up and decided it wasn't a good idea after all, so you chose to go back to being friends."

Not a bad assumption. Wrong, but not a bad assumption.

"No. Nothing like that."

I'm not about to elaborate or dissuade him from his theory. And I'm definitely not about to confess that the entirety of my sexual experience amounts to a single occurrence with Christian during my stay at Bedford Hills two years ago. He must have misread the expression on my face because he keeps apologizing.

"Spencer, stop it already," I admonish. "You didn't do anything wrong. Stop acting as if you dragged me off somewhere and had your way with me. We're good. Okay?"

"Thanks for saying that. I couldn't forgive myself if I hurt you in any way."

"Don't sweat it." I shiver when a light breeze blows. I left my coat in one of the closets in the house. A flared mini skirt, cashmere top and bare legs in heels offer no protection from the increasingly nippy temperatures.

"Are you cold?" he asks. Before I can answer, he takes off his jacket and drapes it over my shoulders.

"That was stupid of me, to come out without my coat. It was hot in the house, with all those bodies. I needed the cool air, but the temperature is dropping fast."

I'm rambling and need to stop. I should heed my own advice and take it easy.

We talk for a bit longer. By now, most of the partygoers have headed indoors.

"Maybe we should head in," Spencer says.

"You go ahead. I'll stay out here for a few more minutes."

"Let me at least get you a drink."

"Okay."

Spencer takes off and returns a few moments later with a cup of water. He says, "I'm heading back inside, but if you're not there within the next ten minutes, I'm coming out to get you."

"Deal," I say and he heads back inside.

I chug down the water in two big gulps and wipe the stray drops from my mouth. I take several deep breaths to calm my emotions and thoughts. I almost got in over my head tonight. I can't allow that to happen again.

My phone vibrates in my purse and I fish it out with one hand. It's a text.

Ty: Where are you? We gotta go. It's late.

I begin to type my response but don't get to finish the message. That's the last thing I remember before my world fades to black.

CHAPTER 26

GONE

"SPENCER, HAVE YOU seen Cooper?"

"Yeah. We were chatting not too long ago. She's in the back yard, said she needed a few more minutes outdoors. Why? What's the matter?"

Ty Rambally's eyes flickered with worry. "We're supposed to be heading out together, but she hasn't responded to my texts."

Spencer thought that was odd. Abbie hadn't said anything to him about leaving the party with Rambally. "I'll go get her. Meet you back here in a few."

"I'll come with you," Ty said anxiously.

When they arrived in the backyard, Abbie was nowhere in sight. In fact, there was no one left in the back yard.

"She said she would only be a few minutes. Maybe she went back inside and we both missed her. She could have gone to the bathroom."

"Let's go back inside," Ty said. "You could be right."

Rambally broke out his phone from his pocket on the way in and called Abbie. After a few seconds, he tapped the screen to end the call. "It went straight to voice mail."

"Why don't we split up? We can cover more ground that way. It's a house, she has to be in it somewhere," Spencer said reassuringly.

"Good idea. I'll see if can find her friend Zahra. Maybe they're together and she didn't hear her phone vibrate."

A half hour later, they met up in the kitchen. A few partygoers were scattered around, but it was all but over. After searching through every part of the house they had access to, still no sign of Abbie. No one had seen or heard from her since Spencer left her out in the backyard. Her friend Zahra said she thought Abbie was with Ty, and was now waiting in the foyer expecting Ty and Spencer to show up with Abbie in tow.

"Did she seem off when you were chatting outside?" Ty asked.

Spencer tried to remain calm although he could feel the panic seeping in. Rambally was already there, Spencer could see it in his eyes and the way he kept raking his hair back.

"She was fine. I didn't have any reason to think anything was wrong."

That answer didn't satisfy Ty. "What did you two talk about while you were out there?"

"None of your business." The words tumbled out of Spencer before he could formulate a more cordial response. The last thing he wanted to do was aggravate Rambally, who was already on edge.

"Excuse me?" he roared. He looked like he wanted to murder Spencer in his sleep.

"Sorry. I didn't mean to come off like a jerk. I just don't

see how what we discussed has anything to do with her not being here." Spencer didn't want to use the word *disappearance*. It was too scary to contemplate.

"All I know is you were the last person to see her, according to your own words. Now I can't find her anywhere."

"There has to be a reasonable explanation," Spencer said. "Abbie is not the kind of girl to renege on a commitment. If she agreed to leave the party with you, then she has a good reason why she hasn't answered your texts."

Spencer didn't like the idea that she had agreed to leave the party with Rambally in the first place, but he had to get over it quickly, even though Ty's attitude got under his skin. What gave him the right to behave as if Abbie was his property while he was sleeping with Kristina Hayward?

"And you know this how?" They both leaned up against the kitchen counter. Rambally's arms were folded against his chest, his stance aggressive, and his stare cold. He blamed Spencer for this turn of events.

"I've gotten to know Abbie," Spencer replied. "She's an incredible girl. She's smart, and funny and sexy."

Although his description was accurate, Spence threw in the last adjective to aggravate Ty. Spencer figured it was time he pushed back.

Rambally took the bait and inched closer. At six foot two, Spencer had three inches on Ty. "If I find out that you've hurt Abbie, that you had anything to do with her disappearance, I will end you. That's a promise."

Spencer didn't flinch, showed no emotion. In the four years he'd known Ty Rambally, he'd come to know him as a stand-up guy. He'd just made a serious threat.

"Back off," Spencer said, his voice low and menacing, all niceties forgotten. "Don't ever threaten me again, because next time I'll take it personally. I'll let it go this time because it's a stressful situation."

"I'm heading to Cooper's residential college. Maybe she's in bed, fast asleep. For now, I don't think it's a good idea for you to be around her. It's obvious she's not safe with you."

"Look, you need someone to blame. I get it. But nobody could have predicted how this evening would end."

"She's never disappeared before, Spencer. How about that? And I meant what I said. If anything happens to her, I'm coming for you."

CHAPTER 27

GONE

B Y 5:00 A.M. Sunday morning, just about four hours since he last saw her, Abbie Cooper was still missing and Spencer hadn't heard anything further from Ty Rambally. He hadn't slept. He had driven back from the party in a daze and remained in his car in the parking lot, where he still sat. He called Abbie's phone several times and left numerous messages and texts. No response. He did the same with Rambally, who grudgingly agreed to let Spencer check in with him for updates, and Spencer in turn would do the same if he heard from Abbie.

Spencer thought back to the previous evening's events. Where could she be? Why wasn't she returning his calls? He made it clear that he was worried and both he and Ty were looking for her. Did she call Rambally, and he didn't bother to loop Spencer in?

He picked up his phone, which sat on the passenger seat, the screen dark and silent. He punched in his password and then dialed Rambally's number. When it went to voicemail he said, "Ty, it's Spencer again. Just checking to see if you heard anything and haven't had a chance to let me know.

147

Don't leave me hanging if you know something. I just want her to be okay."

He clicked off, placed the phone in his jacket pocket, and pushed back the passenger seat so he could stretch his legs. He closed his eyes, just for a minute so he could think. He didn't know how long he had been dozing, but suddenly his eyes hurt. He opened them slowly to blinding sunlight. It was way past dawn. He placed his hands over his eyes to shield him from the bright rays. The dashboard clock said it was 7:45 a.m. He felt for the phone in his pocket and pulled it out. When he pressed the button to light up the screen, he saw there was a recent text message. With trembling fingers, he punched in his passcode.

> **Ty:** Cooper's fine. A little embarrassed, that's all. Said she kissed you and felt awful for pulling back. She couldn't face you so she went back to her dorm and called it a night.

> **Spencer:** What a relief. Thanks for letting me know. Will check in with her later.

While relief seeped through his tired bones, Spencer wondered if he had misread Abbie. She was the one who offered reassurances when he beat himself up over the kiss. She showed no signs that she was upset about it. Then she just disappeared without saying a word to anyone for hours?

Although he was no Abbie expert, Spencer had trouble believing that things went down the way Rambally said in his text. It didn't sync up with what he knew about her. Where did she really go last night? And why was Rambally lying about it?

CHAPTER 28

AFTER

I SIT UP and swing my legs off the bed. I feel my way through the darkness and open the bedroom door. A thick arm grabs me around the throat, almost crushing my windpipe. The pain is excruciating. My arms and legs flail. My body is being dragged, but I don't know where to. It's pitch black. I see nothing. With all the energy I can muster, I plant my heels on the ground, desperate to slow down the backward motion. Then the pressure around my neck eases. I try to scream but no sound comes out. No one comes to rescue me.

I fight with all my might but get nowhere. Then the silent figure picks me up and hurls me through the air. I feel myself falling rapidly, as if going down an elevator shaft, faster and faster. My terror increases as I move faster and faster. I'm afraid when I land, the fall will kill me. I stretch out my arms in a frantic effort to grab on to something that will break the fall. There's nothing but air.

I wake up with a jolt. Sweat drips from my body and I can hear my breathing loud and anguished, piercing the darkness. My eyes slowly adjust to the darkness. I make out a room that looks familiar. I scramble off the bed and flip on the light switch. I'm safe. It was just a nightmare. I'm at Ty's apartment. I return to the bed, sitting at the edge. I raise my hand to feel around my neck. The nightmare was the most intense one to date. I wipe the tears that drizzle down my cheeks. Maybe if I watch a little TV, I can fall back asleep.

I wake up from another terrifying dream, my breathing heavy and perhaps loud enough to be heard by Ty down the hall. He could come banging on my door any second, asking if I'm okay. My physical injuries are on the mend. My cast comes off in a week. But emotionally, I'm a runaway train, zigzagging all over the tracks with no idea where I will end up. I slip off the covers and slide out of bed. For the rest of the night, there's no way I'm giving the boogey man another shot at me.

I barge into Ty's bedroom. I'm surprised to discover a faint glow around the room, coming from a night light. I climb into bed without an explanation.

"It's about time," he mumbles, half asleep.

"What?" I whisper.

"I know about the nightmares, Cooper. I've left the light on for you every night since they started."

CHAPTER 29

AFTER

I CAN'T TAKE it anymore. The nightmares and sleepless nights. The fatigue that follows. The paranoia that he's watching me, still. Even after the assault, his presence is everywhere, even if I don't know who *he* is. I can't sit around and do nothing. Maybe if I sit down and make a proper statement to the police since I was in no condition to do so when they showed up in my hospital room—then I can take back some semblance of control, weaken his grip on my psyche.

I'm keeping my expectations low, however. I've done some research. Most sexual assault cases never go to trial because victims don't file charges. Why? Shame. Fear that no one will believe them. Fear that those who do believe them will cast blame, fear of reliving the crime. The chances of a conviction are slim, and even more diminished in my case since I can't recall the attack.

"Are you okay? Ty asks, both hands on the steering wheel.

"Nervous. I wish we had more to go on."

"You'll do great," he says. "It's the police's job to investigate."

151

My skepticism must be glaringly obvious, because he frowns at me. "Come on, Cooper. We have to give it a chance."

"I'm trying. Otherwise, I wouldn't be here in the car with you, heading to talk to the police in some tiny town in which I spent a few hours of my life. A few hours that changed so much."

We arrive at the Bethany police station, a recently renovated red brick building with white trim and a red, cobblestone path leading to the heavy, white double doors of the main entrance. Armchairs are scattered around a small coffee table to the right of the main desk. Everything is neat, spacious, and well, new. We walk to the front desk and explain to the officer behind the Plexiglas window that we're looking for Detectives Thompson and Nash. He walks us down a long corridor peppered with offices and commendations and awards on the walls.

We're seated in a sparse but comfortable room with a small wooden round table, and three chairs. We're told the detectives will be with us shortly.

Ty looks at me and creases his brow.

"I promise not to shatter into tiny pieces once the questioning begins."

"It's been a rough couple of weeks since you came out of the hospital. It's okay."

The door opens and detective Nash enters, a tall, beefy guy with a cordial smile, thick strawberry blond hair, and a matching moustache. Thompson is right on his heels, thin, fit and stoned-faced in a pretty, pink blouse and matching cardigan sweater. After the shaking of hands and exchange of pleasantries, Nash takes the seat across from Ty and me.

Thompson chooses to stand next to the window.

Nash produces a pen and notebook. "Why don't you start from the beginning and tell us what you remember," he says.

"Well—" I place my hands on the table. "It's like I told you at the hospital. I don't remember anything about the actual attack."

"That's not unusual in cases like these," he says. "You were drugged. The toxicology tests confirm that. They found GHB in your system. It acts fast and can last hours. One of the side effects is memory loss."

I look away from the detective. Does this mean the attacker has done this before, drugged his victims?

"Do you need some water, a little time to collect your thoughts?" Detective Thompson asks.

"No, I'm fine."

"Let's focus on what you do remember then," Nash says. "How did you travel to this party and was anyone with you?"

"I rode with my friend Zahra."

He scribbles something in the notebook. Ty sits ramrod straight in his chair.

"Then what happened?" Detective Thompson asks. She wants me to break down the evening for them.

I told them what time I arrived, describe what I remember about the interior of the house, who I interacted with, and the last things I remember before everything went black and I woke up in the hospital black and blue.

"Ty and I agreed that I would come over to help him do practice runs for his interview with Harvard Medical School admissions," I say.

"Then I texted her so we could leave and I didn't get

a response," Ty said. "That's when I figured something was wrong."

Nash writes in his notebook again and then looks up. "Do you remember anyone lurking around you or any guy who was particularly aggressive?"

He wasn't aggressive, not the way the detective means, but I can't help but think back to the kiss with Spencer, one of the last things I remember. I must look guilty as heck to them.

"Was there someone?" Thompson asks. She draws in a breath then releases it.

"Not really. My friend Spencer texted me and . . ."

"Is Spencer a guy or girl?" Nash interrupts. "You never know these days."

"Spencer is a guy."

A furtive glance passes between the two detectives as if to say now we're getting somewhere. I have no idea where they think this is heading.

"Anyway, Spencer texted, saying he wanted me to rescue him from some girl who bored him. We ended up in the back yard, near a tree. We talked. It was getting chilly, so we decided to head inside but he went on ahead of me. I told him I would be in, I needed a few minutes to myself."

"Why was that?" Nash asks.

I ponder my answer carefully, and the two detectives scrutinize me with an intensity that tells me they think I'm not being straight with them. How do I tell the detectives the truth without casting doubt on an already shaky situation? I'm sure they'll interview Spencer to confirm what I've told them. There's no way to predict whether he will tell them about the kiss. Better to get ahead of that potential storm.

I sit up straighter in my chair. It's no crime to kiss a boy, is it? I hadn't done it in over two years and I shouldn't feel bad about it. In fact, there was a time when I desperately wanted the boy sitting next to me to kiss me. That never happened. It almost did, but almost doesn't count.

"Spencer and I kissed while we were out in the back yard amongst the trees. When it was time to go, I stayed behind because I wanted some time to process my emotions."

I cross my arms over my chest, daring them to make something of it.

They don't. Detective Nash plows on with the questioning. "Do you recall any strange noises, anyone in the shadows, anything like that?"

"I don't."

Do you remember who was out in the backyard?" Thompson asks. She must be tired of standing because she leaves the spot near the window and pulls up a chair next to her partner.

I shake my head. "I knew very few people at the party. I didn't recognize anyone out in the back yard. All the people I did know were inside at that time."

Nash turns his attention to Ty. "You said you texted Abbie because the two of you were supposed to leave together but she didn't respond. Can you confirm the time?"

"It was closing in on 1:00 a.m., a few minutes before."

Nash starts clicking his pen, a pensive look on his features. He begins, "Help us clear up some details here. You arrived at the party with your friend Zahra then agreed to go home with Ty right before you were in the backyard kissing Spencer. Does that about sum it up?"

Shoot me now. I can see it in their eyes, how they arrived at a conclusion: the scenario Nash just outlined plus the fact that I ended up drugged, raped, and at the hospital naked and unconscious with alcohol on my breath. What a picture. I couldn't have made up this scenario if they paid me a million dollars. The detectives think I'm a party girl who got wild and got herself in trouble. I could be wrong, but sympathy isn't exactly oozing from either one of them.

"Ty and I have been best friends for years." I smooth down my skirt and clear my throat. "As I mentioned, I was going to help him prepare for his interview with Harvard, so it was just simpler to sleep over. That's why we planned to leave the party together."

Detective Thompson nods her head slowly. Relief washes over me. I need them on my side. Then a thought occurs to me. I haven't told them about the roses, notes and gifts. After I describe the situation, Nash asks, "Do you still have the notes?"

I remove a manila envelope from my purse and hand it to him. He spreads out the notes on the table. Thompson leans in so she can read too.

After a while, Nash says, "And you have no idea who could have sent these notes?"

"None whatsoever. They seemed harmless at first, although I was uneasy that someone was watching me. Everything changed when the doll arrived."

I explain to the detectives about the doll and the ball at Bedford Hills, and how only someone who was either present at the ball or saw the painting of me wearing that gown would have known about it. I don't mention that I asked Christian about it. No need to rope him into my drama. Poor Ty is already up to his neck in it because of our friendship.

"Oh, I also took photos of the flowers," I say and reach into my purse again to retrieve my phone.

I click on the camera icon on the phone, scroll through some photos until I find the right ones. I hand over the phone to Detective Thompson. Nash leans in as she scrolls through the photos of the flowers.

"These are beautiful roses," Nash says. "I've never seen them before."

"They're rare. I was only able to find out about one of them so far. They're expensive, cost hundreds of dollars.

"So you're thinking this guy, this Humble Admirer is the one who attacked you?"

"Maybe."

My plan has backfired. Nash draws his brows together and clears his throat unnecessarily. Thompson offers up a tight smile and swallows several times. The chain of events I've described offers no insight or clarity into the case. In fact, it makes me look like a hot mess.

"Well," Nash says, "we will do everything we can to catch this guy. But we also want you to be prepared —"

"You don't have to sugarcoat it for me, Detective," I interrupt. "I'm pre-med, and I've done my research. If I'm lucky, the rape kit will get tested in weeks, maybe longer because of the backlog. Less than one percent of perpetrators ever see the inside of a prison cell. Add to that we have no eyewitnesses to the crime, my memory problem…I know it will be an uphill battle."

The mist gathering in my eyes reminds me that my emotions are still raw. The possibility that he may never be caught sends me over the edge. Ty squeezes my hand under the table. If I don't get out of here this second, I may lose it in front of the detectives.

Ty glances at me then says, "We have to go. Cooper isn't feeling well, but we'd be happy to answer any follow-up questions another time."

He thanks them for their time, collects the business cards they offer, and before they make any pronouncements about next steps, I'm halfway down the hall heading to the car in the parking lot, barely able to see through my blinding tears.

CHAPTER 30

AFTER

I CAN'T IGNORE him any longer. Spencer has been texting and leaving messages the past few days, but I haven't spoken to him and have turned down all his attempts at meeting face to face. My responses have been via brief text message.

Keeping the attack quiet is counterintuitive, secrecy being the nemesis of the truth and all that. Believe me, I get it. But I don't know if I'm ready to discuss what happened to me with Spencer. If it were just physical injuries, my arm, bruises and scrapes, it would be much easier.

By the time I arrive in the dining hall, he's already seated and fidgeting with his phone. He serves up a warm smile and enthusiastic hello when I appear at the table. I take the seat opposite him.

"You really know how to scare a guy," he says in admonishment.

"That was not my intent."

He looks down at my arm, alarm in his eyes. "What happened to your hand?"

"I'm clumsy."

He stares at me, his eyebrows squishing together.

I take a deep, long breath. It's only a matter of time before either Detective Nash or Thompson contacts him, so I may as well come clean. "I injured my arm when I was thrown out of a moving car. I can't give you any details because I don't remember anything leading up to that."

In a slow calm tone, I explain to Spencer my ordeal and end by telling him investigators will most likely want to talk to him.

He stares back at me, his gaze incredulous. He says nothing. He doesn't move a muscle. He may have stopped breathing for all I know. Then he turns away for a moment, as if trying to think of the right words. When he finally does, his voice is low and tense.

"Abbie, I had no idea all of this happened. I'm sorry is beyond inadequate. How are you feeling? Is there anything I can do?"

He reaches across the table to touch my hand. I instinctively pull back.

The hurt clouding his face makes me feel like a big old meanie, the kind of person who would kick an adorable puppy for laughs.

"I would never hurt you, Abbie."

"It's not you," I'm quick to reassure him. "Ever since the attack, I'm not myself. I'm jumpy. It's not fun but that's what I'm dealing with."

"I feel responsible in a way."

"Why?"

"If I hadn't left you in the back yard alone, maybe it would have scared off whoever did this to you."

"That's a huge assumption. We will never know."

"Do the police have any suspects?"

"Nope. My memory loss took care of that, or rather, my attacker took care of that when he drugged me. The only evidence is the aftermath."

He shakes his head. "I just can't believe this. I wish I had the right words, Abbie, but I don't. There's nothing I can say that will help you come to grips with such a barbaric crime."

"You don't have to say anything, Spencer. I'll rise above it somehow. I'll be okay. I'm a Cooper. That's kind of our thing."

"You shouldn't have to rise above it." He cracks his knuckles. "It shouldn't have happened at all. When Ty texted me to say that you went back to your dorm to put some distance between us because of the kiss, I was never more relieved in my life. Ty and I both were sick with worry. Never in a million years did I think you were violently assaulted and in a hospital somewhere."

"Yeah, sorry about the lie. I was in no condition to deal with anyone or talk about what had happened. Everything was still fresh and I was struggling, am still struggling with the aftermath."

"So you've been at your dorm all this time?" he asks.

"What do you mean?"

"Well, you need help. You need to be supported. How are you managing?"

"Ty has been helping me."

"At his place?"

"Yes."

"That's good."

161

Something in his tone tells me he's not happy with this arrangement. Those questions were asked on purpose, to confirm what he already suspected.

"I'm lucky to have him. I don't know what I would have done if he wasn't there."

"What about your parents?"

"I haven't told them, and I don't know if I ever will."

Spencer scratches his temple. "Why don't you want your parents to know? I thought you were close with them."

"I am. But telling them will open up a bunch of complications. My dad is a cancer survivor in remission. This news could send him reeling and possibly into a relapse. I can't risk it."

I don't know why I'm explaining all this to Spencer, especially since I have conflicted feelings about him.

He leans forward and says, "That's pretty courageous and selfless, putting your dad's needs ahead of your trauma. Based on what you've told me about your family, I don't think they would want you to keep this from them, though."

"It's not their decision, is it?"

He leans back in the chair. "Ty threatened to kill me while we were searching for you. During our stint as teammates on the crew team, he was one of the calmest dudes I ever came across. When it comes to you though, he's scary. I get it now."

I frown in confusion. "Why would Ty threaten to kill you? That's not like him."

"Like I said, when it comes to you, he's a different person. He thought I had something to do with your disappearance."

This statement offers no clarity to my previous question. "What led him to think that?"

Spencer shrugs. "It was in the heat of the moment. I was the last person to see you. He was just lashing out. Frankly, I think the guy was scared out of his head and so was I."

I steeple my hands together and stay quiet for a moment. Panic I understand. Threatening to kill someone because you think they're guilty of some nefarious deed seems extreme for Ty. Heading back to the party inside the house was Spencer's idea, but he had no way of knowing I would choose to stay behind. Or was it just, as Spencer says, they were both sick with worry and Ty spoke out of fear?

"Abbie, are you still with me?"

"Sorry. I was just thinking."

"About what?"

"Your jacket," I say quickly.

"What jacket?" he asks.

"Are you serious? You don't know what I'm talking about?"

He looks perplexed and swallows several times. "I swear I don't know what you're talking about." His tone is uncertain.

"It's not a trap, Spencer. I was wondering why you haven't asked about your jacket—the one I was wearing the night of the party. I was cold and you draped it around me. I was wearing it when I was taken. But according to the hospital personnel, I wasn't wearing anything when I was found and admitted. I only had a sheet of plastic wrapped around me."

Spencer's face turns ashen and he blinks rapidly. He attempts to speak several times without success.

"You never missed your jacket?"

"I assumed you had it and I would get it back later," he says, the tremors in his voice unmistakable.

"Well, I don't have it. Whoever attacked me has it. He probably got rid of it by now. Sorry to say, but you will never see that jacket again. I hope you didn't have anything valuable in the pockets. I can reimburse you for the loss."

"Don't," he says sharply. "How could you even think I would allow you to do that? Come on, Abbie. I'm not a monster. It's just a jacket, no big deal. I have another one."

He gives off a forced smile. This has shaken him to his core. He recovered quickly, but there was fear in him when I brought up the subject. But why?

"I didn't mean to insult you. You were nice enough to loan me the jacket and now it's gone. I just wanted to replace it."

"It's okay," he says softly. "Can I ask you something, though?"

I gesture for him to proceed with his question. He says, "Have you considered the possibility that whoever attacked you could be long gone by now and out of the reach of the police? I'm just saying, if I did something that horrible to someone, I would not stick around."

"I thought of that possibility, yes. But I've dealt with a psychopath or two before, and there's also a possibility, a very strong one, that he hasn't gone anywhere. He wants to stick around to admire his work, to bask in the glow of how clever he is, how he fooled and continues to fool everybody. If it's the guy who sent me those roses, he's still here."

Spencer furrows his brow. "What roses?"

I give him the abbreviated version of my secret admirer

164

drama. He lights up as if I've just injected him with a shot of adrenaline.

"Do you really think he could be the guy? Did you tell the police about him?" *Why do you want to know what I've said to the police? Are you trying to stay ahead of them?*

I mentally kick myself for allowing paranoia to creep up on me again. "Yes, but all they have to go on are the notes and pictures of the flowers."

"That's something at least," he says. "It's better than nothing."

"Well, he can't hide forever."

"Why do you say that?"

"I don't care how long it takes. There will be payback."

"How?"

"I don't know how. I just know there will be a reckoning."

CHAPTER 31

─◦─

AFTER

I GRAB A seat at the crowded campus café, ignoring the noisy chatter around me. I stare into the steaming cup of black coffee, inhaling the aroma. The top of my hoodie covers most of my face. I can't take any chances. Maybe I came here because I wanted to prove to myself that I still got it, that I can operate right under their noses and they're still ignorant of my presence. It's not necessarily that Abbie Cooper is stupid per se. It's just that she's never encountered anyone like me before, and that has put her world in a tailspin. She's looked into my face, smiled at me, flirted with me, and still she couldn't tell. Well, that's her problem, not mine.

My ear buds are firmly planted in my ears, although I'm not listening to anything in particular. I just have no desire to be bothered. People tend to back off when they see headphones.

I'm curious about how she's coping after things got regrettably out of hand. I had to improvise that night, and that wasn't a good thing. Not after all of my meticulous

166

planning. I didn't expect her to come to and stare me dead in the face. Thankfully, my hoodie disguise was fully in place and she was too drugged up to make any kind of identification. My only consolation is the fact that I was extra careful, leaving no trace behind. They'll find nothing. I'm a phantom, someone who doesn't exist. But one can never be too careful. She's clever and determined, so I will continue to be on guard at all times.

Keeping her clothes was risky, but I wasn't sure if evidence of where she'd been could be detected from her clothing, so it was best to get rid of them. The cashmere sweater and mini skirt were a steaming pile of molten debris by the time I was done with them, along with her underwear and bra. I couldn't very well burn her shoes, so I dumped the expensive designer sandals into the Hudson River, where they will live for eternity. I tossed her phone out of the car when I dumped her near the ER, along with her purse, which I was careful to handle with gloves. Doesn't that prove I'm not a monster? I had to make sure the phone was powered off the minute I had her so no one could track her, but at least whoever found it would have been able to call someone.

"I thought that was you," a female voice says. I snap to attention and knock over the cup of coffee, spilling the liquid all over the table.

"I'll get some napkins," she says and disappears from view. I have to get out of here. But before I can make a run for the exit, she's back and wiping up the mess that was her fault.

"Sorry, I didn't mean to startle you. At first I wasn't sure it was you because of the hoodie, but I was right."

"You got me." I ball my hands into fists. All I want is to get away from her. "Look Kristina, I really have to run. I just came in for a cup of coffee and sat for a few minutes to check my email."

"Come on, you can talk to me. I haven't seen you in a long while. How have you been?"

She takes a seat. I curse inwardly. "I'm good. Thanks for asking."

"Is something bothering you? You seem tense. And what's with the cloak and dagger act? Hoodie up, face covered and staring down at your phone? Are you hiding from someone?"

"I don't know what you're talking about."

She folds her arms. "There's something different about you. I can't put my finger on it."

"You don't really know me, Kristina. Stop pretending that you do."

"Well you don't have to get an attitude about it. Just making an observation, that's all."

"Well don't."

My bad attitude doesn't deter her. "You looked pretty intense when I walked in. What's so interesting on your phone?"

I glare at her. Before I can respond, she snatches the phone from my hand and starts scrolling through it.

"Give that back." She's causing a scene, which I'm trying to avoid.

"Well what do we have here?" She perks up in her seat. "These roses are gorgeous. I've never seen those before. Do you have a secret girlfriend?"

"Give me back the phone, Kristina," I say through gritted teeth.

"Come on, don't be a grouch. I think it's great that you're sending flowers to her, whoever she is. She must be pretty special."

Without thinking about it, I reach over and grab the phone from her hands. "Mind your own business."

I pocket the phone, pick up my bag, and leave the café without a backward glance.

CHAPTER 32

AFTER

AFTER HE ATE the last slice of pizza and downed every drop of Mountain Dew, Spencer headed to the men's room, and splashed water on his face. He wiped his face with a paper towel, tossed the used pieces in the trash, and then glanced at his reflection in the mirror. He wanted to exude a calm and in-control demeanor when he spoke to the detectives who should be arriving at the pizzeria any minute now. When they called to say they just wanted to chat with him in regards to an attack on Abbie Cooper, he wasn't surprised, but it still made his heart beat at twice its normal rate.

When he arrived at the booth he occupied earlier, Spencer spotted the detectives coming through the door. Nash was the huge, redheaded one and Thompson a petite, serious-looking brunette. He waved to them.

"Thanks for agreeing to meet with us," Thompson said. Both she and Nash sat across from Spencer.

"No problem, Detectives. I don't know how I can help, but I'll do my best."

They started out with the usual—how did he know

Abbie Cooper, how long had he known her, where they met and the like. He provided the pertinent details.

"What can you tell us about the night of the attack?" Nash asked, pulling out a small notebook.

Spencer started at the beginning. "I sent her a text message, asking her to rescue me from a boring conversation with another girl. We flirted a little via text and then agreed to meet in the back yard."

Thompson held up her hand. "What do you mean by flirted a little? Were the two of you dating?"

"We spent time together. Abbie didn't call it dating. She made that clear from the beginning. I found her intriguing."

Nash leaned in closer then asked, "Intriguing how?"

Spencer shrugged. "She could have anyone she wanted. When we hung out, I couldn't always get a good read on her."

"So she liked to play games, play hard to get?" Thompson asked.

"You said that, not me. She didn't make any promises, if that's what you're thinking. As I said, she told me up front that she didn't think the two of us in a relationship was a good idea."

"Yet she was flirting with you, via text," Nash said balefully.

"Well, that was no big deal. We've been sending each other flirty text messages for a while now, but I always respected the boundaries she set."

Nash said, "Is that so? Do you have any of these messages on your phone?"

"Am I in trouble?" Spencer asked. His voice went up a notch. "Those messages are deeply personal."

Spencer didn't see what the text messages had to do with anything. It's not as if it was going to lead them to a suspect. There was nothing in those messages to indicate she was scared or nervous about anything. In fact, he was surprised to learn during their last conversation that Abbie had received anonymous gifts and messages of the romantic kind.

Thompson said, "There could be something in those text messages that could help find the perpetrator. Maybe something she said."

He really didn't want to, but he had no choice but to pull up the string of messages and hand the phone over to the detectives. The last thing he needed was for them to become suspicious of him. He hoped they wouldn't tell him they needed to keep the phone for a while. That would really suck.

"Here you go," he said, and handed the phone to Nash.

Nash held the phone between himself and Thompson so she could read the messages, too.

It seemed like they were taking an eternity as Nash scrolled through and read intently. It was hard to get a read on them, but they didn't show any obvious signs of being alarmed by anything they read so far.

Spencer raked his hand through his hair and hoped he didn't sound nervous when he said, "See, nothing suspicious in those texts. Just a boy and a girl having fun." He had to ask again if he was in trouble.

Nash rushed his words. "No, not at all, Spencer. We're just trying to put the pieces together. We want to make sure nothing is overlooked. Can you forward those texts to my phone?"

"Sure," he answered shakily. But he had to think on his feet. With those texts in hand, who knew what kind of interpretation the police could come up with? No offense to them, but he had no desire to speak to either Thompson or Nash, ever again.

"You know, you might want to talk to Ty Rambally," Spencer said.

"We spoke to him when Ms. Cooper came to the station to make a statement," Thompson said. "He didn't have much to add other than to confirm that the two of you were searching for her the night she disappeared."

"Yes, he was freaked out. He was mad that she didn't answer his text message saying it was time for them to leave. When he realized she was truly missing, he panicked. We both did."

The detectives perked up. They locked on to Spencer's comment like a heat-seeking missile.

"What do you know about Ms. Cooper's relationship with Ty Rambally?" Thompson asked.

"Not much. They met in high school, they're close friends. Ty is protective of her. Frankly, I think he's the reason she and I never had a real chance."

"What do you mean by that?" Nash asked.

Spencer took a deep breath. "She's into Ty. Has been for years."

"Was it mutual?" Thompson asked.

"Hard to tell. Sometimes he's her knight in shining armor, the next moment he gets angry because she didn't answer his text. Then there's his girlfriend Kristina. As I said, difficult to tell if he feels the same way about Abbie."

The detectives took a minute to digest this information. Spencer could see their brains clicking away, trying to piece things together and come to a reasonable conclusion.

Thompson asked, "In your opinion, is Ty capable of hurting her?"

"Anyone is capable of anything. As far as I've seen, Ty is a good guy. He has a bit of a temper, but who hasn't lost their cool from time to time? He's solid as far as I know but hard to say. I don't know what the guy is like in private. I can only tell you what I've observed."

They zeroed in on the temper statement and asked Spencer to expand on that point. "I would have done the same thing in his place. Last year, he practically pulverized a drunken freshman who was groping at Abbie and wouldn't take no for an answer. Then he threatened to kill me. He thought I had something to do with her disappearance. But that was just the fear talking. I told Abbie about it."

Both detectives take notes. Nash says, "So he's violent and possessive. Has Abbie ever showed any signs of domestic abuse? Any unexplained marks or injuries? Does he control what she does, who she talks to where she goes?"

"I haven't seen anything like that." Spencer shook his head. "Besides, Abbie is too strong-willed and independent to let that happen."

"You'd be surprised," Thompson said. "Anyone can be a victim of domestic abuse, it doesn't matter their socio-economic status or how things may appear to the outside world."

The meeting had taken a turn that Spencer didn't anticipate. It should have made him uncomfortable but it didn't.

In fact, it worked out to his advantage. If what he told the detectives caused problems for Rambally, Abbie would be more likely to lean on Spencer for support. Make it easier for him to get what he needed from her when the time came. That would show Zach, who always made Spencer feel incompetent, like he couldn't get the job done.

"Did Abbie ever mention a secret admirer slash stalker to you?" Thompson asked.

"She did. The notes claimed he would reveal himself soon, but based on what happened to her, that looks doubtful now."

"Why do you say that?" Nash asked.

"If he was the one who attacked her, then why would he reveal himself after what he did?"

"But Abbie would have no way of knowing that her secret admirer and attacker are one and the same," Nash pointed out. What makes you so sure it's the same person?"

"I'm not. Just making an obvious connection. That would be a strange coincidence if it's not the same guy."

"You mean getting these anonymous messages and then being attacked in a short time span?" Nash asked.

"Yes."

"Then something must have caused him to snap," Thompson said.

"Based on what Abbie told me, he knew a lot about her. He could have seen us together and lost it. It made him angry and he decided to get even," Spencer said.

Nash stroked his chin.

"You've given us a lot to think about, Spencer, perhaps new angles to pursue in this case," Nash said. "This has been very helpful."

"Glad to help in any way I can. Abbie is a terrific girl and didn't deserve this. I hope you guys catch the bastard and lock him up."

"So do we," Nash said.

"WE NEED TO talk," Spencer said anxiously into the phone. He drummed his fingers on the table of the booth. After the detectives left, he remained behind. He needed time to clear his thoughts.

"What's going on?" Zach asked.

"We have to meet as soon as possible. It's important."

"I have classes."

"Skip them. There's a problem."

"Come visit me this weekend then."

"It can't wait that long," Spencer snapped. He was losing patience.

Zach sighed. "The earliest I can get there is tomorrow."

"Fine," Spencer said grudgingly. "Meet me at the Five Guys Restaurant in Norwalk. It's splitting the distance."

"What's this about?" Zach asked.

"Abbie Cooper. And the police."

CHAPTER 33

------◆------

AFTER

SPENCER ARRIVED AT Five Guys, nabbed a table, and waited for Zach to show up. It was lunchtime and the place was hopping. He was too hyped up to eat. The drive to the restaurant did nothing to ease his inner turmoil, and now he was wound so tight, he might pop any minute. Too many thoughts about what could go wrong with the plan to take down the Wheelers, Abbie Cooper's state of mind, and whether he and Zach could really pull this off.

A few minutes later, Zach arrived. Once he was seated, Spencer didn't wait to unload.

"The police talked to me about what happened to Abbie," he said. "It could affect our plans."

Zach removed his hands from his coat pocket, placed them on the table, and said, "What happened to Abbie, and why would the police talk to you about it?"

Spencer stayed silent for a moment when he realized he hadn't told Zach about the attack. He had to rewind to the beginning. No wonder Zach fixed him with a gaze that said he might need a mental evaluation.

Spencer took a deep breath and apprised him of recent events. Zach listened intently but didn't react. Then he said, "I don't see a problem as far as the plan is concerned. All she needs to do is get us those invitations."

Spencer shifted in his seat. He glanced at Zach and then at customers coming through the door. When he refocused on Zach, Spencer said, "Did you hear what I said? She was violently attacked and ended up in the hospital. This is not good. Do you think she's going to help us now, with all that she's dealing with?"

Zach let out an exaggerated sigh and clasped his hands together. "The Wheeler New Year's Eve Ball is eight weeks away. That doesn't leave us a lot of time. The only thing that should concern you now is how to get those invitations, how we're going to legitimately get inside that party. Security is ironclad. You know this."

"Are you deaf?" Spencer asked, nostrils flared. "The ball is the last thing she'll be thinking about."

"Then work harder," Zach growled. "All you had to do was make her fall for you. How hard could it be? Stop whining and do your job. Otherwise, this whole thing falls apart. We won't get another shot at the Wheelers. Abbie is it. She has the access, she has their trust, and that douchebag Christian still has the hots for her. We're being handed this chance on a silver platter, so what is your problem?"

"What is *your* problem?" Spencer's yell drew the attention of several patrons. He lowered his voice. "Her state of mind is a huge obstacle. She just survived a brutal attack. She was raped, Zach. There are consequences. She's living at Rambally's apartment, and that poses another problem. She may decide to see me less and less while she's going through whatever rape victims go through."

Zach scowled and Spencer glared at him. Then Zach said, "Do you have feelings for her? Because that would be a disaster, mainly for you."

"Don't threaten me. I'm not afraid of you."

"Maybe you should be."

"Never."

"Let me lay this out for you one more time in case you lost some brain cells along the way," Zach said. "If we lose this opportunity, we won't get another. Exposing Alan Wheeler's secret to the world is our ticket to the life we deserve. If you let that slip away because you're too weak to do what needs to be done, I'll make you pay."

They both fell silent, each refusing to back down. Then Spencer said, "I warned you about threatening me. I could blow this whole plan apart just to spite you."

"But you won't." Zach radiated confidence. "Don't pretend to be better than me, Spencer. You want the money and power as badly as I do. You want the world to know the truth, and to get revenge on Alan for what he did to your mother." He cocked his head to one side as if in deep contemplation. Then he says, "But I think what's really eating you is the fact that Abbie was Christian's girlfriend, and you couldn't even make it to first base with her. I guess some guys have the magic touch and others don't. No shame in admitting that."

Spencer didn't think about it. In a flash, he reached over the table, grabbed Zach by the throat with both hands and squeezed as hard as he could. Zach had the nerve to look amused for a second or two. Spencer didn't see it coming until it was too late. With a strength that seemed almost inhuman, Zach reached up and punched him hard on the nose. Blood spurted from Spencer's nose. He cursed at Zach and cradled his throbbing nose. Patrons stared open mouthed as blood made its way down Spencer's sweatshirt.

Zach stood up. With a sneer pinned to his features, he looked down at Spencer. "Get your act together. The ball is in eight weeks. We better be in tuxedos at the Wheeler mansion on New Year's Eve. And while you're at it, why don't you work on the speech that will expose Alan Wheeler for the evil dirt bag that he is. Tick tock, Spencer."

CHAPTER 34

AFTER

I T'S BEEN CLAWING at me for days, the sense of impending doom, but I've ignored it like an unwanted diagnosis. The signs were obvious, but I made up excuses. I've been through a horrific trauma. Nightmares plague me so I don't sleep much, which leads to constant fatigue. I lost my appetite because of constant anxiety and stress, wondering if my attacker will ever be caught. I still struggle with the aftermath. All of those excuses make sense. But I can't run from the truth anymore.

"Is it done?" I ask Zahra. I stand right outside the bathroom door of the apartment. My voice is steady, clinical, and matter of fact.

When no response comes, I slowly open the door. Zahra stands next to the sink, hands outstretched and trembling with the object between her thumb and index finger. I take it from her and hold it up in front of my eyes. The double pink lines, sharp and unmistakable, stare up at me. I drop the test, take two steps backward, open the bathroom door and head for the living room sofa, where I slump into the soft leather.

My heart beats dully in my chest as if it's lost the will to pump hard and strong. My head spins at an alarming rate and I'm thankful I'm already sitting.

"Abbie, are you okay? Talk to me, please." Zahra's pleading falls on deaf ears. I'm too numb and mentally fatigued. Suspecting is one thing. Irrefutable proof is another. I know this to be true despite the razor thin possibility that the test could be wrong. It's not. The full weight of what it means will hit me later. Right now, I struggle with the reality that trumps all others: I'm carrying my rapist's child.

Zahra turns my face toward her, forcing me to look at her. "Talk to me, Abbie. Your silence is scaring me."

"What is there to say, Zahra?" The ache in the back of my throat makes my voice sound alien.

Despair is plain on her face. She swallows numerous times before she continues. "This is life-changing, and the circumstances that caused it makes everything ten times worse. I don't know what to say, Abbie. This is messed up on so many levels. No matter what you decide, your life will never be the same."

Tears roll down her cheeks. I look at her with no emotion, no verbal response to the scenario she just summarized. *My life will never be the same again.* All I can do is stare at her like the helpless, wounded creature I am.

She puts her arms around me. We sit in silence, each lost in her own troubled thoughts.

A while later, I tell Zahra I need to be alone. She nods, gathers up her purse, gives me a big hug, and promises to check in on me later. After she leaves, I open the walk-in closet in the living room, slink inside, and shut the door

behind me. I sit in the semi darkness and shake uncontrollably, chill after chill attacking me in a relentless tsunami.
My breathing is labored, but I'm determined to sit in the
enclosed space to exorcise the terror I'm sure is only just
beginning.

CHAPTER 35

AFTER

LATER THAT DAY, when Ty comes through the door waving a piece of paper, excited and grinning broadly, I work overtime to dispense with the air of misery that has followed me all day like an abrasive second skin. I push my confused and painful emotions down deep and pray they don't erupt at the worst possible moment.

He tosses his jacket on the back of a chair in the kitchen and holds up the letter. "Do you know what this is?" His eyes dance.

I grab the paper from him and unfold it. He leans over me. When I see the crimson seal in the top left hand corner of the letter, I know right away. He got in. He got accepted into Harvard Medical School. I scan the opening lines of the letter then turn around.

I pull him into my arms and hug him tightly. He wraps his arms around me with equal fervor. We stay like this, clinging to each other, a silent promise that our lives will always be intertwined. I struggle to hold back the tears prickling at the back of my eyes. They're happy tears, I tell myself. Ty deserves this and so much more. He must have sensed my distress. He pulls away and gazes into my eyes.

"What's wrong, Cooper?"

"Nothing. I'm just happy for you. All your hard work, everything you've wanted is falling into place. Your dreams are coming true, Ty. You're unstoppable, and I for one can't wait to see what you do next. I can't wait to see how you take the world by storm and revolutionize medicine. You will, you know."

"Wow. I don't know about all that."

"I believe in you. You will do that and so much more."

He gets serious, and his eyes fixate on mine. He brushes my cheek with his index finger, ever so lightly, so much so that I almost believe I imagined it. However, my reaction to the gesture is very real. My body floods with warmth, and my heart begins to beat erratically. I will my brain to say something, do something, but it's not cooperating. I stand rooted to the spot in the kitchen. He moves in closer and lowers his head. I close my eyes and when I do, he kisses me, slow and sensual, like a perfectly choreographed love scene with the perfect soundtrack echoing in the background. I lean into him and kiss him back, eager for more. And just like that, it's over.

My eyes fly open, and I want to disappear when I see the emotion dominating his features: guilt.

"Cooper, I'm sorry," he says, backing away. "I don't know what came over me. Please forgive me. I would never take advantage of you, especially what you've been through. I just . . . I just had a moment. I promise it won't happen again. I'm really sorry."

I don't know if I should cry or get angry. How dare he treat me like some pitiful being? Apologizing for kissing me is as bad as being rejected in my book.

Or maybe it's not over with Kristina, stupid, and he feels bad about kissing you while he's still seeing her. Did you ever think of that? Maybe if you weren't too chicken to ask him outright . . .

"Don't make it weird," I say. Anger steadily creeps up on me. "You kissed me and I responded willingly. Am I so pathetic in your eyes? Do you feel sorry for me, Ty? Poor victimized, damaged Abbie. She can't handle a simple kiss."

We both have tempers, and he's not about to back down. He glares at me, his nostrils flaring. "I was trying to be sensitive," he snaps. "I don't want to make things worse. You've been through an unspeakable, life-changing ordeal. And you're not pathetic or damaged. I don't ever want to hear those words come out of your mouth again."

"So you're making decisions for me now, what I can and cannot handle?"

I don't know why I'm so sensitive. He is the last person on earth I should use as a punching bag. I've turned what is supposed to be a special evening into a slugfest that's all about me. I'm ashamed of myself.

I hold my hands up in surrender. "I was way out of line. I shouldn't have come at you like that. You don't deserve that treatment, especially from me."

"I know you're frustrated," he says softly. "Next time let's talk about instead of throwing down like two cage fighters."

I nod and tell him I'm in the mood for a celebratory dinner, but rather than go out, I'll cook. I owe him that at least after my bad behavior. I prepare his favorites: maple glazed salmon with roasted vegetables, pumpkin soup, a Cobb salad, and pineapple upside down cake for dessert.

After we set the table and sit down to dig in, I say, "Your parents must be ecstatic about your acceptance into Harvard."

"I haven't told them yet." He settles a linen napkin on his lap.

This is surprising news. I thought for sure he would have told his mother first. Ty's mother Jenny is originally from the Bahamas and one of the leading reproductive endocrinologists in the country. Mrs. Rambally, or Dr. Whistler (she goes by her maiden name professionally), is what they call a Tiger Mom—a strict, demanding woman who pushed her only child to achieve the highest levels of academic success. Ty's father Bobby, an Indian immigrant from Guyana, is a leading plastic surgeon and what Ty calls the more reasonable of the pair. Dr. Rambally always struck me as a laid back, gentle, caring soul with a sense of humor, who played peacemaker when Ty and his mother got into it, which they've been known to do. Ty and his father are close, a closeness I suspect his mother sometimes envies.

"Oh, I assumed you called them the minute you saw the letter."

"You're the first and only person I've told, Cooper." He spoons his soup.

"It means a lot to me, Ty, that you would share something so amazing and life-changing with me first."

"It shouldn't come as a shock to you. I couldn't think of anyone I wanted to share my news with more than you."

As we continue our dinner table chatter, I wonder about my future and the decision that looms before me. I can't keep this baby. Only one decision can safeguard the future I envision for myself—I have to get an abortion, and soon.

"What's wrong? You have this faraway look in your eyes," Ty says.

"Nothing. Stop worrying. I'm fine."

"No, you're not. You're holding out on me. What is it?"

I put down the fork I was holding and look away from him. He gets up from his seat and comes around to my side of the table. He kneels in front of me and turns my face toward him.

"What is it, Cooper? It can't be all that bad."

Here I go again, dumping my problems in his lap. "It is all that bad."

"Tell me. We'll face it together."

"I don't know if you'll want to face this."

"Let me decide. You can tell me."

"I'm pregnant. Found out today."

His shoulders go rigid with shock, his face contorted into a mask of pure anguish. He stays that way for a few beats, and then gets off his knees. He takes the seat next to me at the table. He screws his eyes shut and then opens them again. I say nothing, giving him the space he needs to process what he's feeling.

"Are you sure?" His voice shakes.

"I took a home pregnancy test. Two pink lines popped up. It was one of those tests that can detect early pregnancy."

"You haven't had time to think about what you want to do, I suppose."

"I can't keep it, Ty. That's just not an option I'm willing to consider."

He shakes his head slowly. "Think about it carefully. Weigh all your options."

"I will, but I don't see any other way."

He shakes his head again. "You have my support, whatever you decide."

"Thanks. I appreciate it."

CHAPTER 36

AFTER

"A RE YOU SURE you want to go today? You just decided last night," Zahra says.

Once again, I've hauled Zahra into one of my schemes, only this scheme is scary, requires medical intervention and a few days off from classes. No sweat. Easy stuff.

We sit in the café located at the corner of Campus Central, a wide, open space that that brings together under-graduate and graduate students from all areas of study. The surrounding area is dotted with dormitories and academic buildings in stunning gothic architecture.

Zahra nibbles on her apple caramel scone and I scan the crowd inside the café, nervous that I might see someone I don't want to talk to, namely Spencer. Or Kristina. She stopped coming around Ty's apartment. I haven't asked him about her, but if I know Ty, he probably told her now was not a good time and they should cool it. *But you don't know for sure, do you?*

"Who are you looking out for?" Zahra asks, following my gaze.

"Nobody."

"Spencer."

"Yes. He's been supportive, but I can't deal with him right now."

Once I refocus on our table, Zahra asks, "Are you going to tell Ty?"

"I already did, last night."

"What did he say?"

"He'll stand by me, whatever I decide. I'm just going to do it without telling him. He deserves a break from my crisis."

"He'll be upset when he finds out you did it without him. You'll have to take a few days off from school. Because trust me, there will be pain."

"How would you know?" I shiver at the notion of more pain. Although I don't know all the details, at the very least I know this is going to be an invasive procedure. Yet another invasion of my battered body after the assault, collection of evidence for the rape kit, and now this. My scarf feels as if it's about to strangle me. I give it a firm tug to loosen it.

"I just know, okay."

"Zahra," I say quietly. "How come you know so much about this stuff?"

She looks away, her eyes traveling to the other students in the café. Then she turns to look at me, her eyes glistening. "You're not the only one who had drama in high school."

"What do you mean?" I lean in.

She swipes her eyes with the tips of her fingers. She swallows hard and can't look me in the eye.

"I see," I tell her.

"It was nothing like your situation. You didn't ask for

this. I on the other hand, I was stupid. My stupidity had consequences."

"Everybody makes mistakes, Zahra.

"Yes, but mine could have been avoided. Anyway, my parents told me straight up that they were done raising kids and I was on my own. They would support whatever decision I made but I shouldn't expect any help from them. I had college to think about. I wasn't ready to take care of a kid. I could barely take care of myself. Maybe if I had help I would have made a different choice, but I didn't see how I could have made a life for me and a kid with just a high school diploma. Not the kind of life I wanted."

"I know what you mean. It's not an easy thing, but I just don't see any other way."

"Your parents would help you, wouldn't they?" she asks.

I frown. "I can't dump this on them. I have to deal with it on my own. And maybe years from now I may have regrets, but right now, regrets are an expensive currency I can't afford."

"Do you know how it works, what actually happens?" she asks.

"You mean the process? I haven't gotten to that part yet. As you pointed out, I only came to this decision last night."

Zahra explains to me the procedure involved in an abortion. When she's finished, I'm horrified and scared, but I know I must stick to the plan.

"What about the future?" I ask. "I mean, you can still have kids, right?"

"I think so. I went to a reputable doctor and the follow up visit went well. She said there was no reason I couldn't."

"Good. I do want kids eventually, just not right now."

"Me too," she says.

"How far along were you when you found out?"

"About eight weeks."

"And how far along were you when you got it done?"

Zahra shifts in her seat and drops her gaze. "Four weeks later," she says quietly.

"Oh," is all I can say.

"Do you think I'm a bad person?"

"No. I'm about to do the same thing, so does that make me a bad person? Does that define me and negate everything I've done in my life up until now?"

She shakes her head.

Silence falls over our table. I ease over to the foremost corner of the booth in which we sit. I place my head down in the cradle of my arm and sob. I hear Zahra sniffling too. I need to pull myself together. If this is going to work, I have to be strong, decisive and fearless.

CHAPTER 37

---◆---

AFTER

TWO DAYS LATER, Zahra and I sit in the waiting room of a clinic tucked away inside a nondescript building twenty minutes from campus by car. There is a separate waiting area and exit for patients. The room is pleasant, with potted plants and paintings on the wall. The receptionist welcomes us with a smile. We take a seat and wait for me to be called to see the doctor. Since I'm still on my parents' insurance, I have to pay cash for the procedure and any pain medications so my parents don't find out.

Someone calls my name, and I look up to see a nurse in blue scrubs.

"Follow me," she says pleasantly.

I scoop up my purse and Zahra gives me the thumbs up sign. I follow the nurse into an exam room with a couple of chairs, bed, a sink, garbage bin, medical supplies and an ultrasound monitor. I'm freezing. I don't know if it's the temperature in the room or naked fear. A few minutes later, there's a knock on the door and I tell whomever it is to come in. A pleasant looking man in his early fifties, with dark hair graying at the temples, introduces himself as Dr. Green. He does his best to put me at ease.

"Would you prefer to have a nurse in here with us?" he asks.

"I'm fine," I say, although I'm not sure. "Let's talk about the procedure."

"Of course, but first let's talk about your options and what may be the right course of action for you."

"I don't need to discuss options," I say coolly. "This is the only option I'm willing to pursue. It's the only option that makes sense for me."

"Are you sure about that? It's my job to advise you not only of options available but also whether the decision you make is the right one for you."

I tell him about the attack. The nightmares and anxiety, lack of focus, how my schoolwork started to suffer, the headaches. He says I might be suffering from Post Traumatic Stress Disorder (PTSD) and I should see a therapist. I think back to the email from Professor Cross. She wanted me to see Dr. Grace Shanahan. I've avoided making the call. I know it could be helpful, but the thought of seeing a professional makes me feel like I'm a broken doll who needs fixing. It means he got the better of me if I can't function without help.

"Don't worry, I'll be fine."

I consent to an exam but ask for a female nurse. After the exam, I make one of my biggest mistakes. I agree to an ultrasound to determine how far along I am. When I see the heartbeat on the monitor, a black image the size of a peanut, and the nurse tells me I'm five weeks along, I break down right in front of her, not caring that she's a total stranger.

I sob uncontrollably, a mist of sadness and helplessness seeping into my bones.

"I know it's hard, honey," the nurse says. "That's why we want our patients to carefully consider all the angles before they move forward."

I thought I had this under control. It seemed so straightforward. My rationalization was sound. My logic made perfect sense. Now I'm all confused again, and my earlier logic is as useful to me as a dead car battery. My life just got exponentially more complicated, and I have no idea what to do.

CHAPTER 38

AFTER

I'M FRESH OUT of answers. I don't know what to do, where to turn, how to fix it. A baby is growing inside of me. A baby I don't want and couldn't possibly love because it was conceived in hatred and violence. I feel nothing for it. It's an unwanted alien that invaded my body and decided to set up shop, growing everyday. I don't take prenatal vitamins or take extra care or stare at my stomach in adoration. I feel no excitement or anticipation. I've often wondered what it would be like to be pregnant with my first child. The shared joy of it, how excited my parents would be to become grandparents, and what it would be like to do all the things parents do when they're overjoyed about becoming parents. But I feel none of that. Only despair.

I'm barely holding on at school. It takes more energy and focus than before to keep up. Now, with this new development, everything may fall apart. If my grades suffer, I will lose my academic scholarship. Once that happens, my parents will have to fork over my tuition. Then I will have to explain everything. How all of it will affect my dad is still a huge question mark, a risk I can ill afford.

The police have no leads. The results from the rape kit haven't come back, nor did I expect that they would. Will the fact that I'm pregnant change that? I don't know. My only solace in this mess is that the tests for sexually transmitted diseases came back negative. Yet, my attacker continues to taunt me. How could I have ended up pregnant? I have two theories: One, if he used protection, it failed. Two, if he didn't use protection, he's confident no DNA match will come back from a national criminal database search.

A knock on the driver side window startles me. I look up to see an older man miming at me. I think he's asking if I'm okay. I give him the thumbs up sign in case he can't read lips. He returns the thumbs up sign, gives me another smile and then leaves. I breathe a sigh of relief. I sit for a few more minutes to calm myself down, and then exit the car.

I enter the massive medical building, take the elevator to the eighth floor, and follow the signs to psychiatry. I arrive in a waiting room, and then an assistant escorts me through a corridor of offices after my name is called. I'm steered into a comfortable office with a couch and two chairs, a rug, a small bookshelf and lamp. Diplomas from Yale and University of Chicago cling to the walls.

A few minutes later, Dr. Shanahan walks in and introduces herself. A tall, elegantly dressed woman with a short Afro and kind brown eyes. I try to hide my surprise. I was expecting an Irish-American doctor because of her last name. That's what I get for making assumptions. I decline her offer of water. She puts me at ease right away. The fact that she came recommended by Professor Cross is a big plus.

Dr. Shanahan sits across from me, crosses her legs, and

says she wants me to be comfortable. Once I assure her that I am, we begin.

"Tell me what brings you to see me. I read your intake form, but I want you to tell me in your own words."

I stare up at the ceiling and lightly tap my feet on the carpet.

"Take your time."

"I'm confused. I'm tired. Sometimes I get angry because it's unfair and I wonder what I did to deserve it. The pressure of school is getting to me, and I feel like giving up."

I cover my face with my hands to get my emotions under control. I can't believe I said that aloud. I wasn't even aware I was thinking it. I'm not a quitter. So why did those words leave my mouth?

I remove my hands from my face and Dr. Shanahan hands me a box of tissue. I dab at my eyes and take a deep breath. "I don't know why I said that, about giving up."

"Have you been thinking about quitting school, perhaps to return later?"

"I'm overwhelmed, Dr. Shanahan. My world is spinning out of control and I don't know how to handle it because this is a different kind of trouble. I've handled difficult situations before, but this time, it's too much."

"The violence you mean."

"Yes. I don't think it was random."

"Tell me about it."

"You don't randomly drug people. You plan it. If it's the person I suspect it is, he sent me flowers and notes before all of this happened. I think he felt like I rejected him and decided to get even. But how can you reject someone you don't even know?"

"That's a reasonable question. But in the mind of someone who believes he's entitled to have access to you, that you should return his feelings, anything could be misconstrued as a slight against him and interpreted as rejection. Something as simple as talking to another man can be interpreted as betrayal. It doesn't matter to him that he was operating in the shadows and you have no clue who he is."

"That doesn't make any sense." I bite the nails on my index finger and stop when Dr. Shanahan looks at me with a bemused smile.

"No it doesn't, not to a healthy mind. You said you wanted to quit school," she says. "Taking a semester off is not unheard of in these types of situations. You've experienced severe trauma that could be with you for the rest of your life. Some time surrounded by loved ones, to heal and gain perspective, could be helpful on the road to recovery."

"I can't afford the time off. I'll lose momentum."

"How do you mean?"

"My future plans." I explain to Dr. Shanahan my timetable for graduating, my plans for medical school, followed by an internship and residency. The many years of training it will take to become a top neurosurgeon. To take time off while I'm only a second year undergraduate student will slow me down.

"But mostly, if I leave school, he will win. I can't let him win."

"Win how, Abbie? What do you mean?"

I take a deep breath. "If I take time off from school, he would have derailed my plans, put me off track. I can't put my dreams on hold because of what that monster did. I have to plow ahead. I can't give in, Dr. Shanahan. And if the idea of him not winning is what keeps me going, so be it."

She shakes her head, as if in complete agreement with me. "You mentioned on your intake form that you have recurring nightmares about the attack?"

"Yes. He's always going for my throat. I can't see him. It's too dark. Then he hurls me through the air and I'm falling, with nothing to break the fall. I always wake up before I hit the ground."

"Those kinds of nightmares are not unusual when one suffers the kind of trauma you have."

"Then how do I make them go away?"

"There is no magic bullet, Abbie. Sometimes, they go away on their own with time. As you get stronger, gain coping skills, and you put some distance between yourself and the trauma, they can go away or continue for years. That's one of the reasons that the support of family and friends is so important for your recovery. How is your family handling the situation?"

I look away from her and clasp my hands in my lap.

"What is it?" she asks.

"I haven't told them, and I'm not going to."

She sits up straighter in her chair. "Why not?"

I explain to her about my dad's illness and how he's in remission and I don't want to stress him out.

"Would you say you're close with your family?"

"We're pretty tight-knit."

"Then Abbie, sooner or later, they're going to know something is wrong."

"Tell me about it. My mother freaks out if I get so much as a sniffle."

"So how do you intend to hide this from them? This is not something you recover from overnight. There could be triggers."

"I don't know, Dr. Shanahan," I say, my voice inching up a notch. "That's why I'm here. I came to you to help me deal."

"I understand. It's confusing and overwhelming."

"Yes, it is."

"Is there any other reason you don't want to tell your parents, besides your father's illness?"

"Of course there isn't."

"Are you sure?" she asks gently.

"What are you getting at? What other reason would there be?"

"You said you and your family are close. The fact that you want to protect your dad tells me that perhaps you're a daddy's girl. Am I right?"

"Yes. So what? What does that have to do with anything? You won't understand," I say finally.

"Try me," she challenges.

I squirm in my seat and keep my eyes downcast. Too many emotions are swirling inside of me. I have the most amazing dad on the planet, and I don't think I exaggerate when I say he thinks I hung the moon. And if I were to tell him, he would mount his own personal manhunt for the perpetrator. Despite knowing this, I can't bring myself to tell him. Mom would be devastated and go into protection mode. She'd try to keep me in a bubble so nothing bad will ever happen to me again, although she knows that's not possible. But my dad, it's just different.

"I tell myself every day that I'm the same person I was before all of this happened. But I'm not so sure. I've changed. It's hard to explain. I don't want my relationship with my dad to change. I want to be the same Abbie he sent off to college. I'm kind of the same but then I'm not. I don't know," I say throwing up my hands. "It's really complicated."

"I think you're doing great explaining it."

"Then there's my little brother, Miles."

"What's your relationship with him like?"

"He looks up to me. He thinks I'm a great big sister. I don't want him to think I've changed either. I just want to be the same for my family. The attack is like this thing that follows me around. Sometimes I wonder if people can see it stenciled on my face. Rape victim. Damaged goods. Tainted. I know I shouldn't have those thoughts, but I do."

"That's a heavy burden to carry around. People have all kinds of different reactions to victims. But that's not your problem. So let's keep the focus on you. What does winning look like to Abbie? You said you didn't want your attacker to win."

"To go on with my life as if none of it happened. He took from me something I wasn't willing to give. I wish I could turn back the clock."

"But we can't, Abbie. We have to figure out a way to move forward."

"Well, even that's more complicated than I thought initially."

"Why is that?"

"I'm pregnant. I want to get rid of it, but I had an attack of conscience, so I'm in limbo."

Dr. Shanahan is visibly taken aback. She almost slumps in her chair, ever so slightly but I notice. She's earning her hourly rate, that's for sure.

"Have you told anyone?"

"Just my friend Zahra. She went with me to the clinic. I also told Ty."

"Abbie, that is a lot on the shoulders of a young girl. I strongly advise you to talk to your family."

No. That's not happening. Ever.

"My mind is made up. I already explained to you my reasons. I have to figure out how to deal with this on my own. Besides, I'm not entirely alone. Ty has been helping me."

"Another girlfriend?"

"No. He's a boy."

"You smiled when you said his name."

"I did?"

"Yes. Tell me about him."

I waste no time gushing about Ty. It takes the focus off me. I give Dr. Shanahan the backstory, how we met in high school and have been best friends ever since. How he has seen me through some of the toughest periods in my life, including now when he took me to his place and cared for me right after the assault.

"It sounds like he's been an anchor for you."

"That's a good way to put it." I nod. "He's always been a safe place for me, as long as I can remember."

"That's great, Abbie. I'm glad you have his support to help you through. What does he say about the pregnancy?"

"He says he will support me, whatever my decision."

"That's great to hear. Do you have romantic feelings for him?"

I stare at my hands in my lap until Dr. Shanahan says we have to stop for the day.

CHAPTER 39

AFTER

THIS IS MY third visit to the center. I didn't even make it in to see the nurse or doctor last time. I left the waiting room before they could see me. When I called for a third appointment, I assured them that I was ready this time and promised I wouldn't waste their time or pull another disappearing act.

I squeeze Zahra's hand so tight I see the anguish on her face.

"Sorry," I say and let go. "This is it. No more hesitating or running away. It's just a few minutes and it will all be over."

I'm talking fast, perhaps trying to convince myself that it's going to be as easy as I envision. Zahra and I sit next to each other in the now familiar waiting room. They've added another plant and some new magazines since my last visit.

"Stop overthinking it, Abbie," she scolds. "You're not that far along. It means less bleeding and fewer complications, hopefully."

"Uh huh. I know that." My gaze lands on the woman across from me, not much older than I am. She looks as terrified as I feel. Our eyes lock briefly then she focuses her attention on her cell phone. The woman next to her looks like she could be her mother or aunt. I can't imagine my mother in a place like this. She would absolutely put her foot down. Another reason I have to do this before I lose my nerve and she finds out. I'm still not in the clear. Mom could still show up out of the blue. I want this over with before that scenario plays out. With my luck, it will. She might even show up with Dad in tow.

Poor Zahra. My name is called, and for the third time, she gives me the thumbs up sign and swears everything is going to be okay.

Ironically, I end up in the same room as when I first visited the place. Nurse Barbara stands and I take a seat.

My cell phone buzzes and I retrieve it from my purse. With the potential for Mom to show up unexpectedly, I need to be warned in advance so I take the call. I apologize and tell Barbara to hang on for a second. She points to the door and mouths she'll be back.

"Two days in a row. I'm beginning to feel special, Lee. Either that or you're bored."

"Sorry. I didn't think you would pick up. I was about to leave a message, figuring you would be in class this time of day."

"Nope, you got me live. What's up?"

"Shelby is taking me to Louisiana in a few days. To see her mother."

"Get out of here, are you kidding?"

"I'm fresh out of jokes."

"Why? What brought this on?"

"Shelby and I have been talking a lot, you know, about the past. Plus, her mother isn't doing so great. She has regrets about not seeing her dad before he died. I think she wants to make peace with her mother about kicking her out when she got pregnant with me. And I've always wondered about the woman who abandoned my mother when she was a child herself."

I place my hand over my chest to calm my tumultuous heart. For the first time in four years, since we found out that Lee was the child Mom gave up when she was fifteen, he referred to her as *my mother*. We've had many fights about Lee's refusal to finally forgive Mom and build a proper relationship with her. Over the years, he's gone from downright hating her to a reluctant acceptance of the facts. Their relationship has much improved, although Lee always kept his emotional distance. He never fully embraced Mom. This is huge, a life-changing event for him. He's going to Louisiana with her. He's going to face our grandmother. And that means he's finally and fully accepted our mother.

"That's great news, Lee," I say, my voice cracking. "That's a miracle I never thought I would see. You and Mom, connecting in such a profound way."

"You did it again, Abbie. This is happening because of you."

"Uh oh. What did I do?"

"You wouldn't let me give up on the possibility of having a relationship with the woman who gave birth to me. You made me see that my anger wouldn't change the past. When I first met you at St. Matthews, I thought you were something special. I've gotten to know you and Miles pretty well, and Shelby did an amazing job. Now I see that if circumstances had been different, she would have done a remarkable job with me too."

"She would have, Lee. She definitely would have, but you turned out great, too. You're half of her, don't forget that."

"I won't. Anyway, I just wanted to let you know. We'll chat soon."

After I hang up from Lee, a wave of emotions swells in my chest, threatening to explode in big torrents and drown me. I sit perfectly still. If I move, even an inch, it's all over.

There's a knock on the door. I don't answer. Nurse Barbara eases into the room and shuts the door behind her.

"Are you okay, hon?"

I remain silent. My vocal cords won't work anyway. Barbara looks at me and all I can do is stare back at her like some petrified, helpless being.

"Do you want me to call someone?"

I manage to shake my head enough to signal no.

"Do you need a few minutes alone to collect your thoughts?"

I take deep breaths and clear my throat. "I'm fine."

"We can do this another time if you're not ready."

"There will be no other time." Then I look her straight in the eyes. "I can't do it."

Barbara doesn't flinch. In an even, unflustered tone she says, "Not too long ago you were sure. You were justified in your reasons for wanting to terminate."

"My mother also had justification. But she didn't take the easy way out."

"I'm confused," Barbara says. I share with her the remarkable story of my brother, Lee. How my mother suffered physical and emotional abuse at the hands of her own mother, who kicked her out of the house and into a cruel world at fifteen.

"Don't you see? Mom had every reason, just like I do,

to get rid of the pregnancy. The difference is she didn't have the privileged life that I have. She didn't have a home or loving parents or the financial resources that I have access to. She was fifteen. I'm a few years older, attending an Ivy League university. She had it much worse. It was tragic. But she fought, Barbara, under the worst circumstances possible. She was homeless until she gave birth. Yet she had Lee."

"Was it Lee you spoke to just now?"

"Yes. I can't imagine my life without him in it. He did something for me, even before we found out we were related, that was so giving and unselfish. We've been tight ever since."

"So what are you going to do?"

"I guess I'm having a baby."

"What about school?"

"I can finish out the current year. If my math is correct, I will give birth in the summer. The rest, I haven't yet figured out."

"I've been doing this for a while now, Abbie. The moment you walked through those doors, I knew you couldn't do it."

"How did you know?" I wring my hands. My stomach churns as my anxiety about the future looms large and scary.

"The way you talked about your family. When you got off the phone with your brother, I knew there was no way you were going through with it. In the end, your desire to live your truth was more powerful than your ambition."

She articulated what I've been too stubborn to recognize all along. I thought I had all the answers. They were logical, justifiable, and complete. I threw everything else out the window, my inconvenient truths: my values, my faith, the very essence of what makes me who I am. What happens next, I have no clue.

CHAPTER 40

AFTER

A STUNNED ZAHRA slowly backs the car out of the parking lot and we head back to campus.

"You think I'm crazy, don't you?" I ask.

"I don't know what to think. I thought we had this plan on lockdown. Then you went in there and blew up the whole thing with dynamite."

"It wasn't that dramatic. You exaggerate."

"It *was* dramatic. You did a complete one eighty," Zahra insists. "Abbie, you're talking about becoming a mother and you have no idea who the father of the baby is. Have you thought about what it could do to you if every time you look at the kid, it triggers bad memories? It happens, you know. Then the kid grows up with a resentful mother, and they never understand why."

"You're just trying to scare me. You don't have to. I'm scared out of my mind as it is."

"You didn't seem scared when we left the clinic."

"Well, I am. A lot. There are tons of questions I don't have the answers to, and I better find out soon."

"What do you mean?" She slows down to allow a couple and their young daughter to cross the street.

"Where am I going to live, where am I going to have this baby? I have to find an OBGYN while I'm still at school. I figure I can finish out my sophomore year since I won't have the baby until next summer."

"Right," Zahra says, shaking her head. "Okay, what else?"

"If I give the baby up for adoption, then it's straight-forward. Give birth in the summer and be back on campus next fall."

"Whoa!" She takes her eyes off the road for a brief second to give me a look. "You said you were keeping the baby, now you're talking adoption?"

"I never explicitly said I was keeping the baby. I only said I couldn't go ahead with the abortion."

Zahra frowns, as if trying to make sense of what I've said. "Okay, it makes sense, I guess. But seriously, do you think Jason and Shelby Cooper are going to allow you to give away their first grandkid to strangers? You must be out of your mind if you think that."

"I haven't thought about all the angles, okay. Including the fact that I'll have to tell them something. Which reason is worse: I fooled around and got pregnant or tell them the truth? I don't know which one would be less painful for them."

"Neither," Zahra says, as if I should know this already. "Either way, they're going to be devastated."

"Okay, let's move on to option two for a minute."

"Which is?"

"If I decide to raise the baby on my own. That would make me a college dropout, but I figure I can ask my dad or mom to hook me up with a job. At least I'll have a steady income. I can pay for childcare and support us both."

"What about housing and transportation?"

"I still have a good amount of money left in an account my parents set up that includes securities and other assets. It's their last financial contribution to my upbringing. Now I need to make sure I use the account wisely."

After a brief pause she says, "Do you really think you can make this work, Abbie?"

"I have to. My mother was in a far more dire situation than I am. Both she and Lee made it. What excuse do I have? I'm not the first person to have this happen to her."

"How are you going to explain this to them? About being pregnant."

"I don't know yet. I'm still working on it."

"Well you better hurry."

CHAPTER 41

AFTER

A FTER CLASSES, I head back to Ty's place and find a surprise waiting for me: Kristina Haywood on the living room sofa. Ty, hands in his pockets, is wearing a hole in the rug. What is she doing here? *You wanted to know the status of their relationship. Maybe you're about to find out.* I want to hit something. More accurately, I want to drag Kristina out of the apartment by her hair, tell her never to come back, and then slam the door in her face. I don't care if the thought is an immature one. *Play nice. You have no say in who comes over and who doesn't. It's his apartment.*

"Hey, Ty. Kristina, this is a surprise," I say.

Ty rushes to offer an explanation. "Kristina heard about what happened and wanted to express her support in person."

"I have a card." She starts digging through her bag. She hands me a thick white envelope and I accept it. "I'm sorry to intrude. I wanted to see how you were."

She must have seen the skepticism on my face, so she launches into a monologue, which ultimately sounds like she feels sorry for me. I grab a spot next to her on the sofa.

She turns toward me. "I know we're not close, Abbie, and there has been some underlying tension between us. But when I heard what happened, I put all that aside because you don't deserve this. No woman does. I couldn't believe this horrible thing happened to someone I know. You seem to be handling it well by the looks of things. If that happened to me, I don't think I could be as strong as you are."

"Thanks for coming, Kristina. That was considerate of you. It's not easy, but I'm coping as best as I can. Ty has been wonderful. This situation has put our friendship to the test. I don't know what I would have done without him."

I smile in Ty's direction. Not because I'm trying to make a point to Kristina but because it's the truth. How would I have coped had he not stepped up?

"What are the police doing to find the attacker?" she asks.

"They've been conducting interviews, trying to gather as much information as they can. They don't have any leads to pursue yet."

"There has to be something they can do. A predator is running loose out there, and he may strike again."

"Especially if he's a student here," Ty responds.

"Wait, you guys think someone from our school did this?"

"We don't know," I say. "We have to consider all possibilities. Don't forget it was during a post-game celebration that I was snatched. Most of the people there were students. Or it could have been someone from the surrounding towns who heard about the party. And since it didn't happen on school property, there's not much campus police can do."

All three of us fall silent for a few beats, then Kristina says, "So that's it then?"

"Gosh no," I say, scorn in my voice. "It's only the beginning. As I told Spencer, I'm going to find out who did this and make him pay."

Kristina's eyes bug out of her head. "How?"

"Working on it. I have to get justice for myself and his potential future victims."

"Good for you," she says. "Let me know if there's anything I can do to help."

Awkward silence.

Then Kristina says, "I'll be going now."

She stands up and I thank her again for the card and for stopping by. Ty escorts her to the door. After Kristina leaves, Ty resumes pacing the living room. He rubs the back of his neck as if trying to erase the skin there.

"What's wrong?" I cross the space and take him by the hand, leading him to the sofa. "Talk to me. What's bothering you?"

"I told Kristina I couldn't see her anymore."

"Oh." I sit up straighter. "When did you break up with her? Today?"

"Last week."

"Why?"

"You know why."

The intensity of his gaze both thrills and scares me. I hold in a breath as I become aware of my heartbeat, which beats as loudly as a marching band.

"She's . . . she's taking it well," I stammer.

"I didn't give her a choice." Then he stands up. "Come with me. This may help you understand."

He heads for the stairs and I follow in silence. Inside his bedroom, he asks me to sit, so I plop down on the queen-sized bed. He stands in front of me. Any minute now, round three of his pacing will commence.

"I've been doing a lot of thinking," he begins.

"About what?" My eyes are trained on him. He starts to pace again.

"About the future. About the baby."

"Well, actually I needed to talk to you about that, you see—"

He holds a palm up. "Let me finish. I have to get this out."

That sounds ominous. I don't like it. I fidget with the sleeves of my sweater.

He stops pacing. "When you told me about the pregnancy, it shocked the heck out of me. I just didn't see it coming, and with everything that's been going on, it made things even more complicated. I've been waiting for you to let me know when you plan to go to the clinic so I could accompany you for support. But I have a better plan, Cooper."

"I don't understand."

He rakes his hand through his hair and clears his throat. I bounce my right knee. Butterflies roil in my stomach. He's going to say I should confess everything to my family and have them help me figure things out. That he's tired of coming to my rescue, helping me with my problems. Whatever he's about to say will change us forever. I can feel it deep in my spirit.

I consider running away. Run out of the room and just keep going. Pretend that we can both go back to our carefree lives of mixed signals, where he would flirt with me one minute and show up at a party with a girl on his arm the next. Recapture those moments where we sent each other silly memes and quotes or laughed non-stop at some joke that only the two of us got. Rewind time so we could confide our hopes, dreams and fears to each other. That's what I want.

He heads to the walk-in closet to grab something. When he turns around, he's holding a huge, life-sized, pink teddy bear, the fluffiest and most adorable stuffed animal I've ever seen. I want to snatch it from him and cuddle it right away, sink my face into its fluffy softness. But Ty's expression erases those playful thoughts from my head.

He's dead serious. My stomach starts to churn again. Everyone loves stuffed animals, but I'm not getting the warm and fuzzies from him.

His next move surprises me. With the teddy bear close to his body, he kneels in front of me. Confusion reigns in my head. What is he doing? For the first time, I notice the teddy bear is dressed in a white t-shirt.

He turns the teddy bear around to face me. In big red letters, emblazoned on the front of the t-shirt are the words:

ABIGAIL COOPER, WILL YOU MARRY ME?

I stare at the letters on the bear's chest. I can barely breathe. I close my eyes and open them again. The question is still there. I didn't imagine it. I open my mouth to speak, but words don't emerge. Ty peeks out from behind the bear, a smile tugging at the corner of his mouth.

"So what do you say?" he asks.

It takes me a second to realize I've been staring at him—or rather at the words on the bear's shirt—and I haven't spoken since I saw the question posed.

"Ty, I don't know what to say."

He holds up three fingers. "The answer has three letters."

"Wow," I say, and extend my hand to so he can get off his knees.

He plops the teddy bear down on the bed and sits next to me. "Are you going to leave me hanging?" His expression is tender, his eyes bright and expectant.

I've dreamed of this day and played this scenario out in my head many times, what it would be like if he proposed. The timing: after we were both finished with medical school. The place: the Bahamas, on a yacht in crystal, clear waters as the sun set behind us with family and friends on board. He would get down on one knee, with the ring in a velvet box, red not black. A light breeze would come off the ocean. Our families would have already planned an engagement party because they knew in advance he would pop the question. He would have asked for my dad's blessing first. A fabulous engagement party would follow, lasting until four the next morning. That's how I saw it in my mind's eye.

But instead of feeling joy, a potent sadness is rapidly snaking its way around my heart. I can feel the mist gathering in my eyes.

"Are you proposing to me out of obligation? Because we're friends and you feel sorry for what happened to me?"

He blinks several times as if trying to understand my strange reaction. He lifts my chin with his index finger and looks directly into my eyes with a laser focus that's so powerful, I'm afraid he might burn a hole through me.

"Your question is disappointing, Cooper. The fact that you asked says you don't know me at all."

I remain trapped in his gaze. He posed a serious query and he deserves a serious response. I owe him the naked truth.

"Sometimes I feel that our friendship is one-sided. That it benefits me far more than it does you. Since the day we met, you've never left my side. No matter what drama was playing out in my life, you were always there—my anchor in the storm.

"When my mother was wrongly accused of murder and sent to jail, you were there to hold me up so I wouldn't fall apart. When my senior year of high school was hijacked by a bully who threatened to use my mistake to destroy me, you were there, my ace in the hole. You're always rescuing me, Ty, and I wonder if it has become second nature to you. Whether this latest debacle has triggered that need in you to protect me, to blunt the sharp edges of whatever life throws my way."

"So you have a problem with me caring for my best friend?" His eyes flare with anger.

"No, that's not what I mean, I just . . ."

"You think I would take something as serious as marriage so lightly, that I would propose to you on a whim because you're in a tough situation?"

My annoyance flares, too. "Ty, you would not have proposed to me if I wasn't pregnant by some vicious, unknown assailant. You're starting a new, exciting journey next fall when you begin medical school. My unexpected and unwanted pregnancy is not your burden to carry or fix."

"Don't you think I know that? What do you take me for, Cooper? Hmm? Did it ever occur to you that I do what

I do because I adore you and there is no person, event, or situation that will ever change that? That I can't envision a future without you in it?"

He slides off the bed and starts to pace again. "I thought you knew me better than that."

"Ty, I'm sorry. I know that we have a special bond, but I always thought my feelings for you had to be kept hidden. Sometimes you kept me at arm's length and frankly, it was confusing. When I showed up to apologize for snooping in your apartment and saw Kristina wearing your shirt, I made the decision to accept things as they were. That we would always be great friends who care for each other and that would have to be enough for me."

He stops pacing and leans against the dresser. He stares out the window. "When you dated Christian Wheeler, that last year of high school, it killed me to pretend I was okay with it. But I sucked it up anyway."

He continues to stare out the window. "Every time some random guy hit on you, I wanted to punch him in the face and yell, *she's mine.* And when you danced with Spencer that night at the party before the attack, I wanted to rip his head off. I didn't like the way he looked at you or tried to touch you. I almost lost my mind the night of the attack, when I couldn't find you and nobody knew where you were. I thought, if anything happens to her, my life would be empty. When I saw you in that hospital bed all bruised and battered, part of me almost died."

My skin tingles and my heart thrashes around inside of me, as if seeking a way out, to ease the intensity of my emotions because they're too much to handle right now. I breathe in and out a few times to calm myself.

"I didn't know," I whisper. "I swear I didn't know."

He leaves the spot against the dresser and joins me at the edge of the bed once more. "I didn't want to scare you with the intensity of my feelings. I did my best to keep it under control and hidden away from you, to keep our friendship uncomplicated and fun. I was afraid if I told you how I felt, it would ruin everything and get awkward between us."

He felt the same way all along. I completely misread him, but maybe that was the point. As he said, he was keeping it under control. I'm so happy I could cry. Why didn't I know this? Why couldn't I see through his act instead of torturing myself every time he dated someone new, which wasn't that often to begin with? I convinced myself I would always be just Cooper to him, his best friend, never anything more.

I excuse myself and tell him I'll be right back. I bolt out of the bedroom and sprint all the way downstairs, to grab my bag and find what I need. I take the stairs two at a time and re-enter the bedroom, where I find him in the same spot on the bed where I left him. I grab the teddy bear and sit. I turn it over, remove the cap from the sharpie and write in big letters on the bear's t-shirt:

YES

The most dazzling smile I've ever seen lights up his face. He squeezes my hand. "Thank you, Cooper. You've just sentenced me to a lifetime of happiness."

I lean over and plant a kiss on his cheek. I linger for a bit and then blow raspberries, and he laughs and laughs.

"The bear has another surprise for you," he says. "Try not

to pass out. You looked like you were about to when you saw the proposal."

"I promise not to pass out," I say giddily.

"Lift up his shirt in the back and slide your fingers through the opening," he instructs me.

I do as he says. At first, I only feel the stuffing and filling, but when I push a little more, I feel something hard and circular. I pull it out of the bear and toward me. I shriek with delight at the gorgeous engagement ring. It seems that all the light in the room has gravitated toward the princess cut diamond in the center of the ring and the smaller stones surrounding it. The brilliance almost blinds me, so I hold the ring out, and away from my eyes.

He takes the ring from me and asks me to extend my left hand. He slides it unto the third finger with ease. It's perfect, around three carats by my estimation, conspicuous but not ostentatious. I squeeze him tight. I can't help myself. However, I must address the giant pink elephant in the room.

"Ty, I've decided to keep the baby. I couldn't go through with the termination."

Without missing a beat he says, "I know."

"What?"

He picks up the pacing again. "I think you wanted to do it because it made sense at the time, the logic of it. In the end, it went against everything you stand for."

This was not the proposal I conjured up in my fantasies. I had planned everything out, the perfect timeline for my life, with little or no room for deviation. Although this did not align with my plans, it's perfect. There are far worse things in this life than marrying one of the good guys, even if we're both still very young.

I reveal to him the oh-so-brilliant plan I concocted with Zahra on the drive back from the clinic.

"It's not a bad plan," he says. "My parents had an UGMA account for me too. How else could I afford this apartment or your ring? If we pool our resources together and plan well, we should be fine. My parents are paying for medical school. We could get an apartment near Cambridge or a surrounding town no more than twenty or thirty minutes away by car."

"Lexington or Belmont could work, but both towns are far away from my parents."

"That's the point, Cooper. We have to do this on our own. It's our life, our family. We can't ask our parents for any more help."

My heart lurches when he says *our family*. That's what we are now, from this moment on. An instant, readymade family.

"What do we say when I start to show?"

"We say it's *our* baby. Our family and friends know our history. This may actually not surprise them. For the rest of the year, we say nothing about the pregnancy. I don't think you'll start to show anytime soon. Even if you do, we can fudge the timeline. I don't want anyone thinking this has anything to do with the assault. It's *our* baby."

"And our parents?"

"Your father is going to kill me when I tell him I got you pregnant, but I'll have to take it like a man. That's why we need a foolproof plan when we tell them. My dad will be okay. My mother won't like it, but I can handle her."

"I know you can." I stretch out my palm and gaze at the ring. "And you're right. My father *is* going to kill you."

CHAPTER 42

―◦―

AFTER

W HEN SPENCER ENTERED the mid-campus café later that afternoon, Kristina was already seated. His ears burned from the frigid November temperature. He plopped down opposite her and removed his scarf. He could do with a steaming cup of hot chocolate or coffee, but he was too wound up to bother ordering. The minute Kristina had texted him saying that she had news, he ditched his late afternoon class. His future was at stake. If things went as planned, he needn't worry about classes.

"I went up to the apartment," she began. "She came in a few minutes after I arrived. I gave her the card. She seems to be coping as well as can be expected under the circumstances. Ty is very protective of her."

"Tell me everything she said." Spencer leaned in, not wanting to miss a single morsel of information.

Kristina eyed him suspiciously. "You're still not going to tell me what happened to your nose?"

Why did she have to bring that up? Spencer was still raw with hatred toward Zach for fracturing his nose. Okay, the truth was, his rage stemmed from Zach's comments, although being punched also made him angry.

"Never mind about that. I got into a fight. I don't want to talk about it. So, what did Abbie say?"

"She's not giving up. She wants to nail whoever did this to her, and I don't blame her. That animal must be caught and neutered."

"Whoa." Spencer leaned back in his seat. "You and Abbie are best friends now? I thought you couldn't stand her."

"We don't have to be friends for me to sympathize. That guy is a predator. It could have happened to me or any other girl at the party that night. For whatever reason, he picked Abbie."

"Did she say how she plans to catch this guy?"

"Not really."

"Well good for her that she's determined to seek justice," he said.

"I thought you and Abbie were so-called friends," Kristina said. "Why don't you ask her directly what's going on with her?"

"She's been through a lot, and I don't want to be that guy. I'm giving her the space she needs."

Kristina made a show of clearing her throat. "Really? What are you up to, Spencer?"

"Nothing. I wanted an objective point of view about how she's really doing. I care about Abbie."

This was great news. It meant that he could soon broach the subject of the Wheeler New Year's Eve Ball with her. If she was recuperating and coping well, he'd approach her soon. He hadn't figured out the catalyst for that conversation yet, but when the time came, he would. He and Zach hadn't spoken since their brawl at Five Guys Restaurant four days ago. Zach's threats gave Spencer the chills. He knew better than anyone what Zach was capable of.

Kristina glowered at him. "Why are you acting all weird?"

"I'm not. I miss Abbie and I want her to be okay. As I told you last time, I wish she gave me the chance to be there for her."

"You keep saying that, but I don't believe you," she said. "Why are you obsessed with her? You graduate in the spring. She's not your type, so what's up with the strange behavior?"

"What do you mean she's not my type?"

"She takes herself too seriously. She's not exactly the up-for-anything type, if you know what I mean. You would need to have unicorns flying out of your butt before she would let you see her naked."

"You're being too dramatic. And how do you now we haven't hooked up?"

"Because she tells Ty everything. He let it slip when I asked him about you and Abbie a few weeks back. Are you upset that she turned to Ty for comfort and not you? Is that it?"

"Something like that," he mumbled.

"Wow. You really like her, don't you?"

He leaned in again. "Look, I don't know how to explain it. She did something to me, like she flipped a switch and I started to see the world in a different light. She's actually funny once you get to know her, and she's not as serious and intense as you think. You should see some of the text messages she sent me."

"Show me." Kristina rubbed her hands together with glee.

"I don't kiss and tell."

"Please. You're no gentleman, but you're certainly a liar. There's more to the story than you're saying. I know how you treat girls. You're being extra careful with Abbie Cooper, acting as if she's some fragile flower. She's not. I don't trust her. She's sneaky and manipulative."

"Where is this coming from? Weren't you just praising her?"

"She convinced Ty to dump me. That little witch isn't all sugar and spice. She's just good at hiding how conniving she is. Don't waste your time."

This was an unfortunate turn of events, and Spencer didn't like it one bit. If Abbie convinced Ty to let go of Kristina, that could only mean one thing—she was staking her claim and things between them were heating up. Once that happened, the Wheelers would be the last thing on her mind. Kristina was genuinely upset. How could he use that to his advantage?

"I didn't realize you had strong feelings for Ty."

"What do you mean?"

"You're mad that he dumped you on Abbie's say so. It wouldn't bother you this much if you didn't care for the guy."

She hunched over and a sob escaped her. In the almost four years he'd known Kristina, he'd never seen her get emotional over anything, let alone a guy. Girls could be so complicated. Half the time he didn't get them at all, not even his own sister. They were like thousands of tiny puzzle pieces with no way to solve, no picture on the box that showed how the completed picture was supposed to look.

He reached out and stroked her hand. She looked up at him and snatched her hand away from his. "I don't need your pity, Spencer."

"Sorry. Just trying to help."

"Don't," she said. "I'm peeved. Ty and I clicked. He was the whole package: gorgeous, sexy, ambitious, and kind. And super generous too."

Spencer feigned interest. He would rather have a power drill tunnel through his eyeballs than listen to this drivel. But listen he must if he wanted to stay on Kristina's good side. He hadn't yet figured out how she could be useful to him, if at all.

He rubbed his temples. His head spun. He didn't have the stomach for this type of thing. Zach was the one who was good at handling complicated situations, but he would rather cut off his hand than ask for Zach's help with this end of things. He should talk to his sister Brynn. She knew how women thought. She could help him untangle this mess without Zach finding out Spencer needed help. He would see her over Thanksgiving. That would still give him a month to work on Abbie and secure those invitations to the ball.

"So do something about it," he suggested.

"Like what?"

"Go after what you want."

"Oh I get it. If I go after Ty, that causes problems between him and Abbie, which works for you when she comes running to you for a shoulder to cry on. Thanks for making my pain about you, Spencer."

"You're taking it the wrong way, Kristina. I've just never seen you like this. You're not the shrinking violet kind of chick."

She narrowed her eyes at him and tilted her head. "I'm not but I'm also a realist. We're about to go our separate ways in a few months anyway, so is it worth it?"

"There's no reason you couldn't continue your relationship

afterward. Assuming you can pry him away from Abbie's clever clutches."

"Reverse psychology? Really, Spencer?"

"You're the one who confessed that Ty dumped you for Abbie. I was simply pointing to facts. She snatched him from right under your nose."

"She didn't play fair. She exploited the damsel in distress cliché. Don't give her too much credit," Kristina crossed her arms and rolled her eyes.

He really needed to speak to Brynn, Spencer thought. If Kristina decided to cause problems, what would that mean for him? He would be there to help Abbie pick up the pieces, that's all. He could start laying the groundwork by asking her about her holiday plans. Yes, why didn't he think of that before? Start with Thanksgiving, talk about her mother being a celebrated TV chef and how great it must be to have a Thanksgiving meal prepared by her. Then ease into Christmas and New Year's Eve.

"Okay, I'll give you that, but still, he broke up with you. That's the bottom line."

"What an eager beaver you are. You just can't wait to have another shot at her, can you? I still don't trust you. You're up to something."

On that note, Kristina picked up her jacket and left the café.

Another idea occurred to Spencer after Kristina left. He Googled *Shelby's Kitchen* Thanksgiving Recipes on his phone. It was a good conversation starter. Next, he searched Abbie Cooper + Wheeler New Year's Eve Ball. Several hits came back. He scrolled through the first result, a series of photos. He began to fume and eventually felt that fuming boil to white, hot rage. A few of the photos were of Abbie in a stunning, white off-the-shoulder gown and Christian Wheeler draped all over her. Zach's cruel words echoed in his ears. *She was Christian's girlfriend, and you couldn't even get to first base with her.* He hated Zach. He hated all the Wheelers. He hated that Zach was right.

CHAPTER 43

AFTER

M Y EYES SCAN the section of the library where Justin and I are scheduled to meet up. I spot him in a corner of the library peppered with rows of large bookshelves lining the wall, and leather chairs and tables in the center, and along the sides.

"Are you okay, Abbie?" he asks. He nudges his glasses further up his nose as if he needs to see me more clearly.

"Fine, Justin. Don't I look fine?"

"You always look great, but you seem troubled the last few weeks. I just want to know if I can help you in any way."

"It's the usual." I pick up my bag to take out my laptop, notes and textbook. "Sometimes it gets too much, you know what I mean?"

"I know exactly what you mean. There are times I worry I won't make it to graduation. We still have two more years to go, and it'll only get harder."

"Nonsense," I say. "It's supposed to be painful, remember? You'll get there."

"We both will, Abbie."

His innocent remarks strikes a melancholic chord within me, the kind that makes me want to crawl into a hole and drown in a pool of my own tears. *I won't make it, Justin. I don't know if I'll ever graduate from Yale University.*

But I agree with him, and we get down to reviewing lecture notes and testing each other's knowledge on the latest module. I begin to type an addition to the study guide we've created when something strikes me. I didn't pay attention earlier, but now it's jabbing at me. I look at Justin, who's deep in concentration as he looks at his screen—the screen of a brand new laptop, an expensive brand that costs at least two thousand dollars. He got rid of his old computer, a cheaper brand with a different operating system. Why am I making a big deal about his laptop? People upgrade all the time.

I start checking out everything about him to see what else I may have missed. I'm plagued with doubts again. What if my secret admirer and my assailant are two separate individuals? What if Justin *is* the secret admirer, although I haven't heard from him since the assault?

I look down at his feet and see brand new sneakers, the ones that cost two hundred dollars a pair. I look up again and run a quick scan. It wasn't visible before because the sleeves of his sweater covered it, but he's sporting an Apple watch. Under normal circumstances, I wouldn't think twice because it's none of my business. Now, however, everyone I interact with is my business. Mr. Humble Admirer could afford expensive gifts. Now I wonder how Justin can afford these high-end items.

Stop being paranoid. Maybe Justin got a job and has been saving up. He looks up and catches me staring at him. So embarrassing. He smiles at me, totally misreading the situation. He thinks I was checking him out. I was, but not for the reasons he thinks. I'm so busted.

"Nice watch," I say.

He looks down at his wrist. "Thanks. I just got it."

Awkward silence follows. *Say something, anything.*

"So, heading home for Thanksgiving?" I ask.

That did the trick. "Yes. I can't wait to see my family. And eat too much."

"I'm looking forward to that too."

"You know Abbie, you don't have to be nervous around me. I would never do anything to hurt you." He pushes the laptop aside and focuses on me.

"Why do you think I'm nervous around you?"

"I don't know. You seem tense. You said it was the usual stuff, but I caught you looking at me strangely. Not in a good way."

"Was I? Sorry if I've offended you."

"Don't sweat it. For a minute, I thought it was because of that guy you're dating. The one you were with at the pizzeria. What's his name, Spencer? Dude had major attitude."

Why is he bringing up Spencer? "First of all, I'm not dating Spencer. Secondly, nobody tells me how to treat others. And third, do you and Spencer know each other and how?"

I notice a slight quiver of his lips. He looks behind him, as if expecting someone.

"Justin, do you know Spencer? I got the sense that the two of you did, that night at the pizzeria."

"Nah." He waves his hand. "Just didn't like the way he was disrespecting you."

"What do you mean?"

"Just a vibe I got. He was acting like you were his property. I know that's not how you roll."

Confusion must have registered on my face because he adds, "It's a guy thing. I could be overreacting. Just watch your back. I don't trust him."

"Are you trying to scare me?"

"Just saying guys like that always have a scheme going."

"What are you talking about? You just told me you don't know Spencer, so how would you know he has a scheme going?"

He leans forward. "Saw him scoping you out before he came up to you at that frat party a few weeks back. He was on the phone with somebody and right after he hung up, he *accidentally* ran into you."

I slink back into my seat. A chill runs up my spine. I feel physically ill and place my hand over my stomach.

"Are you okay?" he asks. "Do you want me to get you some water?"

He doesn't wait for my response. He opens his bag and produces a unit of bottled water. I accept it gratefully, break the seal, and take a few sips. Justin's eyes land on my hand rubbing my stomach. A strange look comes over his face, and then it vanishes as quickly as it appeared.

I remove my hand from my belly and place it in my lap. "Justin, I want you to tell me everything you remember that night as it relates to Spencer. It could be important."

"Did that jerk do something to you?" he asks, raising his voice.

"Nothing like that. Can you tell me what you recall?"

"Saw him arrive at the party with some chick. He ditched her the minute he saw you across the room. It was as if he didn't expect you to be there, but because you were, he had to change plans. That's when he made the call and then swooped in. Like I said, watch your back."

I rewind that evening in my head. I remember how charming Spencer was when he asked me to dance. Ty formally introduced us. During our conversation, Spencer received a call. He said it was from his annoying sister. A couple of days later, as I was leaving the library, he caught up to me. Got pushy about wanting to see me. I remember thinking he was behaving like someone who had a goal in mind. I asked him about his sister again, and he said she'd called for something mundane that she could have texted him about. Was it a story concocted for my benefit? What does Spencer Rossdale want from me? Who really was on the other end of those phone calls?

"Thank you for telling me, Justin," I say softly.

I would be wise to heed his advice and watch my back. I don't know what Spencer's game is, but I can't let on that Justin may have clued me in to something sinister.

CHAPTER 44

AFTER

ZAHRA AGREES TO meet up at mid-campus café. I'm excited to share my news with her, but that excitement is tempered by what Justin revealed to me yesterday. Ty and I were up until two in the morning discussing what it could mean. The only solid conclusion we came to was that Spencer cannot be trusted and we should keep an eye on him.

I arrive at the café before Zahra and grab us a spot near the window with a great view of the park. I whip out my phone, remove my gloves and snap a photo of my ring finger, and text it to my dearest friends Callie and Frances. Within seconds, my phone pings. I know it's Callie and I can't help but smile. She's a student at Fashion Institute of Technology in New York. Frances is at Northwestern in Chicago.

When I pick up the phone to confirm my assumption, the message I see is not from Callie. I gasp, drawing the attention a few curious eyes. For a moment, I feel dizzy and disoriented. I squeeze my eyes shut to regain my equilibrium. I stare at the message again but it's still there, bold and threatening:

Stop searching. I'm watching you!

I clutch my belly in a protective gesture. I didn't think about it. It happened naturally, as if my body wants to remind me that I have a life growing inside of me. As if I could forget. The message is from an unknown sender and most likely untraceable. A criminal who has been silent since his crime wouldn't risk being caught by communicating with me. He must be confident he won't be tracked. Why threaten me now? Why not when the police were asking questions?

Outside the window, big, fat fluffy flakes fall from the sky, pelting the ground. It's the first snow of the season. When I was little, I always looked forward to it. It didn't matter if the first snowfall was twelve inches or one inch. I would bound up the stairs to grab my mittens, hat, jacket, and sled until Mom gently mentioned that we needed a lot more snow for the sled to work. She would bribe me with candy to stop me from wailing with disappointment.

Zahra finally arrives and plops down opposite me. She doesn't bother to wipe the snowflakes from her hair after she removes her jacket and rests it on the back of the chair.

"Let me see it," she says, bouncing in her seat.

I extend my left hand so she can examine the ring.

"It's perfect. Don't blind anybody."

Zahra makes me recount every second of the proposal, and I'm glad to give her the details, all the while nervous my attacker will send another text. I ask her if she wouldn't mind getting me some tea and anything that seems healthy on the menu. The minute she leaves, I put my experiment into motion. I pull up the text from unknown sender and respond. One of two things will happen. Either we'll end up in a bitter exchange or the message will bounce back, like one of those "do not reply" emails that are set up to send out messages, not receive them.

I type the following message:

Watch all you want. I won't stop.

My hand shakes as I wait for a reply. I can't allow this coward think that he can continue to terrorize me. Once was enough. If I don't stand up to him, how can I teach my son or daughter to be courageous in the face of unrepentant evil?

Sweat breaks out on my forehead. I tug at my scarf, loosening it, and place the phone on the table. Zahra arrives with a tray and puts it down in the center.

"Did something happen while I was gone?" she asks.

"It's nothing."

She takes a seat. "It's something. You're agitated."

"Why would you say that?"

"For one, you won't stop tapping your foot. I can feel the vibration under the table. Plus you're sweating."

"It's hot in here."

She continues to gaze at me with skepticism, arms folded.

"Fine. I got a text."

"What text? From whom?"

"From him. My attacker."

"Please tell me you're joking. It's not funny, Abbie."

"I wouldn't joke about that."

Zahra clasps her hand around the cup of coffee and tries to take a sip. She rests the coffee back on the table without removing her hands from it, as if cradling it for comfort.

"What did he say?"

I show her the text message. She shivers and takes another sip of coffee.

"You have to go to the police with this," she says.

"Maybe."

"This guy straight up threatened you. Now you have proof that he's out there."

"Yes, going to the police would be the right thing to do. And I will."

"But?" she asks, sensing my hesitation.

"He's outsmarted us all so far. Now he's doing something he never did before, using electronic communication, which can be tracked."

"So you're thinking he knows he can't be tracked?"

"Exactly. Why else would he take the risk, knowing I would go straight to the police? He does not want to be caught."

"So he could be a tech genius or something?"

"Possibly. The message could have been sent using a disappearing text app. The message would self-destruct after it's been read, as if it never appeared in the first place. If he's using a burner phone, forget it."

"Let's see then."

I pick up the phone and my prophecy has come true. The message is gone. I hold up the phone so Zahra can see.

"Like magic," she says.

"Yeah, like magic."

"How come you know so much about technology?" she asks.

"I took computer science in high school and had a STEM (Science, Technology, Engineering, Math) Fellowship as part of my curriculum. My mother was also a scientist and knows a lot about technology-related tools. And I may or may not have done a little cyber spying in the past."

"You have to tell me." She scuffs her chair closer to the table.

"I remotely installed keylogger software on someone's computer because I thought they were threatening me and I needed proof. I can't do that now because I don't know who the boogey man is."

Her eyes go big in wonderment. "Whoa. I had no idea you could do that kind of stuff. You're a total bad ass, my hero."

"It's not cool to do that stuff. I only did it because my future was hanging in the balance. I told you what happened senior year of high school. However, I don't think I would ever do that again. Besides, it's illegal. Next time he sends me a text message, I'll take a screenshot before it disappears. That way I'll have something to show Detectives Thompson and Nash. In the meantime, I have to do something."

"What are going to do?"

"Make him come to me."

Zahra's confused look is wreaking havoc with my bravado. "I responded to his text. He hasn't replied yet, but I let him know I'm not afraid of him. That will set him off for sure."

"Abbie, the man kidnapped you, drugged you, raped you, and threw you out of a moving car. What if he tries to kill you this time?"

"He could. But either I fight back now and have a shot at stopping him or I stay his victim the rest of my life. If you were me, which option would you choose?"

We both fall silent. Zahra continues to clutch her coffee. I tense up, afraid he will make another vile threat. I must train myself not to react with anger or fear, because this new game is as much about mental stamina as it is about the potential for more violence. He could be criminally insane for all I know. He could have done this many times before and gotten away with it, and that's why he has the guts to threaten me. He's sure he won't be caught because he hasn't been caught.

"I have to think about the people in my life too, Zahra. He knows a lot about me. I have to assume, depending on how crazy he is, he could come after them to get back at me. People like that don't like it when you fight back. It sends them over the edge and makes the crazy ten times worse."

"I never looked at it like that. You could be right."

CHAPTER 45

AFTER

MY PHONE PINGS and I practically jump from my seat. My eyes dart all around the café, trying to identify a man, any man who might be texting on his phone. I know it's a ridiculous idea. Most of the people in here are college students who text as much as they breathe. So much for my little peptalk.

I force my gaze to focus on the message and breathe a sigh of relief when I see it's from Callie. Her message reads:

At last!

I close my eyes and rub my temples, trying to get ahold of myself.

"Abbie, are you okay?" Zahra asks, alarmed.

I shake my head and hold up my index finger to indicate I need a minute. It's overwhelming, the seesaw that my life has become, oscillating between paranoia and fear one minute and dizzying happiness the next.

After a couple of deep breaths, I open my eyes to find Zahra staring at me, about to burst into tears. I assure her that

I'm fine and explain Callie's text. Her shoulders slump with relief. "Good. I thought that nut job had sent another threat."

"I'm sure he will. He's just biding his time."

I respond to Callie's text, telling her we have much catching up to do. She says she doesn't care if Frances is up or not; she's going to call her and share the happy news. I've barely touched the food Zahra brought to the table earlier—a fruit cup, yogurt, a whole wheat bagel, and tea. Stress isn't good for the baby, I remind myself. Then an awful thought pops into my head: *What if I don't want to know who he is?* If I uncover his identity, will it give me nightmares forever? What if the baby comes out looking like him or worse, he wants to be part of the baby's life?

I absently take a sip of the tea. Zahra hasn't touched her food either. I force myself to take a few bites of the bagel and fruit. I need all the calories I can get.

"Have you told your parents about the engagement?" she asks.

"Not yet. We'll tell them over Thanksgiving."

"What about Spencer, does he know?"

I shake my head. "I'm in no hurry to share the good news with him."

"Why not?"

I explain my conversation with Justin and the suspicion that Spencer pursued me on purpose as part of some sinister plot.

"That's crazy and then some," she says. She takes another sip of coffee. "What are you going to do about it?"

"Nothing for now. I can't let him know I'm suspicious. I have to behave as if nothing has changed. It's another reason

I can't wear my engagement ring openly yet. And nobody can know I'm pregnant. Only you, Ty, and my therapist know. Obviously, my family will once we make the big announcement, but that's it."

"That's a lot of stress to carry around."

"I know," I whine, and then slump in my seat. "The whole Spencer thing is making me uncomfortable."

"You think it may have something to do with the attack?"

"I don't see how it could, but I can't discount anything at this point. At the very least, he might know something. I don't see how, though."

"What then? What does he want with you?"

"Only Spencer knows the answer to that. I thought he was coming on too strong, but I told myself to relax and have some fun. College wasn't all about studying. I should have followed my intuition. But now that Justin has warned me and I think back to the whole shoe incident, it gives me a headache."

"What do you mean?"

I remind Zahra of our previous conversation regarding Spencer's reaction to the Louboutin pumps when I mentioned Christian had purchased them as a gift for my eighteenth birthday.

I lean forward and grab Zahra's arm. "Oh my goodness. The shoes. I was wearing them that night."

"Abbie, you're going to leave a mark, ease up," Zahra says, looking at her arm and wincing in pain.

"Sorry." I let go of her arm.

"What are you talking about?"

"The night I was attacked. I wore those Louboutins to

the post-game party. Coincidence?"

Zahra scratches her head as if searching for answers. "I don't see the connection."

"He said he was jealous after the incident at the movies, where he brought up the shoes in the first place. His reaction when I mentioned that Christian bought them as a gift was stronger than just jealousy. You and I have speculated a lot as to whether or not he knows Christian and if so, why he never mentioned it."

"Right. Has he mentioned the shoes since the movie incident?"

"No. But I wore them a second time while in Spencer's presence. The post-game party."

"You've lost me again," she says.

"It's about the shoes. Sort of."

"I don't follow."

"The shoes represent something to Spencer, and I think it has to do with Christian. Seeing me in those shoes again could have set Spencer off. If he had anything to do with the attack."

"I think I see where you're going with this. When he said he was jealous, we assumed it was a general kind of jealousy about an ex who could afford to buy you expensive gifts when he couldn't. Guys are competitive about stuff like that. But maybe Spencer was being more specific, as in jealous and possibly angry about the fact that you dated Christian."

"Precisely. But why? What's his problem with Christian?"

"Whatever it is, it's serious enough that he may have been involved in assaulting you, guilt by association kind of thing."

My phone pings, and both Zahra and I cease our conversation. Neither one of us moves a muscle.

"This is ridiculous," I say. "I can't panic every time a text message comes in."

"Okay. See who it is."

I slowly pick up the phone as if it were a dangerous object. I peek at the message:

Spencer: Need your help.

"It's Spencer," I say to Zahra. She makes a funny face and I chuckle.

Me: With what?

Spencer: Thanksgiving recipes for my mom. Can you meet?

Me: Can't meet but what kind of recipes do you want?

Spencer: Does your mom have a top ten hits or something like that?

Me: Sure. Just Google Shelby's Kitchen Top Thanksgiving Recipes.

Spencer: Totally makes sense.

Me: This year's Thanksgiving episode already aired, so your mother can watch it on YouTube if she wants more ideas.

Spencer: You're the best. Heading home soon?

Me: Yes.

Spencer: Me too. Can't believe the year is almost over. Next thing you know, it's New Year's Eve.

Me: Yeah, time flies.

Spencer: Are you big on New Year's celebrations? Does your family throw a big party?

I stare at the screen as my mind races. He just gave me the perfect opening, and I'm going to take it.

Me: Mom and Dad usually throw some shindig. But a couple of years ago I went all black tie, high society.

Spencer: How so?

Me: Attended the Wheeler New Year's Eve Ball with Christian.

Spencer: Oh, really? I bet that was a blast.

Me: Yes it was.

Spencer: Are you going again this year?

Me: Maybe. Need to talk to Katherine Wheeler first.

Spencer: She'll roll out the red carpet for you.

Me: Why do you say that?

A pause. The responses aren't coming as quickly as they were before. Did he just tip his hand, gave me a clue that he now regrets? How does he know Katherine will roll out the red carpet?

Spencer: Just guessing. Everyone loves you.

Me: I have to go. Catch you later.

Spencer: Okay.

"What was that all about?" Zahra asks.

"He's clever. He didn't take the bait. I saw an opening to mention the New Year's Eve Ball and he deflected. Made his comments sound generic, innocent. But I know I got his attention. He's intrigued."

CHAPTER 46

AFTER

ARE YOU OKAY?" Ty asks, taking his eyes of the road for a second as traffic slows down.

"Sure. Why do you ask?"

"You're nervous about the trip. Thinking about exactly what we're going to say to your parents."

"As long as we stick to the script, everything should work out. My dad is going to be upset, but he will come around. It's better than explaining the truth."

"That's a positive perspective," he says, interlocking our fingers while his other hand is firmly on the steering wheel. A driver cuts in front of us and Ty taps the brakes. Both hands are now on the steering wheel.

"Geez, what a jerk," he says.

"People go extra crazy around the holidays. Let's get to Castleview in one piece."

"I won't let anything else happen to you, Cooper," he says, his face grave. "I already screwed up. If I were keeping a better eye on you, none of this would have happened."

"What? Ty, that's nonsense. Bad things happen to

people. Any place, any time. I'm not a child. How can you blame yourself for this?"

"I just do, okay."

I fold my arms and gaze at him. "Okay then. Tell me what magical powers you possess that were supposed to prevent this from happening to me."

His jaw ticks. He allows the question to percolate. "It took me too long to start searching for you. Too long to realize I hadn't seen or heard from you in a while. If I wasn't so busy with . . . well, I just could have done better."

He was about to say if he weren't busy with Kristina, he would have looked for me sooner. I can't allow him to carry that burden. It's unfair and unnecessary.

"Don't do this, Ty. The situation is complicated enough without you throwing yourself on the martyr sword. This is not your fault. There is nothing you could have done or not done to prevent it."

"We don't know that. Just a few minutes could have made a difference, Cooper. Seconds even."

"Not so. We don't know exactly when I went missing. It happened right after you texted me. I saw your text come in and I don't remember anything after that. You were waiting for my reply and when you didn't get it, that's when you became concerned. That scenario could have happened to anyone."

Traffic slows down again. A couple on a motorcycle pulls up alongside us. The roar of the engine disturbs me somehow. I remain silent until they take off. Then I turn to Ty.

"You feel guilty because you were with Kristina. I don't know why you would. I don't see what hanging out with your girlfriend has to do with me getting attacked."

"She was not my girlfriend. We were just getting to know each other." His response is swift and firm.

I frown. "But you wanted us to get along."

"I didn't want her getting jealous of my relationship with you. There were signs that things were heading that way. We had a couple of arguments. It was easier to tell you I wanted the two of you to get along. That way, you wouldn't be tempted to respond if she provoked you."

His confession surprises me. He has always put my feelings ahead of his own and hasn't stopped. I cling to him at night because of the bad dreams. A death grip, if I'm being honest. I've seen the marks on his body, the result of my episodes, when I do battle with the dark phantom that's always trying to get me. He hides them from me but I know they're there.

I've also caught him taking cold showers in the middle of the night. I suffer from insomnia because of the attack. I can hear the slightest noise, aware of every movement. I scurry back to bed before he finds out I know his secret. I don't want to embarrass him.

"Thanks for having my back, as always. But can I ask you something?"

"Sure," he says, slowing down.

"Why do you hide the wounds from me?"

He tenses. "What wounds?"

"You know the ones. I didn't want to bring it up because you go through a lot of trouble to hide them from me. I'm sorry, Ty. I'm sorry I hurt you, even though I don't know I'm doing it. Maybe it's time I take up Dr. Shanahan on her offer. She can write a prescription for me so I can sleep, so I won't hurt you. Obviously, I would be medically supervised to make sure it doesn't harm the baby."

He goes quiet, a pensive look overtaking his features. Then he says, "I don't think that's a good idea, Cooper. We have to put your health and that of the baby first. You've been doing great, working through everything with Dr. Shanahan and me. I think that we should continue on that course."

"But—"

"Come on. Every drug has side effects. There's no way to predict how it will affect you, medically supervised or not."

His jaw tightens and his hands stiffen on the steering wheel. He doesn't like the idea and doesn't want to discuss it any further.

"What about you?" I probe.

"What about me?"

"The injuries. I don't know how long these nightmares will last. I can't keep hurting you in my sleep."

"Let's focus on your recovery."

"Are you dismissing my concern?" I ask acidly. "Ty, it bothers me. It hurts me to see the scars on your body, knowing I put them there."

Snowflakes are coming down hard. We still have thirty minutes before we arrive in Castleview. Traffic is at a standstill. I decide to wait him out, force him to give me answer I can live with.

"Don't you worry about me. I don't feel a thing if that makes you feel any better."

He pats my knee in a gesture meant to calm my anxiety. Even as he does so, I know he's lying. Those nightmares are intense. In every one of them, I'm fighting for my very life. The injuries he sustains because he sleeps next to me are no small thing.

CHAPTER 47

AFTER

I T'S ALWAYS GREAT to have my daughter home," Dad says. "Ty, thanks for keeping an eye on her."

We gather around the island in the kitchen. Mom has made her famous hot chocolate using pure Peruvian chocolate bars, and we're all sipping our cups, savoring the rich, delicious smoothness. Miles prattles on about his class trip to Barcelona next spring, and Lee is the most relaxed I've seen him in a long time. He was actually teasing Mom earlier. Dad looks like the Jason Cooper I've come to know, strong, confident and in control. In his early fifties, he still looks terrific in spite of a few extra gray hairs. Our family is picture perfect, and I'm about to shred the image into a million little pieces.

"Ty got accepted into Harvard Medical School," I announce. I don't know why I blurted out the news. Perhaps I'm just nervous about delivering my own news.

A wave of congratulations and best wishes circulate around. We all clink our mugs in a toast to Ty.

Dad slaps Ty on the shoulder. "Way to go. That is a huge

accomplishment. Your parents must be so proud."

Ty beams at the compliment. "Thanks, Mr. Cooper. I think my mom is still calling her relatives all over the country and the Bahamas to brag. She's saving Aunt Meredith for last. They still try to one up each other. Now it's about whose kids are most accomplished."

We all have a good laugh.

"Well, tell your mom she has her sister beat," Dad says.

"Is that why you're glowing, Abbie?" Mom asks. "Because of Ty's good news?"

I have no clue how to answer that question and I hope the guilt that just landed a blow in the pit of my stomach doesn't show on my face.

"Sweetie, are you okay?" she asks.

"Well of course, I'm happy about Ty's great news," I say. "He worked hard and it paid off."

Ty inches closer to me, indicating it's show time. Mom gave us the perfect opening, and we can't wait any longer because it's wreaking havoc with my emotions.

"Actually, Cooper—I mean Abbie—and I have some news of our own," Ty begins.

I fiddle with the ring I dumped in the left pocket of my sweater before we entered the house, and manage to slip it on to my finger. Silence falls over the kitchen. All eyes are focused on the two of us.

"Well, out with it Ty," Dad urges him.

Ty looks at me, and I give him an encouraging nod. All we can do now is watch the fireworks pop after we light the fire.

"Abbie and I are getting married."

"And we're having a baby," I add quickly.

My younger brother Miles gapes at us open mouthed. Mom and Dad look at each other in confusion, not sure if they heard right. Lee chugs down his remaining hot chocolate, places the mug on the counter, and rubs the back of his neck. I take my hand out of my pocket, the ring now secure on the third finger.

"I know this is a shock—"

My mother cuts me off.

"Lee, Miles, please excuse us," she says to my brothers.

After they leave, I have a seat at the kitchen table and so do Ty and my parents.

"Ty, what have you done?" my father asks with steely calm. "What have you done to my daughter and the promising future she had ahead of her?"

"How are you guys going to take care of and provide for a baby?" Mom asks. "What about school?"

"Mr. and Mrs. Cooper, it was a shock to us too," Ty says. "Obviously, we didn't plan to get pregnant. Abbie still has two years left to earn her degree, and I just got into medical school. But we talked it over and have a plan for how we're going to handle things."

But neither one of them is listening to us. Mom gets up from the table and starts pacing from one end of the kitchen to the other, muttering repeatedly that she can't believe this is happening, and asking herself where she went wrong. Dad remains glued to his chair at the table, looking like he's about to cry. They're devastated. All the hopes and dreams they had for me have disappeared in one evening, with two damning sentences.

"Abbie, how could you have been so careless with your

life, with your future?" Mom looks at me, accusation thick in her voice. "And Ty, this is how you repay our trust?"

Dad still hasn't said another word. Ty is struggling. He wants to be respectful, but he won't take the jabs lying down either.

"Mrs. Cooper, the truth is, Abbie and I would have ended up this way eventually. It just happened sooner than we planned. You know we've had feelings for each other for years. We made a mistake and we're taking steps to address it."

"Really? And how are you addressing it?"

Mom won't back down. I thought Dad would be the one to blow a gasket.

"Where will you live?" she asks, her gaze directed at Ty. "Who's going to help Abbie with the baby while you're at school? How are you going to support a family? Medical school is a full time endeavor."

She turns to me. "Do you honestly think you will return to college to finish your degree with a child to raise and a husband in medical school for four years, plus an additional five to six years of training? And what about your dream of becoming a surgeon? Is that over now?"

"Mom, it's our life, our struggles and triumphs to endure. We'll handle whatever comes our way. We're still young. Don't write us off just yet."

Mom bursts into tears, walks over to me and pulls me into her arms. "My brave girl, you're taking on way too much too soon. But you've always been fearless, even as a child. I know you'll handle this but I worry. I just wish it wasn't happening before you had a chance to experience life."

After our embrace, I whisper to Mom and Ty that I need

to speak to my father alone. After they leave the kitchen, I pull up a chair across from Dad.

"I know you're disappointed. I'm sorry I let you down."

He remains quiet, not looking at me. I won't let his silence stop me, though. "This is hard for Ty and me too. We've taken everything you and Mom said into account. We know life isn't perfect, but we can make a go of it."

Still no response.

"I've known Ty since I was fourteen, and in many ways, he's always looked out for me. You can't deny that, Dad. This time won't be any different. He will be a wonderful father to our baby. As for providing, we'll make the numbers work. We'll have to make sacrifices, but who doesn't?"

"You don't understand what it's like to watch your first born child's promising future go down the toilet," he says bitterly. "The first time I held you in my arms as a newborn, I promised myself to do everything in my power to make sure you had an amazing life."

"And you kept your promise, Dad. I had a great childhood. You and Mom raised me well. To work hard, take responsibility for my choices, to be kind and respectful to others. An amazing life doesn't mean free from challenges and difficulties. Ty and I will be fine. I'm not saying it will be easy, but we'll make it."

As I look into my father's fearful eyes, I wonder if we have it all wrong. My parents' reaction was the same as mine after I got over the initial shock of discovering I was pregnant. What will become of my goals and dreams and all the things I had planned in between? But I think I've already answered my own question. An amazing life doesn't mean there will never be trouble. It just means we have to fight harder to have that life. I'm marrying a man who will never quit on me. And isn't that a wonderful gift in itself?

Dad steeples his hands and place them on the table. "I'm not happy about this, Abbie. I hear your arguments, but this is not what your mother and I wanted for you. You're not even out of your teens yet, for goodness sake. In one fell swoop, you're taking on marriage and motherhood. You have no idea how difficult it can be. All of this is too soon in my book. You're still a child."

I look away. His heartache is more than I can bear. No matter how many times I tell him it's not the end of everything, he will still maintain that my future has been compromised. I'll find way to deal with my parents' disappointment. I'll find a way to hold it together, not to let the truth swallow me whole.

"Dad, no matter how old I get, you and Mom will always see me as a child, *your* child."

"You're right about that. None of us saw this coming and it's troubling."

"I know there's nothing I can say that will make this easy for you. I just hope in time you will come to believe that things will work out, so you won't worry so much. Please don't worry so much," I plead.

"You ask the impossible," he says, his voice faltering. "I will worry about you and your brother until I take my last breath."

Don't lose it in front of him. He's struggling as it is. Think about something unpleasant, something that makes you angry. Hold it together for his sake.

The tears are circling, and I stare down at my hands

resting in my lap. My chest aches with a heaviness that won't soon go away. There's nothing much left to say. Dad asks about the wedding. I explain that we haven't had time to think about setting a date. He says he can't wrap his head around the fact that he's going to be a grandfather. He gets teary-eyed when he says so.

"You're thinking about your long-term prognosis, aren't you?" I deduce.

He shakes his head. "As disappointed as I was to hear that you'll have to drop out of college for a while, it also reminded me that there's always the possibility that I won't be around to see my grandchildren grow up."

"Dad is the cancer back?" I ask, panicking.

"No, not at all," he's quick to reassure me. "But there are no guarantees in life. And maybe I should start looking at this baby as a blessing."

Oh Dad, if you only knew the backstory you wouldn't say that. And that's why for the rest of your life, you can never know the truth.

I CURL UP on the couch in the family room next to Lee. It's late and I'm tired, but I couldn't go to sleep without chatting with him first. Besides, it's his turn to yell at me, after I get the details of his trip to Louisiana with Mom. After all, it was his call to inform me of the trip that was the turning point for me, the moment I realized I couldn't go through with the abortion.

"Was it weird meeting Grandma Betty face to face?"

"Yes, it was awkward. She didn't have much to say to me. I think she may have regrets but wouldn't admit them."

"That doesn't surprise me. Mom had a similar experience when she went to visit her after Grandpa Richard died a few years ago. Mom wanted to know why Grandma was physically abusive toward her, couldn't love her, and then threw her out of the house when she got pregnant with you. All Grandma would say was that she was grieving. Apparently, she gave birth to twins. Mom's twin sister Maddie died right after she was born. Grandma Betty was mad at Mom for surviving, or some crazy thing like that. I guess our mother reminded her of the loss. Did you know that?"

"Whoa," Lee exclaims. "I had no idea it went that deep. I knew about her being abusive, but not that our mother is a twin."

"Do you feel like you have closure now?"

"I don't know. I mostly did it for Shelby. It was important to her. Since I had no emotional attachment to Betty Lansing, there really wasn't any closure to be had."

"Well, I'm glad you went anyway. Family is important, even the crazy ones."

"What about your family, Abbie? The one you're creating with Ty. What's that about?"

"I don't know what you mean."

"What are you and Ty hiding, little sister? You expect me to believe that you guys suddenly got careless? Last time I checked in, you two were still just friends. What brought about this life-altering change?"

"Come on, Lee. I expected this from our mother, not you."

Lee has a sixth sense about me. I was so worried about my parents' reaction that I didn't include him in the equation. He's always had my back, and I know that anything

I confide in him, he will never repeat to another soul. But this, I cannot tell him. The seriousness of the situation, the brutality of it, will have his head spinning while he makes a beeline for Mom.

"You're a smart girl, Abbie. I have a hard time believing that this just *happened*," he says, using air quotes.

"What do you think happened, Lee?"

Do you really want him to answer that question?

He cracks his knuckles, a nervous habit. "Something brought this on."

"Yes, it's called sex."

Lee narrows his eyes at me. I should just shut up now. This false bravado isn't working, and if I sit here too long with him, he's going to squeeze the truth out of me.

"Now I have proof. Something is definitely wrong with this picture. You never talk like that."

"Maybe I've changed."

"You have. Don't think I haven't noticed." Then he moves closer to me.

"What is it, little sister? You can talk to me and it will go no further than this room. I'm worried about you."

"I'm getting married and having a kid, and I'm not even out of my teens yet. Isn't that enough?"

"You're not going to tell me, are you?"

"No, I'm not."

He eases back into his sitting position. He says, his voice strained, "Okay. I'll respect your decision."

"Thank you, big brother."

CHAPTER 48

AFTER

I SIT IN one of my favorite rooms in the house, the westerly facing sunroom. It's heated in the winter and I like to curl up on the antique sofa with a good book. It's late morning on Thanksgiving Day. All everyone could talk about during breakfast was how Ty and I hit them with a double whammy, and they're still reeling from it. It's slowly sinking in for everybody. At least Miles is happy that he's going to be an uncle. I love that boy. He thinks his big sister can do no wrong. I filled in Ty on my conversation with Dad. He had one of his own with his mother. She was quite unhappy. Big surprise.

"Mrs. Cooper kept looking at me strangely," Ty said to me earlier. "Like she thought I was hiding something. We need to be careful around her. She has some kind of special secret radar. She might push you hard. You have to stick to the script. I almost messed up the math when she asked how far along you were, I was so nervous."

Mom made sure I had a big, healthy breakfast, one of the reasons I'm hiding out in the sunroom. I need time to digest it. She insists that I should have a regular OBGYN here in Castleview and one at the medical center near campus. Dad must have spoken to her last night because she was much calmer this morning.

I toss the book I'm reading into the basket across the room, loaded with old books and magazines. The basket topples over, and I let out a frustrated sigh because I have to leave my comfortable spot to pick up the spilled contents. As I stuff the contents back into the basket, one magazine in particular catches my attention. I place the basket upright and take the magazine with me to the sofa. *Art & Architectural Monthly*—a global publication that features high-end art, top architects and their work, and the best in travel and luxury. The house on the cover looks very familiar.

My heart beats at a frantic pace as I turn the pages, looking for the cover story. I find it in the middle of the magazine. It looks familiar for a reason. It's Bedford Hills, Christian's family estate.

My thoughts collide with each other, creating a storm cloud of emotions: Spencer and his odd behavior; Justin's revelation that Spencer targeted me at the frat party back in September; Spencer's overly cautious responses during our New Year's discussion, not to mention the doll. Has Spencer been to Bedford Hills before? Did he see me the night of the ball? If so, what does he want with me two years later? And what does that have to do with my secret admirer and the assault?

CHAPTER 49

AFTER

H ONEY, YOU LOOK sad," she said. "Are you upset that Zach couldn't join us for Thanksgiving this year?"

"I don't care if he's here or not."

"Did you two have a falling out?"

"Zach went skiing in Vermont with his douchebag friends. Don't make a big deal about it, Mom."

"Sorry, honey. I hate to see you so upset."

"I'm not upset. Why do you have to blow everything out of proportion?"

Spencer almost regretted coming home. His mother's excessive prodding about his emotions and continuous attempts to bond with him were beginning to irritate him. He only came home because he wanted to see Brynn. He should feel guilty about the way he sometimes treated his mother, but he was in no mood for self- reflection. She did the best she could, yet he still found it hard to forgive her.

His mother worked as an executive assistant to some hot shot at a multi-national energy company. She made a good salary and had great benefits since she'd been working for the company for almost fifteen years. He guessed she must have dipped into her 401k and cashed out some of her stock to supplement financial aid. How else could she afford to send him to an Ivy League university? Things could have been so different if she had the guts to stand up and speak out. Force Alan Wheeler to step up and take responsibility for his actions instead of using his power and influence to hide the truth. How different would his life have been if she had the courage to make Alan own up to the truth about what went down when she worked for him?

"Mom, stop worrying about Spencer. He can take care of himself. Now, can we please have a peaceful Thanksgiving without the two of you sniping at each other?" Brynn said.

"Thank you," Spencer responded gratefully.

"I worry about my kids. That's what a mother does," Diana Rossdale protested. Spencer noticed she fingered her favorite necklace that she broke out on special occasions.

"Does worrying ease your guilt?" Spencer asked, his tone hard.

"Honey, you shouldn't say such things."

"Why not? It's the truth, isn't it?"

"You can't hate me forever. It won't do any good."

Spencer knew she was right, but the anger still burned hot within him, as searing as it had when he discovered the truth this past summer. His mother had lied to him all his life. Now he had to set things right. He had already lost too much. His father had walked out on them because of what she did. He was despicable too, and weak in Spencer's eyes.

He couldn't believe what he had read in that note last summer. When he confronted his mother, she didn't bother to deny it. It explained a lot, though. There were two instances growing up he could remember Alan Wheeler visiting his mother at their home. All he knew back then was that Alan was his mother's boss. He never made a big deal of the fact that on a couple of occasions, Alan handed his mother a thick envelope, and he was not happy when he did so. Even at six years old, Spencer clearly remembered the look of disgust on his face as he exited the house.

Then over the summer, he found the note. His mother had been blackmailing Alan for 15 years, right after Alan fired her from her job as his executive assistant. To make matters worse, his father, Kurt Rossdale, left them once he discovered the blackmail. Spencer had called Zach right after he made the discovery. The discussion had included Alan's not so subtle threat that he would have Diana eliminated if she continued to be a problem.

Spencer and Zach had hatched a plan after the revelation. The plan to expose Alan—drop the bombshell secret that would change everything. In order to do that, they needed access to the man himself, which was near impossible. That was until Spencer remembered a chance sighting two years earlier—a girl he couldn't get out of his head. Never in a million years could he have predicted that his awe-filled moment would pay off two years into the future. At least he had the presence of mind to snap a picture on his phone back then.

"What are you two talking about?" Brynn asked.

Both Spencer and their mother looked up guiltily. Spencer mentally kicked himself. He was so busy being angry that he forgot Brynn didn't know what went down last summer.

He smiled at her. "It's nothing. You know Mom and I have stupid arguments all the time."

Their mother picked up the hint and added, "Spencer's right, Brynn. Being mad at me is his life's work. Some of his anger is justified, though."

"Why?" Brynn asked, and looked at their mother.

Diana Rossdale gave them both a blank look. She wouldn't meet their eyes. She reached for her glass of apple cider with trembling hands. Spencer took control of the situation before it got out of hand.

"Mom was supposed to talk to her boss about recommending me for a paid internship on the Global Initiatives team at Exaron next summer. It was a big deal, highly competitive. The pay was great and with the hands on experience, it would have been a nice set up for my first real job out of college. But she screwed that up too. She forgot to talk to her boss about it. One phone call from him and I would have been in. Now, there are no more open spots left."

"But it's only November," Brynn protested.

"Late November. Like I said, it's a highly competitive program. People apply from all over the country and the spots get filled early."

"Mom, isn't there anything you can do?" Brynn asked, her eyes pleading.

"I tried, honey. The director of the program wouldn't make an exception. He said all the other candidates got their materials in on time. The timeline when he could have made an exception and squeeze Spencer in came and went."

Brynn's shoulders slumped with disappointment. Spencer stayed silent. She was always in his corner. Brynn was only two when their dad left and ever since, the two of them have been fiercely protective of each other.

"I'm done with this farce," Spencer said. He left the table not caring what anyone thought. Brynn followed and begged him to come back to the table. Their mother had worked hard to prepare a special meal in anticipation of them coming home, and the least he could do was act civil. He ignored her pleading.

"WHAT'S THE REAL reason you're mad at Mom?" Brynn asked. "I'm not an idiot, you know. That story about the internship may be true, but that's not why you're hostile. Come on Spencer, what's the big secret?"

Spencer sat in a comfortable armchair in the basement. He continuously threw and caught a yellow nerf ball he bounced off the wall. Brynn stood beside him, arms folded, waiting on an answer.

He stopped bouncing the ball and looked up at her.

"What is it, Spencer? You can tell me. I can keep a secret."

He adored his little sister. She had this way of making him want to be a nicer person. Her dark hair hung loose past her shoulders in thick spirals. Her round, innocent face always made him smile, even when she was upset and complained to him about some friend of hers who was a backstabber. There were late night discussions about which guy she had a crush on, and how Spencer was going to convince their mother to allow Brynn to go to some party that was suspect. He knew he could trust her, he just had to be careful what he said and how he said it.

"Actually, you could help me with this," he said. "I need your advice."

Her eyes went big. "Really?"

"Yeah, sure. But you have to promise to keep this quiet. You can't tell anyone, especially Mom."

"You can trust me," she said. Her face brimmed with eagerness and excitement. She grabbed an old folding chair from the corner near a pile of boxes and sidled up next to him.

He recounted the story to Brynn—the note he found, confronting their mother about the truth, and how it affected him. He told her about Abbie Cooper and why she was critical to the plan's success. When he was finished, Brynn's mouth fell open and her eyes bulged once again.

"Whoa," she said, and held up a hand. "Whoa. I need a minute to process all of this. Are you serious?"

He nodded. Brynn walked over to the pool table in the center of the basement, picked up two balls, and began juggling to gather her thoughts.

"I just can't get my head around this, Spencer. This is huge. I mean, world spinning on its axis huge."

"Yeah."

"A lot of lives are going to be turned upside down. Are you sure you want to do this?"

"I've never been more sure of anything in my life. They've gotten away with it for too long. It's time for action."

"What about this Abbie girl? What's going to happen once she finds out you were just using her?"

"By that time she does, it won't matter. She'll see it was

for a good reason. I wouldn't have involved her if there were another way. I'm never going to get this close again. All she has to do is send a text message or make a quick phone call and we're in. I just have to convince her to do it."

Brynn stopped juggling and walked over to Spencer. She tugged at her hair the way she did when doing some hard thinking. "There's no guarantee she will cooperate. You need a backup plan."

"This is it. There is no backup plan. We need an audience to do maximum damage. The ball is it. Zach and I need to enter that mansion free and clear, with invitations in our hands and our names on the guest list. I can't show up as subcontracted, hired help like two years ago. Back then, I didn't know what I do now."

"Are you sure there isn't someone else who can get you in?"

"If there was, I wouldn't need Abbie."

"Well, based on what you said, she is the perfect candidate. Is there some incentive you could provide that would make her agree to the idea?"

"None that I can think of. Time is running out, Brynn. I bet those invitations have already been sent out. *She* doesn't need an invitation if she tells them she's coming to the ball, but they would provide her with a few if she had guests."

"They would," Brynn agreed. "Maybe the direct approach would be best."

"What do you mean?"

"Tell Abbie you want to go to the ball. For research and networking purposes."

"I don't follow."

Brynn returned to the folded chair she occupied earlier. "Tell her what you told me at dinner, how you lost that internship opportunity. Say that you want to go to the Wheeler New Year's Eve Ball for networking purposes, to see if Levitron-Blair has any openings. They have locations all over the world. I'm sure you would run into several of their executives at the ball, right?"

What a brilliant idea. He had stayed awake many nights, trying to figure out how to get those coveted invitations. He thought with Abbie Cooper, the subtle approach was best. That strategy had been a miserable failure so far. But his sister was on to something. Sometimes you had to grab the bull by the horns.

"Brynn, you're a genius," he said.

"I am?"

"Yes. Now get out of here. I have work to do."

CHAPTER 50

AFTER

T HIS IS HOW he could have seen the painting," I say,
       pointing to the magazine photos.
Ty joins me on the sofa in the sunroom after I had fired off
an urgent text message. "Think about it. You can walk into a
bookstore and pick up this publication."

Ty starts pacing again, hands in his pockets. "Okay.
Say you're right. It still doesn't explain how he would know
about the painting. It's not part of the spread."

"True. But what if he was part of the crew that did the
photo shoot at the Wheeler mansion?"

Comprehension dawns on him. "All we would need are
the names and addresses of all who were there that day.
Find out if any of them is a student at Yale."

"That really narrows it down."

"Assuming your attacker goes to Yale," he reminds me.
"We still don't know that for sure."

I let out a deep sigh. "I know, but it's the best lead we've
had so far. We have to see it through."

He returns to the sofa. "I don't want you to be disappointed if it doesn't pan out. He could have seen the painting some other time, especially if he was at the mansion for a social occasion. The Wheelers host many events. Or he could have been there as part of the support staff for the ball. This guy, whoever he is, could have seen you at the ball and become obsessed with you."

"That's creepy. But why wait until now to strike?"

"That's a great question. Perhaps he only made the connection at the beginning of the fall semester. What if he's a transfer student, for example? If he only saw you back in September for the first time since the ball, that would answer the question of why now."

I shiver at the prospect and Ty strokes my arms. "I'm going to call Katherine, see if she can give us the names of everybody who worked the ball and their photos. I also want to find out about the photographer who did the spread for the magazine. Between those two leads, we're bound to find something."

AFTER A WONDERFUL Thanksgiving dinner in which Mom outdid herself yet again, we gather in the family room to watch the traditional Thanksgiving Day football game. Mom asks me to join her in the kitchen. Her secret detection radar is working overtime, and she hasn't had time to interrogate me because of preparation for the big dinner. Now that it's over, she's jumping on the opportunity.

I don't bother to ask her why we're in the kitchen and just take my seat at the kitchen table. We've had many serious talks over the years at this very spot, including conversations about my feelings for Ty.

She sits in the chair across from me. "What's going on, Abbie?"

"I already told you. I told the whole family."

"There's something you and Ty aren't saying."

"So suspicious, mother. Isn't it enough that we dropped two bombshells on the family on one night?"

"I'm still reeling from those. But there's something else. You and Ty have been whispering a lot, you're both anxious."

"You're just a worried mother, that's all."

"I know when something is off with you. I sensed it when we FaceTimed a few weeks back, when you were at Ty's place. You said you had the flu."

"I did. And I recovered."

"There was a sadness about you that had nothing to do with the flu. I also saw it in your eyes last night."

I'm about to lose it in front of her, and that would be very bad. I bite down hard on my tongue. It hurts and I focus on overcoming the pain to stop myself from crying.

"What is it, sweetie? You used to be able to tell me anything under the sun, and you still can. You're not yourself. Something about you has changed, something fundamental. I don't mean the pregnancy."

I grab her hands and look her straight in the eye. "I'm just tired and stressed. Having a kid is a huge responsibility. Although Ty and I have it handled, it's still scary."

"Why are you having nightmares, Abbie? Nightmares so bad that you need Ty to console you?"

"Um . . . I don't know what you're talking about."

"Don't lie to me, sweetie. You're terrible at it. I heard

you and Ty discuss sleeping arrangements last night, which I thought was odd since you were supposed to sleep in your old room and Ty in a guest bedroom."

I can play this one of two ways. Continue to outright lie, which she already knows I am, or throw her a morsel, some little tidbit that sounds plausible. But what? What would make a mama bear who's convinced her cub is in trouble back off?

"I have these dreams where someone steals the baby. I flip out, because they seem real. That's why Ty consoles me."

"Well, pregnant women have all kinds of crazy dreams. It's not unusual." She looks at me for a long time and then says, "How did this happen, Abbie? Did you do this on purpose, to hold on to Ty?"

If it were possible for my mouth to hit the floor, it would have. But I recover quickly. I'm seriously offended by her question.

"How could you say that to me, Mom? Is that what you think of me, that I would get pregnant on purpose to manipulate a man into staying in my life? That's diabolical and desperate. You think I'm that kind of person?"

She apologizes profusely. "I know you're not that person, Abbie, I'm sorry I said that. I was just shocked. You were on the pill to help with those horrible cramps associated with your period. I just don't understand."

"I got off the pill last year," I say quietly. "The cramping got better and I didn't need to take them anymore."

"Oh, I didn't know that. So Ty didn't use protection then."

"For crying out loud mother, stop it!" I'm yelling now and my reaction stuns her. She jerks back, the sound of the chair scraping the tile floor evidence of how flabbergasted she is. I want to run to my room and cover my head with a pillow.

"If you insist on knowing the details, here goes. Ty and I only had sex one time and I got pregnant. Yes, he used protection. It failed. Slim chance, but it happened to us. And we haven't had sex since that one time. Anything else you would like to know about how I got pregnant?"

I don't know how much longer I can keep up the lie. I can't face my mother another minute without breaking wide open, so I leave the kitchen table and head up the stairs as fast as I can. I slam my bedroom door and collapse on the bed, the tears I've been holding back breaking free like a river damn.

Later on, Mom knocks on the door and I let her in. She asks me to forgive her. She said she and Dad spoke and we have their full support, both emotional and financial. I tell her Ty and I want to make it on our own but we'll take advantage of any offers to babysit. She says I should come work for her on a schedule that will suit my soon-to-be new life. I agree to give it some thought and discuss with Ty.

CHAPTER 51

AFTER

I PLACE THE phone on the end table next to the sofa and head to the kitchen to get a drink. My cell phone rings, halting my movements. What if it's *him* calling? He has my number and warned me he was watching me. What if my attacker is finally responding to my text? I can hardly breathe. I slowly release the refrigerator door and take tentative steps toward the sofa. I look down at the phone screen to see that it's Katherine Wheeler calling. What a relief.

I snatch up the phone. "Hello."

"Abbie, it's Katherine Wheeler."

After we exchange pleasantries about family and school, she explains the reason for her call.

"I got a hold of the photographer who did the photo shoot for *Art & Architecture Monthly*. I will email you his details. I told him you might pay him a visit. His studio is in New York."

"That's great news. Thank you, Katherine."

"Well, I'm not sure I have great news with the caterers. I've used them for a few events, but for the New Year's Eve ball two years ago, they subcontracted out some of the wait staff. If some staff was paid under the table, it would be hard to track them down."

"I understand and appreciate everything you've done."

"No problem, Abbie. Can I ask you something?"

"Sure."

"Is everything all right with you?"

"Yes. Why do you ask?"

"Your voice when you asked for the information. It was unsteady, and tinged with sadness. Not your usual upbeat and animated way of speaking. You said your mother's show was looking for local vendor recommendations to staff an upcoming event here in McLean, but I suspect the Cooking Network has people who can do that for her. If you were in trouble, you would tell me, right? Mr. Wheeler and I care about you, even though you and Christian aren't together anymore."

"It's sweet of you to worry, Katherine, but I'm fine. I just wanted to do this small favor for Mom, that's all. I'll let you get back to your day, and tell Mr. Wheeler I said hello."

After Katherine hangs up, I make a quick phone call. He doesn't pick up, and it goes to voicemail. "Justin, it's Abbie. I have a question for you about what you told me the other day, when we were studying. I need you to clarify one particular detail. It's very important. Please call me back ASAP."

I grab my keys and head out the door. Today, I have a session with Dr. Shanahan. I intend to ask her some tough questions. Depending on her answers, there is a chance I might get my memory back. A chance I will recall everything that happened that night.

CHAPTER 52

AFTER

IT WAS EASY to follow her midnight blue Audi Cabriolet. I hang back several cars, driving a beat up, old tan Chevrolet that has seen better days. It's the kind of inconspicuous ride I need to get around. I paid a guy at a rental place a hundred bucks to take it off his hands for a couple of days and convinced him to avoid doing any paperwork. I gave a fake name, of course. If anyone runs the plates on this car, it will lead back to Roy's Car and Truck Rental Service.

After a couple of miles, she turns into a street clustered with several huge medical buildings. She pulls into the parking lot of the third one, St. Luke's Medical Center. I adjust my sunglasses, pull the baseball cap lower, and straighten the wig as I watch her park and exit her car. She heads toward the entrance of the building.

I follow at a safe distance. She walks past the front desk and head toward the bank of elevators. She turns around, and I dart into the gift shop. My heart thunders in my chest. I fear she might discover she's being followed.

I scurry out of the gift shop as quickly as I darted in. I reach into my jacket pocket and pull out my phone. I get close enough to see her approach the elevator. I pretend to be engrossed in something on my phone but strain to see if she's heading up or down. She pushes the up arrow.

After she takes the elevator up, I walk over to the directory to see what offices and medical specialties are on the upper floors. A woman in a white lab coat frowns at me. After she passes by, I continue snooping. Psychiatry is on the eighth floor. Several doctors' offices are listed. It doesn't take a genius to figure out she's seeing a shrink to deal with what happened. For some reason, it doesn't move me. Not in the least.

CHAPTER 53

AFTER

D
R. SHANAHAN OFFERS me water from the cooler in her office before she sits down for our session. She hands me the drink in small paper cup and I freeze. A flash of memory, sudden, piercing and vivid. I don't know why it's important but it is.

"Abbie, are you okay?" she asks. "What just happened?"

I slowly take the water from her and she has a seat. I drain the contents and dump the empty cup in the trash bin nearby.

"I don't know. I think I had a flash of memory. When you handed me the water just now, I remember someone giving me a drink the night I was attacked."

She sits at the edge of her chair. "That's good. Do you remember where you were? This could be a breakthrough. Close your eyes and lean back."

I oblige.

"Now, think back to the night of the party, what you remembered before your memory went blank," she says in a soothing voice.

I relax my shoulders and close my eyes. I understand why she's so excited about this. I am too. Most of our sessions have been focused on my emotional and psychological state. We haven't addressed my memory problem.

"I see acquaintances, people I know from my classes, intermingled with people I've never met before. My friend Zahra and I drove to the party together."

And what else?" she asks in her still soothing voice.

"It was the usual—yelling, laughter, drinking, loud music."

"Did anything seem out of the ordinary to you, anything that didn't seem right. It could be a person or an object. Do you recall any details about the place?"

"It was a house in Bethany."

I explain to Dr. Shanahan about running into Ty and Kristina, and how Ty and I agreed that I would leave with him because I was going to help him practice for his second interview with Harvard Medical School admissions.

"Did you talk to anyone else during the party?"

"I spoke to Eric and Hak, two of Ty's friends who were there."

"You know them well?"

"Yes. We spent time at Ty's apartment before. They liked it when I cooked or baked. We joked for a bit and they told me to watch out for drunk frat boys who might hit on me because they would have to beat them up."

"Do you think that may be important?" Dr. Shanahan asks.

My eyes open. "Are you thinking they might have had something to do with the attack? No way. They treat me like their little sister. They're good guys. They've been friends with Ty since freshman year. Ty's careful about who he invites into his private space. Trust me, there's nothing there."

I close my eyes again and continue. "I received a text from Spencer asking me to save him from the world's most boring conversation."

"Tell me about Spencer and your relationship with him, how he fits into this puzzle. We've only discussed him briefly as the last person to have seen you before you were kidnapped and assaulted."

"Do we have to?" I ask.

"No. But is there a reason why you don't want to discuss him?"

How can I explain that I can't let go of what Justin told me, that Spencer may have had nefarious reasons for pursuing me, and I think those reasons might be connected to the assault?

"I just have this uncomfortable feeling."

"What brought on those feelings?"

I explain how Spencer almost choked when I mentioned Christian was my ex, and repeat what Justin told me a week ago.

"I see. What do you think it means?"

"I may have cause for suspicion but no proof of anything. I'm not saying he attacked me, just that his actions speak to some secret motive where I'm concerned. I don't know what that motive is yet. The flash of memory I just had, of someone handing me a cup of water, well that someone was Spencer."

Dr. Shanahan knits her eyebrows together and then scribbles in her notebook. "How well do you know Spencer, Abbie?"

"What do you mean?"

"What do you know about him besides the fact that the two of you attend the same university?"

"He has a sister named Brynn, he grew up in Bethesda. He was captain of the crew team, his parents are divorced, and he's an international relations major."

"How much do you know about his past, his upbringing? Have you ever witnessed any violent tendencies from him?"

I shake my head. "No. I don't know much about his upbringing, except that he doesn't like his father. What are you getting at, Dr. Shanahan?"

"He was the last person to see you before you were abducted and attacked. You just had a memory that involved him."

"That's strange. I didn't remember that at all. I recall kissing him, and then I pulled away. I apologized and let him know I wasn't leading him on or anything like that. We talked for a while then I got thirsty. I remembered he headed inside to get me some water but not that he brought it out to me, not until this memory surge."

"Did he ever pressure you to take your relationship further?"

"It depends on your definition of pressure. He would make inappropriate jokes sometimes, and I responded in kind. Some of it was quite funny. There were a few instances of his hand "accidentally" ending up on my knee. A casual brush up against me that seemed innocent when it was anything but, or the time he asked me about my bra size. That was an oddball question, but I figured he was just trying to keep me off balance."

"How did you feel about those occurrences?"

"I thought he wanted to see how far he could push the envelope, perhaps curious about what my reaction would be."

"Did he ever buy you gifts?"

"He bought me a pair of gold earrings, a new cover for my tablet, and a designer sweater. I returned them all and explained it would be inappropriate to accept gifts from him."

I've never spoken of this until now. I never even told Zahra.

"I see," she says. "And how did he take it when you returned his gifts?"

"He was disappointed. I felt terrible about it. I think I hurt his feelings."

"Why do you think you hurt his feelings?"

"It was easy to see the hurt in his eyes. And he didn't contact me for several days, which was out of the ordinary for him. I think he wanted to put some distance between us to lick his wounds."

I felt guilty then but not now. I found the timing of the gifts odd. It was right after the incident at the movie theatre. At the time, I didn't think much of it. However, once new information was revealed, thanks to Justin, all the little things I let slide started to add up into a disconcerting portrait of suspicion.

I shift in my seat. I cross and uncross my arms and legs several times. I start biting my fingernails, although I haven't given in to the habit in a while. That portrait has now grown ten-fold. Rejection can be a powerful motive for revenge.

Dr. Shanahan notices my unease. "I'm not suggesting that Spencer had anything to do with the assault, Abbie. His recollection of that night could be the truth."

"I want you to hypnotize me," I blurt out. "I don't see

any other way for me to recall what happened. And as we discussed in previous sessions, I won't put this completely behind me until I know what happened and how."

The idea has been circulating in my head for some time. Great strides have been made in brain and memory research. If scientists have figured out how to block traumatic memories, they should also know how to retrieve them.

Dr. Shanahan goes silent for a beat. Then she says, "Hypnosis can be a useful tool in some scenarios but can be problematic in others."

"What do you mean?"

"For one, there's no hard scientific evidence that hypnosis helps us to remember things any more than other methods. But the biggest challenge with this method is that it can cause patients to recall memories that are false."

"So I'm supposed to do nothing?"

"Abbie, your memory could come back, let's not give up on that possibility. The brain is funny. It protects us from memories that are traumatic, we forget. It also has the ability recall those same traumatic events."

"What about drugs?" I told her about my research into drugs that can erase memories of trauma and my theory that there should be a therapy out there for the opposite, recalling traumatic memories.

"You're right. Researchers have identified a specific brain mechanism that has the ability to hide traumatic memories in the brain—and to retrieve them. It's called State-Dependent Memory."

Disappointment courses through me. It means this is still in the research phase and they're a long way off from developing any drug therapy based on the findings.

"What happens if my memory of the attack is never recalled? What am I in for, worst case scenario."

Her face turns grave. "Over the long-term, serious psychological problems could occur; anxiety, depression, dissociative disorders."

"Aren't there brain exercises that can help with memory?" I ask. I can't give up so easily. I can't accept that for the rest of my life, I may never recall what happened to me that night.

"Abbie, the fact that you remembered that someone handed you a drink the night you were attacked is great news. Don't underestimate what that could mean. You recalled that on your own, without any prompting, without any intervention from me."

She's right. There is hope, no matter how small. However, it chills me to the bone that Spencer Rossdale may be the key to finding out what happened that fateful night.

CHAPTER 54

AFTER

THE NEXT MORNING, my phone buzzes on the way out of the apartment. I dig it out of my bag and look at the screen. It's a text message. I consider ignoring the text, but answering may be in my best interest.

Spencer: How was Thanksgiving?

Me: Great. How was yours?

Spencer: Couldn't be better.

Spencer: I need to see you. It's important.

Me: What's up?

Spencer: Internships.

Me: Huh?

Spencer: Will explain. Lunch in the dining hall?

Me: Okay.

Spencer: See you then.

I dump the phone back into my purse as I hurry to catch the shuttle. *Internships? What kind of game is Spencer playing?* There's only one way to find out.

At 12:00 p.m. sharp, I arrive in the dining hall. I'm not hungry, although I should eat something. I find a table and break out an apple I carry around for snack. My ring tone goes off and I grab the phone on the second ring. It's Justin.

"Thanks for calling back," I say.

"What do you want to ask me?"

I do a quick sweep of the dining hall to make sure Spencer is nowhere in sight. I bend my head down and cover my mouth as I speak into the phone.

"Did Spencer make that phone call before or after he spotted me the night we met? You said he ditched his date and made a phone call, but I can't remember if it was before or after he saw me."

"After."

"Are you sure?"

"Yes. First, he saw you. Then he ditched his date and then made the call. Right after he ended the call, he approached you. That was the sequence of events."

"Thank you, Justin."

I click off and gasp when I look up. Spencer is at the table, looking right at me. Oh crap, how much did he hear? I can't tell by his expression. Best to play it cool.

"Don't sneak up on me like that," I say calmly. "I'm still paranoid because of what happened to me. I get jumpy."

"Sorry," he says, taking a seat. "I didn't mean to scare you. Was that Justin you were talking to?"

"Yes. What about it?"

"Nothing. I heard you thank him."

"He helped me out with a project for our probability & statistics class. I was thanking him for saving my skin."

"Oh," Spencer says. But I don't think he believes me.

"So, what did you want to see me about?" I ask.

He rakes his hand through his hair and clears his throat. "I need a huge favor. I hate to even ask, and I wouldn't if it wasn't important. If you say no, I will totally understand, no hard feelings. I swear."

"What is it Spencer? Just say it."

"Okay, I had my heart set on an internship with this major energy company for next summer, but the person who was supposed to help me didn't. It fell through."

He stops as if gathering the courage to continue.

"Go on," I say.

"Anyway, I was doing some research . . . I'm a little embarrassed about this part, I hope you don't get mad."

"About what?" I ask, my impatience growing by the minute.

"Remember when I said I was jealous about your ex?"

"Yeah."

"I Googled him. Well, I Googled you and added the name Christian to the search."

I cross my arms over my chest and scowl at him. "And what did you find?"

"I was shocked when the search came back with photos of you and Christian Wheeler. I didn't realize that's who you were talking about."

Liar!

"What does that have to do with an internship, Spencer?

290

I have to say, this is very upsetting. You went behind my back to gather information about me? Why would you do that when you could easily have asked me?"

I ball my hand into a fist. A tension headache is coming on, and I battle to keep it at bay. I can't get too angry. He'll retreat and it will make it harder to know what he's up to. Play nice, I remind myself. You can catch more flies with honey than with vinegar, or however the saying goes.

"I'm really sorry. I wasn't thinking straight. It was a stupid, immature thing to do, and I would never do anything that dumb again. Please forgive me."

He's appropriately remorseful with his crumpled body posture and pleading eyes. I'm sure it's all an act, but I want to hear the rest of the story.

"The internship, Spencer. Tell me about the internship."

"Right. Well, Christian's dad is Alan Wheeler, right? Chairman and CEO of Levitron-Blair? I read that their executives are big on mentoring and coaching new college graduates. So I thought, maybe, perhaps I could get to talk to some of those executives in a relaxed environment."

"O-o-okay. I'm still not sure I follow. What do you mean by relaxed environment?"

"The New Year's Eve Ball. There were a lot of articles about it."

"Let me see if I get this straight. You want me to score you an invitation to the Wheelers' New Year's Eve Ball so you can hob nob with Levitron-Blair executives in the hopes of getting an internship?"

"Something like that," he says softly.

"So that's why you asked me about my plans for New

Year's just before Thanksgiving?"

"I didn't know how you would feel about it, so I didn't want to mention it in a text."

There are plenty of companies that offer internships, so why Levitron-Blair?

"The ball is for charity, Spencer. The people who attend donate a lot of money to the Wheeler Foundation. That's a prerequisite for attending. Deep pockets. Invitations are tough to come by because Katherine is picky and strict about who attends. I'm not being snooty, I'm just laying out the facts."

"I understand." He slumps in his chair like a deflated balloon.

I almost feel sorry for him, yet something about this isn't right. Why Levitron-Blair? Why did he freak out when I mentioned Christian? Why does he want to attend the ball? He can check out the company's website and learn how to apply for an internship. It's a very strange request. But it might be the clue that unlocks this puzzle.

"I'll talk to Katherine. Don't get your hopes up, though."

"Really?" he asks, his smile big and wide.

"Yes. Keep your expectations low. As I said, Katherine is stingy with the invitations, which I'm sure have already gone out."

"Thank you, Abbie. The fact that you're willing to try means a lot to me."

"You're welcome. And don't ever go behind my back again," I say. "There's no reason to do that."

"I won't. I promise."

CHAPTER 55

AFTER

I APPROACH THE doorman at the Metro Crown apartment building as "Dean", the FedEx guy. With a FedEx cap pulled low, glasses and a fleece FedEx vest I purchased online, I look the part. I offer a generic greeting to the doorman and head straight for the concierge. I keep my voice even and friendly, but not overly so.

"Delivery for Apartment 8F," I say to the concierge, a burly man in his fifties with a neatly cut beard and dark jacket.

"Does it require a signature?" he asks.

"No." Better to keep my answers short.

But the concierge is in no hurry. "How about that snow, huh? Makes the job a lot tougher in this weather, doesn't it?"

"I guess," I mumble. The concierge makes no move to pick up the box from the counter and put it away.

"Well, gotta go. Don't want to be late for my next delivery."

"Totally understand that," he says. "Sorry for keeping you. I guess I do tend to go on. My wife says I should put a muzzle on it sometimes. Well, have a good day then."

I move away from the desk and head for the door. I'm almost out of the lobby when I hear, "Hold on just a minute."

I'm sweating now. My hands are clammy and shaking. I want to rip off the cap, but that's a bad idea. I force myself to remain calm, and then turn around slowly to face the concierge.

"There's no return address on this box," the man says accusingly.

"There isn't?" I take the box from him and make a show of giving it a thorough look over. "Strange. Tell you what. I'll call in to the office the minute I get into my truck to let them know. I'm just the delivery guy."

The concierge studies me with skepticism, as if wondering if he should believe me or not. After a few painful seconds, he walks away from me with the package in hand, without another word.

THE CONVERSATION WITH Spencer yesterday dominates my thoughts. I can't believe he fed me that story about an internship and Googled me behind my back when he could have just asked me. I was disappointed at first to discover his underhanded move, but it turned out to be an important clue. He does know Christian and has been pretending he doesn't.

I do not intend to ask Katherine for an invitation on his behalf until I find out why he wants to go to the ball, what his obsession with the Wheelers is all about. I heard back from Katherine's photographer. That lead turned out to be a dud. The photographer had a crew of three for the Wheeler mansion shoot: himself and two female assistants.

It's dark at 5:30 in the afternoon and freezing cold. I dig for my favorite winter hat—a pale pink, cable knit beanie with a bright pink pompom on top. I pull it over my head and slip on my gloves. The snow crunches beneath my feet as I make my way to the shuttle stop. I pat the side pocket of my bag to make sure the Taser gun Ty purchased for me is still there. I can't forget the threat from my attacker. *I'm watching you.* I find it strange that he hasn't responded. That text was sent two weeks ago. What is he up to?

I hop on the shuttle, which is usually crowded this time of day. Students, staff and faculty are heading back to their dorms, off-campus residences, the bus or train station. I grab one of the handles to stay balanced once the shuttle starts moving. The doors open and more passengers pile on.

Someone taps me on the shoulder and I spin around, only to come face to face with a man in a black hoodie and black jeans. His face is mostly hidden. Full tremors take over my body. My quick, rapid breaths cause me physical pain.

"Stay away from me," I shout.

But he keeps coming, his hands curved, and ready to grab me around the throat. He wants to choke me again, in the darkness, like always. I won't let him. I gather my strength and kick and scream as hard as I can. I can't tell if I'm connecting with his body. He grabs both my arms and applies intense pressure. I try to twist my way out of his death grip, but to no avail.

I bite him hard on the arm and a series of expletives follow. Good. But my gratification is brief as two more hands clamp around my legs, holding them in place. *He has help.* I'm too exhausted to fight them both. Then I realise something odd. I'm not sailing through the air, in the darkness like before. In the distance, I hear my name being called. I gasp for air. The voice calling my name gets increasingly louder. I'm afraid to open my eyes but I don't want to be a coward.

When I do open my eyes, the sight before me stuns me. The shuttle has come to a complete stop. Passengers stare at me like I belong in a psych ward. Others have sympathy in their gazes, and a third group looks as terrified as I feel. Most distressing of all, I'm on the floor of the shuttle, cradled in Spencer Rossdale's arms.

Out of embarrassment, I scramble away from him and stand up. Luckily, there's still a handle available, and I grab on to it for dear life.

"Abbie, are you okay?" Spencer asks. "I think you had some kind of episode. You didn't seem yourself."

All eyes are on me, waiting for a response. "Do you want me to call someone, young lady?" I turn around to see the shuttle driver. My humiliation is now complete. The driver pulled over when I was having my "episode", as Spencer put it. How bad was it? What did I say? I'm holding up the shuttle. They're going to throw me in a psych ward and put me in a strait jacket. I lost it in front of a bunch of strangers. Oh crap, what if someone recorded the whole thing with a cell phone camera?

"I'm fine," I say hurriedly to the driver. I apologize profusely to Spencer and the other passengers. I assure the driver as best as I can that I was fine and my stop would be coming up soon. He returns to the driver seat slowly, as if he's not sure he won't have to pull over again soon. I turn to Spencer.

"What happened?"

"I tapped you on the shoulder to say hello and you went berserk. Started yelling that I should stay away from you. You attacked me, and a fellow passenger had to help me restrain you so you wouldn't hurt yourself."

As I gape at him, I know everything he just said is true. "I'm sorry." My voice shakes. "I don't know why I flipped out like that."

I know exactly why I went nuts, but I'm not about to explain to him or anyone else. Only Ty and Dr. Shanahan know about the episodes. Not even Zahra knows about them.

"You're suffering from PTSD, aren't you?" he asks, as if he knows this for a fact.

I look around the shuttle for signs that fellow passengers heard what he just said. The last thing I need is a bunch of strangers judging me or throwing pity my way. I don't want it. If I'm going to fight the psycho who hurt me and find out what Spencer is up to, I can't afford to show weakness, although I just did.

"You can't go tossing around words like that unless you know it to be a fact, Spencer," I say, my voice low.

He frowns. "I didn't mean to insult you, Abbie. PTSD is common in people who've suffered through traumatic events like war, disaster or what happened to you. It wasn't a stretch to think that you could be suffering from it, given your violent reaction to a simple tap on the shoulder."

My hands tighten around the holder. If it were a pencil, it would have snapped in two by now. At this moment, I don't like Spencer Rossdale. I hate his sneakiness, his assumption that he knows me well enough make pronouncements about my situation, and his crack about my violent reaction. Did he just reprimand me?

"Well Spencer, if you're such an expert, you should know you don't creep up on someone who, according to you, is suffering from PTSD."

His nostrils flare and his face turns red. "I know you've had a hard time of it, Abbie, but I'm not the enemy. I want to help you. All you have to do is ask."

I ignore this and instead I say, "Why are you dressed in all black with the hood covering your face?"

He looks down at his sweatshirt and then at his pants as if seeing them for the first time. "I didn't plan it that way. I just grabbed the closest thing that was semi clean."

He looks up at me with a sheepish grin. That still doesn't explain why the hood was up and covering most of his face, though.

Okay Abbie, get it together. Not everything is a pre-meditated plot to get you. You've sat in classes with people who hadn't showered in days. If the guy grabbed the closest outfit he could find that was clean, you can't blame him for that. Plus, it's freezing cold and windy. He was just trying to protect his head and ears.

"Maybe I overreacted," I concede. "You should be able to wear whatever you want without fear that some chick is going to flip out on you."

"Don't worry about it," he says. "But I think I should walk you home."

"It's less than a block from the shuttle drop-off. Thanks for the offer, though."

CHAPTER 56

AFTER

I ARRIVE AT the apartment emotionally and physically exhausted. All I want to do is curl up into a blanket
and forget this day ever happened. Every time I think I'm
making progress to move past my trauma, something pops
up, setting me back. I toss the FedEx package I picked up
from the concierge on the kitchen counter. Weird. There's
no return address on it. After I make some tea, I grab the
package and park myself on the living room sofa.

I shake the box. I can hear something moving inside, an
object of some kind. The label has my name on it with this
address. The people who know I'm staying with Ty wouldn't send
me a package via FedEx, so who is this from and what is it?

I rip the box open, and for the second time today, terror
seizes me. The sound of my heartbeat thrashes in my ears. I
clench my jaw to prevent myself from hyperventilating. Inside the
box is another replica of me wearing the dress from the Wheeler
New Year's Eve Ball, but there's something different about this
one. The gown is shredded and blood-stained. I slowly lift the
doll out of the box and take a close look. Her throat is slashed.

My hands shake so badly that I drop the doll. I look inside the box again to see if there's a note. There is. I pick it up carefully, with trembling hands, as if it will reach out and bite my fingers off. It reads:

Stop searching or you'll end up like her.

My legs weaken and I suddenly feel claustrophobic. I swallow hard and fight the urge to run out of the apartment into the frosty New England air. I force myself to pick up the doll at my feet where she landed. I must be a sadist. I consider the slash of her throat and notice her arm barely hanging on to its socket. He has recreated my injuries in the most horrifying way possible. I choke up and hot tears spill forth. I gently lift the shredded dress and have a peek. It's been slashed with a knife or some sharp object.

Full-on body tremors overwhelm me. I stare at the wall, unable to blink. Keys jangle in the door and my flight or fight response kicks in, but I must be in shock because I just sit there, shaking. My eyes haven't left the spot on the wall. I sense someone walk in.

"Cooper, what's wrong?" I recognize Ty's voice through my blinding fog. I register alarm in his voice but not much else. In a flash, he's beside me.

"Cooper, talk to me, what is it?" He gently shakes my shoulders to bring me out of my stupor. My eyes finally focus on him. Then I look down at my hand. I'm still clutching the doll. He follows my gaze and attempts to pry the doll from my grasp. He succeeds eventually and has a look for himself. He understands the not so subtle threat. I hear him sniffling.

He pulls me into his arms. "I got you Cooper," he says, his voice breaking. " I got you."

300

CHAPTER 57

AFTER

O N MONDAY MORNING, both Ty and I skip class. We have something much more important on our agenda. We make our way down to the security office to view the tape of the day the violated doll was delivered. Depending on what we see, we will also put in a call to FedEx, although I have a pretty good idea what they're going to say: There was no delivery scheduled for apartment 8F on that day, and they don't have anyone named "Dean" who makes deliveries for the area.

Jim Bailey, the head of security ushers us into the carpeted office. At least a dozen flat screens with various images of the building fill up the room. Several desks with additional monitors, phones, a wall calendar, and a large digital map of the area occupy the space. Jim already cued up the video of the day in question.

Ty and I sit on either side of him. He plays the video, and we see the black and white image of residents entering and leaving the building.

"There he is," Jim says freezing the frame. "The guy with his head down and the cap."

Ty and I lean in closer. "We can't really tell much," I say. "Can you enlarge the image?"

"Sure." Jim presses a couple of buttons on the keyboard and the image fills the screen. Not the best quality. The guy was keeping his head down. He wore glasses. Looks like he had dark hair, wearing a FedEx fleece vest and dark long-sleeved jersey. "That's it? That's all the camera captured?" a disappointed Ty asks.

"Well, there was the small incident Mike already told you about."

Jim clicks a couple more buttons and pulls up the image of the same guy leaving the building, and being stopped by Mike the concierge. The exchange is brief. The guy looks at the package given to him by Mike and then gives it back.

"That's all we have," Jim says. "Whoever he is, he knew what he was doing. He made sure his face wasn't in clear view and the glasses could have been part of his disguise."

"It's easy enough to get the FedEx uniform. You can pick one up from eBay for thirty bucks. Sorry I couldn't give you more to go on," Jim says.

"Thanks all the same," Ty says.

After we leave the security office, we go for a walk to get some fresh air and a new perspective on the hunt for my attacker. Downtown is a five-minute walk from the apartment and made up of the central business district, restaurants, shopping and nightlife. The air is crisp and I adjust my coat, making sure it buttons all the way to the top. I don't like being cold although I don't mind the cold weather. We walk along the sidewalk, packed with cars and patches of snow from the last snowstorm.

"Why did he risk coming out in the open like that?" I say. "He had to know it would be risky."

"What if he's an adrenaline junkie? Criminals like him get a high from evading authorities, so they taunt their victims. A catch-me-if-you-can kind of game."

I stay silent for a beat as I digest Ty's perspective. Then I hear an irritated, "excuse me." I turn around to see a young guy carrying a messenger bag slung around his hip glaring at me.

"Sorry," I say and quickly get out of his way.

"Let's get off the sidewalk," Ty says, taking my arm in his.

We enter Anabelle's, the restaurant across the street, and are seated immediately, despite a robust breakfast crowd. The smell of food floats in the air. I'm thankful that this pregnancy has been uneventful so far. No barfing at the smell of food for me. I remove my hat, scarf and gloves and place them on the seat next to me.

"What if he finds out that I'm pregnant?" I ask, as Ty sits across from me.

"That won't happen. Stop worrying. He won't emerge from the shadows to claim responsibility."

"I'm just worried about what he might do if he finds out and gets angry. He's capable of anything."

"We're not telling anyone, and when you start to show, we'll confirm that we're expecting."

"He knows where we live, Ty. Doesn't that frighten you?"

"Of course it does, but we're not going to turn our lives upside down for this jerk. Why do you think I insisted on the both of us taking lessons at the gun range? My aim is almost perfect," he adds, with pride.

"You're liking those shooting lessons too much for my

comfort," I tease. "It still freaks me out, holding a gun I mean. Do you know how many of them go off by accident?"

"That's why we're being trained by professionals. Let's hope we never have to use them."

Our waitress comes over and I order right away. I'm starving. "A spinach omelet with whole wheat toast for me, and a small orange juice. I hear it's freshly squeezed."

"That's right," the waitress confirms. "It's pretty popular."

After she takes Ty's order of scrambled eggs, bacon, pancakes and coffee, I ask him, "Are you actually going to eat all that?"

"Yes. I'm starving, too. I'm having sympathy cravings."

I laugh. "Well, get ready to have sympathy weight gain, too. I can't wait to see that."

Our waitress is back at the table in no time with our drinks. We hardly notice her. My heart does a summersault when Ty levels that dazzling smile at me. The waitress quickly disappears again. We're absorbed in each other, but that comes to a rapid and unwelcome end when I see Kristina Haywood approaching our table, with Spencer not too far behind. What is going on? Not that I'm paranoid or anything.

I give Ty a heads up by nodding in their direction and he sees them too.

"Hi guys," Kristina says stiffly, her smile not quite reaching her eyes. Spencer stands next to her and extends cheerful greetings.

"Good to see you out and about, Abbie," Spencer says. "I'm glad you're okay after the situation on the shuttle bus."

Ty looks at him sharply and then from me to Spencer. "What situation?"

I can't believe I forgot to mention it to Ty. How embarrassing. By the time I got home and discovered what that sicko did to the doll he sent me, the whole episode on the shuttle flew out of my head. In fact, receiving a doll in my likeness carved up to replicate the injuries my attacker inflicted on me was one of the most painful experiences of my life and far worse than what happened on the bus. Why did Spencer mention it? Is it out of real concern or some passive aggressive move?

I force myself to remain calm and take a sip of orange juice. The table is eerily quiet, despite the chatter of patrons and busy waiters tending to them. Ty is still waiting for an answer and Spencer hasn't responded. Then I understand why. He's gawking at the third finger of my left hand. Someone should just haul me away to the loony bin because I'm forgetting even the simplest things, like the fact that I haven't told Spencer that I'm engaged.

"Ty just proposed," I explain. "It was a surprise, but obviously I said yes."

Kristina's mouth twists into a sour expression. "Wow, Abbie. Great job. You know how to go after what you want and get it. Congratulations."

Spencer won't look me in the eye although I observe his poker face. He extends a hand to Ty and congratulates him, too.

Kristina isn't about to quietly fade into Ty's past, however. "It's kind of sudden isn't it? What brought on this craving for commitment?"

None of your business, Kristina.

"It's what we both wanted," Ty responds. "Cooper and I have been friends for years. What better partner for life than your best friend? And why wait when it's right?"

"You're the man, Ty," Spencer says. "Taking on that responsibility."

"What is that supposed to mean?" I ask.

"Nothing. I'm just saying it's great that Ty is helping you deal with the aftermath of your attack. The trauma could be with you for the rest of your life. There aren't many guys who would sign up for that."

I reach for the orange juice again, mostly because I need to stop myself from attempting to punch Spencer in the throat for that condescending remark. But I don't need to, because Ty has my back.

"Don't be ridiculous, Spencer. You don't need to feel sorry for us. I could tell you stories about Cooper's iron will. He thought he would break her. I guess the joke's on him, isn't it?"

Spencer flinches as if Ty's words caused him physical pain. It was fleeting; a nanosecond in time, but it was there. It doesn't make sense. Why would Ty's words about my resilience upset Spencer? Perhaps he's disappointed that I didn't tell him Ty and I were getting close. What a mess I've caused. My earlier white lie that Ty just proposed didn't do any good.

Wait a minute. Why am I feeling guilty about this when I suspect Spencer had ulterior motives for his romantic pursuits, that there's something sinister going on under the surface of his Mr. Nice Guy routine?

"I didn't mean anything negative by it, Ty," Spencer says. "Glad Abbie has you in her corner. The news is sudden, out of the blue as Kristina said."

"It's not out of the blue," Ty says. "It's been years in the making. She could have died that night. Life is fragile, and we didn't see any reason to keep waiting to begin our lives together."

Kristina taps her foot then says, "Could you guys excuse us, please? I want to have a private word with Abbie. It will only take a minute."

The request takes the guys by surprise but not me. Spencer leaves and Ty heads to the men's room. Kristina dumps her car keys with a clang on the table and plops down in the chair across from me.

"I didn't think you were the type," she says.

"What type is that?"

"The type who would move in on another woman's man. You knew Ty and I were seeing each other. Obviously that didn't matter to you. I thought you were a classy girl. Guess I had it all wrong."

Well, there it is. That jealousy Ty mentioned. So, are you going to respond to her provocation?

"Careful, Kristina. Your claws are showing. Ty made his choice. You can't blame me for that."

She leans forward, angry sparks shooting from her eyes. "Can't I? We were doing just fine until your attack. I wonder how much it had to do with your quickie engagement? Don't get me wrong, I'm not implying that Ty offered to marry you out of pity or anything like that, but the timing is curious."

Do not take the bait. You know you want to curse her out.

"Insulting me won't change a thing. I thought you were a classy girl. Guess I got it wrong. I'm sorry that your heart is broken, Kristina, I really am. But the cold hard truth is, Ty is no longer your concern. He chose to begin a new chapter in his life."

"I knew you were conniving from the moment I met

you. You had everyone fooled with the good girl act, but not me. You used your assault to manipulate Ty. Enjoy your temporary victory. It won't last."

"Bitterness is an ugly look on you, Kristina. Just saying. In spite of that, I wish you well with your future endeavors. I know you will be successful in whatever you pursue."

"I won't soon forget this, Abbie," she promises. "I won't." She snatches her keys from the table and stomps out of the restaurant.

After she leaves, Ty reappears and takes a seat. "What did Kristina want?"

"She was less than enthusiastic about our news and wanted me to know."

Ty sighs. "Well, she's never been shy about expressing her feelings."

Before I can ask him to elaborate, the waitress arrives with our food. I don't feel like dining here anymore. "I'm sorry, do you mind if we take the food to go?"

"No problem," the waitress says pleasantly. "Let me grab a couple of takeout containers."

After she returns with our takeout containers, Ty wraps up the food, settles the bill and we exit the restaurant.

"That was utterly strange," he says.

"You can say that again. I feel guilty that I didn't tell Spencer and he had to find out this way."

"You owe him nothing," Ty says as we wait for a city bus loaded with people to pass before crossing the street.

"I know, but he tried so hard."

"We should be worried about what he's up to, not his hurt ego," Ty says.

CHAPTER 58

AFTER

S HE DID IT again. Abbie Cooper had managed to blindside Spencer, and he didn't like it. He was beginning to resent her. How could he have allowed himself to fall for her lies instead of keeping his focus one hundred percent on the plan? She got engaged right under his nose. Not a word, not a hint, nothing. Didn't she just promise to get him those invitations to the Wheelers' New Year's Eve Ball? Was that even real? She could lie with the best of them, he concluded.

"Take it easy, man. You're going to pop a vein," his friend Roger complained.

He didn't care. He was too wound up. Spencer stood in the middle of one of the workout centers on campus with Roger holding the punching bag. He couldn't hear much of anything, not the other co-eds working out at the vast, state of the art gym, not the TV screens tuned in to various news and entertainment channels, not the work-study students carrying around baskets of fresh towels and spray bottles to wipe down the machines. He was a raging bull, and he only saw red.

He wanted to punch Ty Rambally in the mouth, and Abbie too. They were just a little too smug for his liking. If they thought he was going to let them sail into the sunset, they were mistaken. After he stopped her from completely humiliating herself on the shuttle (everyone on board could see how caring and attentive he was), she dismissed the gesture like it was nothing. She didn't look happy to see him at the restaurant earlier.

"You want to take a break?" Roger asked.

"No. I want to keep going."

"Well I can't. I have to get my own workout in. See you around," he said. He let go of the bag and then disappeared into another section of the gym.

Spencer was drenched in sweat. He wiped his face with a towel. He didn't know how long he had been punching the bag, so he took Roger's suggestion to take a break. He collapsed in a corner near his gym bag. He removed the boxing gloves, pulled out the bottled water he had brought along, and chugged it down in one go.

"Hey, Spencer," Jill Montgomery from his global governance class called out. "Want to hang out later?"

He wasn't in the mood for company. "I'm busy," he said rudely.

"Oh. Okay. No problem. Maybe we can hang out next week."

He gave no response. Jill took the hint and went off on her merry way.

He needed to calm down. What did he care if they got married and had a bajillion kids? What did he care that Abbie never felt for him one iota of what she felt for

Wheeler or Rambally? He didn't care that she always had an excuse whenever he tried to touch her, but she had no problem with Wheeler slobbering all over her when they met up in New York. She used him, that's all. It didn't matter that he was doing the same to her. He was no sucker, yet he got played.

She used him as a distraction and crawled into Rambally's bed at the first opportunity she got. Kristina was right. Abbie Cooper was conniving and manipulative, and he should have seen it before.

He rummaged through his gym bag for his phone. He punched in the password, hit the favorites icon, and tapped the person he wanted to call.

"She's engaged to Rambally," he said, when Zach picked up on the third ring.

"We have bigger problems. I don't like what I discovered in her browser history."

"What?" Spencer asked.

"Research on recalling traumatic memories."

"Damn it!" Spencer said. "That's not good."

"No, it isn't. What's the latest on the invitation to the ball?"

"She said she would talk to Katherine Wheeler, but it doesn't look good."

"I don't believe her and neither should you. Especially since Justin Tate has been running his mouth. It's time to shake things up."

"I agree," Spencer said, and hung up.

311

CHAPTER 59

AFTER

S PENCER WAITED UNTIL Abbie was out of sight before he approached Justin. Their little study group had disbursed and Abbie was well on her way to Rambally's apartment by now. How the thought sickened him.

"How's it going, Justin?" he asked. He startled the pain in the butt sophomore when he fell in step with him. Justin sped up, but Spencer had no problem keeping up with him.

"What do you want now?" Justin asked, his tone hostile.

"What were you and Abbie talking about two days ago on the phone? She was in the dining hall when she took the call."

Justin stopped dead in his tracks and peered out at Spencer from behind his hoodie.

"Are you stalking her? That's low, even for you."

"Just answer the question," Spencer snapped.

"Man, forget you," Justin said, contempt in his tone, and continued his brisk walk.

Spencer tugged at Justin's backpack. "I asked you a question, and you're going to give me an answer."

Justin turned around to face him. "It's none of your business. Now, I really have to go. Get a life will, you?"

Spencer shoved Justin.

"Back off," Justin warned, and shoved Spencer right back.

"Don't make this difficult," Spencer said with phony niceness. "I'm just looking for some information."

"Why don't you ask Abbie yourself?" Then Justin smirked. "Ah, she didn't tell you what we discussed, did she? The lady is smart."

"How about I head to the dean's office first thing tomorrow morning and have a conversation about your extracurricular activities?"

Justin sighed loudly and dug his hands into his pants pockets to keep warm. "That tired old threat is just that, tired. But guess what Spencer? If I'm kicked out of here, I can transfer to another school with two years left to go. But what about you? What school is going to take a senior one semester away from graduating? You would lose ground wouldn't you? A lot of ground. Don't threaten me. I keep meticulous records."

Spencer considered what Justin said. Though he was fuming, he conceded that Justin was right. He couldn't afford to get kicked out of school, not at this stage in the game. But even more disconcerting was Justin's reference to records. What did he have on Spencer? What was the best way for Spencer to get his hands on those records?

"That's really dumb. Keeping a record of all the people involved in the Aces Club."

"It's my insurance policy against clowns like you. If I go down, we all go down. And now that I've given it some thought, maybe I should tell you what I said to Abbie."

Though eager to hear, Spencer had to remain cool. "Oh yeah? Who did you rat on?"

"You, Spencer."

Spencer's jaw began to hurt from clenching and grinding his teeth. His heart pounded in his chest so loudly, he feared it would explode.

"And what did you tell Abbie about me?"

"The truth. That you chasing her was all smoke and mirrors. I told her what I saw at the party. How you pretended that the meeting was an accident after you ditched your date and made that call. She knows you're up to no good, bruh."

Spencer began to tremble with rage. He wanted to punch Justin, drop him like a stone. But it wouldn't do any good. They were getting closer and closer to the ball, and with this latest development, he had proof that Abbie Cooper's scheming ways once again thwarted his attempts to execute the plot against Alan Wheeler that he and Zach had spent months planning. She never had any intention of asking Katherine Wheeler for those invitations. He needed time to cool down and refocus, so he simply walked away from Justin without saying another word.

CHAPTER 60

AFTER

WHEN I ENTER the apartment, Ty is on the phone and he's agitated. I wave to him and head to the kitchen. I scan the countertop, just in case any weird packages were delivered. The counter is clear, and I breathe a sigh of relief.

"Well it's my life," he says, his jaw tightening. Just a wild guess. His mother is on the line.

I grab my laptop and give him some privacy by heading upstairs. I enter the bedroom and plop down on the bed with the computer on my lap. Some online research on Spencer Rossdale is overdue, negligence on my part. I pull up Google and type in his name. The first three results include a story on how devastated pop star Gwen Stefani was about her now ex-husband Gavin Rossdale's alleged affair, which led to their divorce; a David Spencer Rossdale from the UK, and a Spencer Rossdale, husband and father of three from the Midwest.

I'm about to type in Spencer's name in combination with Bethesda, MD when Ty burst into the room. "I swear my mother hates me sometimes. She can be such a raving b—"

GLEDÉ BROWNE KABONGO

I give him a sideways glance and he stops mid-sentence.
His face blazes with anger as he paces the length of the room.

I close the laptop and slide it behind me. "Come sit
down and tell me what happened."

He plops down next to me. I rub his shoulders in an
effort to calm him, something I've never done before. I like
it, and it's working. He turns to me.

"Another lecture about why I'm getting married when
my life hasn't even begun yet and whether or not you
pressured me to do this. The worst part is, she now refers
to you as *That Cooper Girl*. She knows it hurts me when she
says it, but she doesn't care. It's her way of punishing me for
making choices that don't align with her vision for my life."

I always knew his mother didn't care for me much. I
don't know what her problem is, but whatever.

"She loves you and wants the best for you. Parents go
nuts when they think something is threatening their kids.
You saw how my parents reacted. They pretty much said I
went and ruined my life, but not in those exact words. You
mother will calm down, believe me. Once she sees you have
things under control and this is what makes you happy, she'll
come around. In the final analysis, that's all parents really
want, for their kids to be happy. Are you happy, Ty?"

He takes my hand in his and pauses for a moment. "I
don't want to wait any longer to make you my wife. Let's go
down to City Hall and file for a marriage license."

I gawk at him because my brain is incapable of forming
words. He strokes the back of my hand and it's doing all
sorts of things to my insides. I think my heart just did a
back flip.

316

"Well, what do you think?" he asks grinning.

"You're just full of surprises, aren't you?"

"It's one of my favorite pastimes, surprising you. So, are you ready to switch last names?"

"Nope."

He's crestfallen, like a kid whose favorite toy was taken away by the playground bully. "What are you saying? You changed your mind? You don't want to marry me anymore?"

"I didn't say that."

"What then?"

"I'm keeping Cooper."

"You don't like my last name?"

"It's fine. I just think it sounds better with Cooper in the mix."

"You enjoy torturing me, don't you?"

"It's one of my favorite pastimes."

THREE DAYS LATER, I become Mrs. Abigail Cooper Rambally in a civil ceremony at City Hall, officiated by a pastor who was able to accommodate our request at the last minute. Ty is decked out in a sapphire blue three-piece suit with white dress shirt and pale pink tie. He looks quite dashing. As for me, I keep it simple with an ivory, A-line dress under a matching princess coat with gold buttons. No fuss on the flowers. I picked up white calla lilies from a local florist for my bouquet. The only witness is a courthouse clerk. We ask her to take a few photos, and then we walk out of the building hand in hand into the cold December air with snowflakes raining down on us, wishing us luck.

CHAPTER 61

AFTER

THE ALEXANDRA ROSE Inn and Spa, an exquisite country retreat surrounded by two thousand acres of nature preserve, comes into view. A little over an hour away from campus, the gorgeous landscaped gardens and woodlands are breathtaking, even in early December. Another lovely surprise from Ty and just what we needed, to get away from our problems for a while, to forget everything and everyone.

Our suite boasts a massive king-sized, four poster bed with canopy, a crackling fireplace, and dozens of bouquets of red roses. The intoxicating aroma of jasmine saturates the air. He didn't forget my favorite scent.

"I know what you're thinking," he says. "You were running all kinds of scenarios in your head on the drive up."

I stand next to the large window, taking in the breathtaking view of the property. He wraps his arms around my waist and kisses the back of my neck. Heat floods my body and I shiver involuntarily. I slowly turn around to face him.

"You never told me that psychic powers was one of your gifts," I tease, barely able to get the words out between breaths.

"Oh, Mrs. Rambally, I have many gifts," he whispers. His eyes blaze with sensual promise.

My hands tremble as I remove his suit jacket and let it slide to the floor.

"That's quite a claim, Mr. Rambally. I'd like to see some proof. Perhaps it's best if you show me."

As if he'd been waiting his whole life to hear those words, he scoops me up in his arms and strides toward the bed.

Cool, satin sheets caress my skin when he places me in the center and leans over me. His concerned expression is touching, but the desire raging in the depths of his eyes is unmistakable. I reach up and run my index finger across his soft, lush lips. His body tenses, his breathing heavy. He wraps a hand around my wrist, and one by one, he sucks each of my fingers, as if it were a succulent, delectable feast. A lopsided grin appears on his lips when I respond with unintelligible words.

His voice is thick with emotion when he says, "I don't want you to be afraid or nervous."

I gaze deep into his eyes and lick my lips. "I'm not afraid."

"I'll never hurt you, Cooper. That's a promise."

"I'll hold you to it."

His long, elegant fingers interlock with mine as he looks down at me with such tenderness, I just might melt. He trails light kisses down the length of my arms. I gasp, the warmth of his mouth burning through my skin. I think he might go for the other arm, but instead he lifts my foot and nuzzles the bottom against his cheek. When he moves his mouth erotically across the arch of my foot and down my legs, I shiver with pleasure.

GLEDÉ BROWNE KABONGO

"You have the most perfectly shaped legs I've ever seen," he says dreamily. "And they're so long. This might take a while."

By the time his caresses reach my bare inner thighs, I clutch the bed sheet as if it's the only thing keeping me from being completely consumed by this ravenous fever.

I reach up to touch him, to pull him into a kiss, but he clasps my wrists together and shakes his head. Message received.

His tongue moves in circles over my neck, creating sparks of electricity that drive me insane. I tremble when his tongue plunges into my ear, hot and slick in a sensual rhythm all its own. My senses are firing on all pistons, my body ablaze.

"If you want to stop, just say the word. Nothing happens unless you're comfortable. Okay?"

No, I don't want you to stop. I've waited for you for so long.

I nod because I'm incapable of speech. I close my eyes and force myself to slow down my breathing, thinking of ways to gain control of myself before the main event.

He misunderstands my silence. "Open your eyes, Abigail. I want you to know it's me and no one else."

"I know it's you, baby. It's always been you."

His eyes lock with mine, and in their depths, I realize that I've found the place I belong, now and until the end of time.

He rolls off the bed and unbuttons the dress shirt he wore to the ceremony, casting it aside. I can't take my eyes off his ripped torso, adorned with the tattoo I observed that fateful day when I went to apologize—the half naked man

320

and woman wrapped in a passionate embrace. He removes his pants and let them slide to the floor. Seconds later, his briefs are off and on the floor, too. He peels off my dress and tosses it behind him.

I moan in ecstasy when he palms my breasts and showers them with exquisite kisses. "Please . . . I need . . ."

He understands the state I'm in and gives me what I want. I fall to pieces in our all-consuming dance of unrestrained passion and a tenderness that nearly stops my heart. When it's over, I collapse in a satisfied, exhausted heap and sob uncontrollably. He cradles me in his arms until I have no more tears left.

CHAPTER 62

AFTER

I T'S FRIDAY MORNING and we have no classes to attend. Ty timed this getaway perfectly. Though I'm exhausted from our all night sessions, we managed to order breakfast, boot up our laptops, and get some work done. Despite the excitement of being newly married, the unpleasant realities of finding my attacker and mistrust of Spencer inevitably follow us around like some evil mist that won't go away.

While Ty flips through the channels on the large flat screen TV, I resume my Google search for information on Spencer. I plug his name into the search bot and added Bethesda, MD. The results focus on a prep school, Bayridge Prepatory Academy. I click on the link, and a photo accompanied by a story from the *Bayridge Echo*, the school's online newspaper pops up.

BAYRIDGE CLAIMS VICTORY OVER BENTLEY ACADEMY the headline screams. However, it's the photo that accompanies the headline that captures my interest. The crew team, with team members in dark blue and gold unisuits, a lake in the background and the oars with the school flag at their tips.

In the first row is a face I would recognize anywhere because he has sat across from me many times. In this photo, he's a few years younger, but it's undeniably Spencer Rossdale.

I should move on from the article but I can't. I'm not sure what I'm looking for, but I continue to eyeball each team member, row by row, and match up their names with the photo. When I get to the back row, I freeze. An identical image of Spencer stares back at me. The main difference here is the caption identifies the face as belonging to Zachary Rossdale.

I rub my eyes with both hands and then refocus. Perhaps I'm seeing double. My eyes dart between the front and back row again, to confirm I'm not mistaken. I'm not. My eyes blink rapidly at the screen. I'm lightheaded so I hold on to the desk, even though I'm already sitting. Spencer has a brother, one who looks exactly like him. I continue to stare at the screen, trying to get my brain to accept what my eyes tell me is true. Why didn't he mention he had a brother, an identical twin brother? He only said that he had a sister, Brynn. Was that a lie too?

"Ty, get over here."

He scoots off the bed. "You found something?"

He stands over me and I point to the photo of Spencer in the front.

"Yeah, he was on his high school's crew team."

"But look at the guy in the back row." I point to the right face.

323

Ty squints. "He looks just like Spencer."

"Identical."

"What the heck is going on?"

"He never mentioned a brother, not even in passing while you two were on the university's crew team?"

"Not that I recall. He and I weren't close, but I think I would have remembered him saying he had a brother. Who goes years without mentioning they have a brother?"

"Maybe they don't get along or had some huge falling out. Siblings sometimes do and vow never to speak to each other again."

"Could be. Let's keep searching."

Ty grabs his laptop and pulls up a chair next to me. We agree I will continue searching the school's website, and he'll search Facebook. I plug in Spencer and Zachary Rossdale in the search bar of the school newspaper's web page. More photos and articles pop up, mostly crew team related. Then I come across some yearbook photos. The yearbook is dedicated to the memory of Jamie Reynolds, who according to the write up, was found dead in the woods behind the school while a student at Bayridge. How sad.

Ty exclaims, "No freaking way."

"What is it?" I peek at his screen. He turns the computer around so it's in my line of vision. He's pulled up a Facebook page with a photo of Zachary Rossdale, his arm around Jamie Reynolds. The post reads:

Miss you, baby. Best girlfriend ever.

The person who posted the message was Zachary, or Zach as he identified himself.

I show Ty the yearbook In Memorium photo of Jamie. "I want to know how she died."

"It doesn't mean he had anything to do with her death."

"I didn't say that."

"But you're thinking it."

"The local paper would have published a story on it," Ty says. "That's not something the school could have kept under wraps. The local police would have gotten involved."

We're using only his computer now, and he searches for Bethesda newspapers. Several pop up. We go one by one, typing in Jamie Reynolds and Bayridge Prep in the search bars. Several articles detail the sad story. Jamie was an honors student at Bayridge, a volunteer at the local animal shelter, and avid runner. By all accounts, she was well liked. She went missing after a party five years ago. A search was mounted and the local police were called in. After three days of searching, her body was discovered in a ravine, deep in the woods behind the school. An autopsy indicated death by strangulation, and that Jamie was sexually assaulted but no DNA was found on the body. To this day, her murder remains unsolved.

I pull away from the screen as if the story will reach through the computer, snatch me, and make me part of the tragedy.

"I'm confused," I say.

"You're not alone." Ty leans back in the chair with his hands clasped behind his head.

"Then we should clear up our confusion," I say. "Let's call the police detective who was the lead investigator. The article says he's Detective George Gaines."

CHAPTER 63

AFTER

THREE HOURS LATER, after we leave the Alexandra Rose and stop at the apartment for a change of clothes and to pack an overnight bag, we're on our way to the airport. Detective Gaines was surprisingly talkative on the phone. But in order to learn what he knows about the murder of Jamie Reynolds, we have to make it to Bethesda by 6:00 p.m. and meet up with him at Mel's Bar & Grill. If we miss him, we'll have to wait because he's leaving tonight to go ice fishing with pals.

Ty is at the wheel, and I nibble on a pastry leftover from this morning's breakfast. I'm always starving these days, and it could get ugly if I don't eat when I'm hungry. Ty says the baby is probably a boy. I'm reserving judgment until an ultrasound tells me if we should be shopping for mostly pink or blue.

"So what do we do with the information we get from the detective?" I ask.

"It depends on what he tells us. Right now, all we have is scenario eerily similar to what happened to you, minus the dying part. Thank God."

"You have to admit the circumstances are suspect. Jamie attended the same school as Zach and Spencer. She dated Zach, ends up dead and sexually assaulted. My stalker made death threats."

"But you don't know Zach."

"True. But what if they have each other's backs, he and Spencer? What if they've each done something similar in the past? We should find out where Zachary goes to college. Maybe there's a clue on the Bayridge website or in the yearbook. I never got to finish searching once you discovered the picture of Zach and Jamie on the school's Facebook page."

"Let's see what Detective Gaines has to say first, then we can decide if it's worth pursuing."

I go quiet for a beat as the car eats up the miles on the highway.

"What is it, Cooper?"

I look out the passenger window with trees and traffic whizzing by.

I turn toward him. "What if it's Spencer?"

"Don't get yourself all worked up. We have no evidence that points directly to him, nothing concrete anyway."

"I know. I was just thinking that if it is Spencer, then the baby . . ."

I trail off. I can't bring myself to say it. Ty squeezes my hand.

"It doesn't matter. He or she will be ours, one hundred percent ours."

My text message ring tone goes off. I hope it's not Spencer. Please, don't let it be Spencer following up about the invitations he won't be getting. In my current state, I don't know if I'm capable of carrying on a civil text exchange with him. I remove the phone from my purse and look at the screen.

Zahra: Call me. It's urgent!!!

"Who is it?" Ty asks.

"Zahra. She says it's urgent."

I call her right away and she picks up immediately.

"Where are you?"

"On the road. What's up?"

"So you're sitting down, good."

"What's going on, Zahra?"

"Bad news, Abbie."

"About what?"

"Not what, who."

"You're scaring me." I look at Ty and inhale sharply. "Okay, who is the bad news about?"

"Justin Tate. He's in a coma, Abbie."

"What?"

My scream is so piercing that Ty loses control of the wheel for a split second and almost jumps into the other traffic lane. A horn blares in admonishment.

"How did this happen?" I stutter because I can hardly believe what I just heard.

"He was hit by a car downtown New Haven. Horrible accident. They don't know if he's going to make it."

My hands cover my mouth to suppress a sob. Ty looks at me concern plastered on his features.

"Do they know who did this?"

328

"No. It was a hit and run."

"Where are you headed?"

This is not the time to fill in Zahra on where we're headed and why, or the fact that Ty and I are married. Those can wait until we get back. "I have to go. Please keep me updated if you hear anything further today. We'll meet up soon, I promise."

I click off from Zahra and share the terrible news with Ty. He's stone faced as he continues the drive. We'll arrive at the departure terminal in less than ten minutes.

"I don't believe in such coincidences," he says.

"Me neither."

"So the Rossdale twins are playing hardball?"

"It looks that way. We've been playing checkers while they were playing chess. Always several steps ahead."

CHAPTER 64

———◦◦◦———

AFTER

B Y THE TIME we arrive at Mel's Bar & Grill in a busy section of town peppered with strip malls, retailers, restaurants and office buildings, it's 5:15 in the afternoon.

We recognize Detective Gaines from his photo and approach the booth. He stands to introduce himself. He's lanky, mid-fortyish, with a neatly trimmed beard and bald head. After the introductions, Ty and I sit next to each other across from the detective.

"Thank you for agreeing to see us," I say. "As I mentioned over the phone, we're trying to find out if there's a connection between the Jamie Reynolds case and an event that occurred recently."

"Why don't you describe the details of this 'recent event'?"

When I'm finished, the detective strokes his chin. "I'm sorry to hear this happened to you, Abbie. Unfortunately, it's a crime we see all too often in law enforcement. The sad fact is, very few cases get prosecuted."

"That's what I've learned as well, which is why we're hoping you can help our cause by sharing what you know about the Reynolds case. It could be a stab in the dark, but it's worth a try."

He reiterates what we discovered on the school website, that Jamie went missing after a party and was found murdered three days later in the woods behind the school. But things get interesting when he starts to discuss the investigation.

"For obvious reasons, Bayridge tried to keep this as quiet as possible. Didn't want a bunch of scared parents yanking their kids and dimming their prospects for new enrollment. But it became a state-wide story."

"Were there any suspects?" I ask.

"At first no. Everyone we talked to said the same thing. They couldn't think of anyone who would want to hurt Jamie. She was well liked. In cases like these, we always look at the boyfriend if the victim had one."

"Did Jamie?" I grip the edge of the table.

It was time to verify whether Zach Rossdale was telling the truth when he claimed Jamie was his girlfriend in the Facebook post.

"Yes. At the time, she was dating a fella by the name of Zachary Rossdale. Zach and his twin brother both attended Bayridge."

"You interviewed Zach?" Ty asks.

"Yes, my partner and I did. He said they had been dating for a couple of months, there were no issues in the relationship."

"Did you believe him?" I ask.

"Hard to say," the detective says. "We didn't have much to go, on but it always bothered me that Zach was the last person to see her alive after they had that fight."

"What fight?" Ty and I ask at the same time.

"According to witnesses, Zach and Jamie had a big fight at the party the night she disappeared. When we asked him about it, he said it was no big deal. Said he was just jealous over some guy he thought was coming on to her. He had accused her of cheating on him."

"Did they leave the party together?" I ask.

"Zach went after her, and that was the last time anyone saw Jamie."

"What did Zach say about that?" Ty asks.

"He said they talked it out and they were fine. It was getting late, so he dropped her off at her dormitory."

"About what time?" I probe.

"Close to midnight. But the funny thing is, nobody could verify this chain of events except for Zach's brother, Spencer. He claims his brother texted him that he left the party with Jamie, and he had just dropped her off."

"But that can be easily verified, the text message I mean."

"You are correct. It would be a matter of getting the records from his cell phone carrier, but we were blocked."

"Blocked how?" I click my fingernails against the table.

Detective Gaines sighs. "Apparently, some higher-ups didn't like that we were looking at the Rossdale brothers."

"Higher-ups who?" Ty asks.

"The headmaster received a call from a very powerful man asking them to make sure the Rossdale boys didn't get hassled in anyway about the case. Then our Chief of Police got a similar call. The murder was blamed on some local criminal or drifter who was prowling the woods at night. The theory goes Jamie must have gone out for a walk to clear her head after Zach dropped her off at her dorm. She wandered too far and got caught by this unknown assailant who raped her, killed her, and dumped her body in the woods."

"Who was this powerful man who ordered the police to drop the case?" I enquire.

"Alan Wheeler, CEO of Levitron-Blair."

I begin biting my fingernails. Ty is just as stunned as I am. He finds a spot on the table and concentrates hard on it.

"I see you've heard of him," the detective infers.

"I used to date his son," I admit.

"No kidding," the detective says.

"We attended the same boarding school in Massachusetts. But why would Alan Wheeler stick his neck out and use his influence to halt an investigation of Spencer and his brother?"

"And it wasn't the first time Mr. Wheeler went to bat for them."

"What do you mean?" Ty asks.

"He paid their tuition for all four years they attended Bayridge."

Ty rubs his temples, and I just sit there staring at Detective Gaines like he suddenly sprouted a second face. I'm in shock.

"That doesn't make any sense," I say.

"It does if you consider the fact that their mother was his secretary for years."

Wow! This rabbit hole keeps getting deeper and deeper. Where does it end?

"Does their mother still work for Alan?"

"No. She moved on to another job, I heard."

"Do you know if either Spencer or Zach ever visited Bedford Hills, the Wheeler Estate?" I ask.

"It's possible. I can't say for sure, though."

"What did Jamie's parents have to say about all this?" Ty asks.

"The Reynoldses never got justice for their daughter, and they will never know what happened to her. Obviously that didn't sit well with them, but they didn't want to get crushed by a five-hundred-pound gorilla either."

"You mean Alan's power and influence," I acknowledge.

"That would be accurate," the detective agrees.

The thought that Alan helped cover up a possible murder is mindboggling. He was always a stand-up guy in my opinion. My dad played golf with him. Just goes to show you can't always read people by outside appearances. This whole scenario is baffling.

Detective Gaines has to leave for his ice fishing trip, so we wrap up the conversation. He gives us his business card in case we have follow-up questions.

I wonder about the connection between the Wheelers and Rossdale brothers as we leave the restaurant. Does that connection have anything to do with why Spencer wanted to attend the ball, why he came up with that lame internship story? If Alan paid their tuition, and their mother worked for him, why didn't Spencer press his mother to get the invitations from Alan? I throw the questions out to Ty as he opens the front passenger door for me.

"Unless there's bad blood," he says as he slides in the driver side. "Something must have happened. They don't have the connection to Alan they once did; otherwise, Spencer wouldn't target someone with access to the Wheelers, meaning you."

I grab my phone from my purse and make two critical phone calls. It's time to checkmate Zach and Spencer Rossdale.

CHAPTER 65

AFTER

S PENCER SAT ACROSS from his brother at a bookstore
minutes from Zach's New York University campus.
Zach had his computer open, and for the past hour, they'd
been following Abbie Cooper's digital footprint, thanks to
Zach's superior computer skills.

"Now that the Justin problem has been neutralized, I say
we get both Abbie and Rambally, but not before we get the
invitations," Zach said.

"I thought we agreed that the invitations were a hoax.
She never talked to Katherine Wheeler, and I still don't feel
good about the Justin situation. That's a complication that
could come back to bite us later. It wasn't supposed to play
out this way. Things are getting out of hand. I didn't sign up
for this."

"He saw my face," Zach roared. "He saw us together
and overheard us. You don't have to be a genius to figure out
he would have gone blabbing to Abbie. He had to be dealt
with. He won't be talking to anybody soon. Hopefully never."

"She found out we're brothers anyway, didn't she?"

Spencer declared with cynicism.

"So what? She doesn't know we're on to her. Let her dig her little heart out. She can't link anything back to us. As far as I'm concerned, we move ahead with the plan, and I know just how to do it."

"How?"

"When is New Year's Eve?"

"A little less than three weeks away."

"Right. The semester ends next week and everybody goes home until next year."

"And your point?"

"You have three days to get those invitations. We've come too far to give up now. Did you work on the speech like I asked you to?"

"You were serious about that?" Spencer mumbled.

Zach looks him square in the eye. "I don't kid around when it comes to the Wheelers. Get the speech ready, and get a tuxedo. Alan Wheeler is going down."

"I don't know about this plan," Spencer griped.

"Are you getting cold feet? If you are, I can finish this alone. It wouldn't be the first time I've had to bail us out because you went soft."

"You dare say that to me after all the times I've had to back you up?" Spencer snarled. "You have no control or self-discipline. Everything has to be extreme with you."

"Don't be mad at me because she played you."

Spencer wanted to throat punch his brother in the worst way but had to settle for curling and uncurling his fists at his side. He and Zach stared each other down like two prize fighters before the big match.

Zach relaxed and his voice took on a different resonance, one of reason. He said, "Come on, Spencer. Don't you think what Abbie Cooper did to you was cruel? You were a perfect gentleman, and she rewarded your attention and kindness with betrayal and contempt. She had to be punished. She got what she deserved. Stop feeling guilty about it."

"Are you sure about that? Snatching her was never part of the plan."

"We had to improvise. It happens."

Spencer pondered his brother's statement. Zach had a way of making things crystal clear whenever Spencer had doubts. But what if his brother was wrong this time? Sure, Abbie had toyed with him, manipulated him, and that made Spencer angry. Yes, he wanted payback. But did she deserve such brutal vengeance?

CHAPTER 66

AFTER

I DIDN'T SLEEP much last night. Most of my time was spent tossing and turning, and stealing the covers in my restlessness. Poor Ty ended up on the floor at one point. After our conversation with Detective Gaines, I called both Katherine and Christian. Katherine can help make the connection between the Rossdales and Alan; at least, that's what I'm hoping.

Christian and I agreed to meet at a coffee shop within walking distance from the hotel. I have to tell him the truth, face-to face. It would be awkward to show up at his home with a husband in tow. I spot him and approach the table. I'm decked out in a winter dress coat, scarf and gloves. I'm ten weeks along, just shy of three months. I still look the same, no sign that I'm pregnant.

He sees me and stands up to hug me. I sit down and remove my scarf and hat but not the gloves. "Thanks for meeting me," I say. "Katherine said you were home this weekend, so I took it as a sign."

I may as well not beat around the bush. I don't know

why I'm nervous but I am.

"We could have met at the house. Now you have me thinking something's up. Why are we meeting here, Abbie? Are you okay?"

His concern for my well-being is touching and stirs up in me something resembling guilt.

"I'm fine." My eyes do a quick scan of the shop. Patrons are scattered throughout, enjoying their hot beverages and pastries, conversing or engrossed in their phones.

"Abbie, what is it? Are you in trouble?"

Well, it depends on your definition of trouble.

I smile at him weakly. He picks upon my nervousness. "I knew it. You are in trouble."

He reaches across the table to hold my gloved hands. I slowly remove them from his touch. The hurt reflected in his eyes is heartbreaking but I press on.

"I wanted to see you because I have something to tell you. I would have sooner, but it's been a crazy couple of months."

"Is it bad news?"

"Not really. Yes and no. It depends on your perspective."

"I don't like the sound of that." He rubs his hands repeatedly. "But whatever it is, you can tell me. We have always been open and honest with each other."

"I'm off the market," I blurt out. It sounds so cliché and stupid, but I'm nervous and it's the first thing that comes to mind.

He leans back in his seat. His mouth twitches for a second or two and then he says, "What do you mean?"

I remove the glove from my left hand and extend it to

his line of vision. He stares at my hand as if it's some strange creature he wants to escape because he's sure it's meant to cause him pain. When he looks up at me, his eyes are welling up.

"When did this happen?"

"Ty and I got married yesterday."

"Why?" he asks.

I'm taken aback. When a woman announces to a friend that she got married, why is not the go-to-question. "I don't understand. Why do people get married?"

"There's more to the story. We saw each other three months ago and you never mentioned that you were dating Ty or that the two of you were serious."

"That's because we weren't."

"Then what changed?"

I squirm in my seat. He's right. We've always been straight with each other. "You know this was always a possibility. You know the history."

"There was no guarantee that the two of you would have ended up together."

I've upset him and now he's giving me the third degree. I have to be calm and patient. "I love him, Christian."

"But you were never sure how he felt about you."

"My heart knew. He showed me all the time. I just didn't want to acknowledge it out of fear."

"So when you told me that . . ."

"Of course I meant it. It was a big deal for me to say that to you. I had never said it to anyone before, not even Ty."

His eyes twinkle with mischief. "Well, at least I have that memory to cling to. No offense to your new husband."

"Really?" I chastise him in jest.

He smiles. "Ty is a good guy. How are the two of you going manage being married when you live in two separate cities? I mean you still have a couple of years left to go, and Ty is graduating in the spring, right?"

"Yeah, about that," I begin.

I explain the whole story to Christian, about the assault, my hospitalization, the threats, the strength it took for me not to fall apart completely, and how if it weren't for Ty, I would have. I tell him I've kept the truth from my parents and why. I describe the shock of discovering I was pregnant, and the soul crushing anguish of debating if I should keep it.

He sits perfectly still throughout, his face knotted in a mix of anger and horror. When I'm done, he doesn't say a word. I beat back the tears prickling at the corners of my eyes. The pain is still fresh as if it happened yesterday.

He looks away from me and pinches his nose. He doesn't look at anything in particular. He just can't look at me. When his gaze returns to our table and my face, I can see the sadness roaming his features.

"I'm so, so sorry, Abbie," he says, his voice cracking. "I'm going to help you catch the bastard. First Sidney and now you. We couldn't save Sidney, but . . ."

"You're not cursed if that's what you're thinking. It's a rotten, unfortunate coincidence that this happened to two women you dated. Don't make it a burden, Christian."

"How can I not?" he asks glumly.

"Because it's stupid to think that this happened because of you. It's not rational thinking."

"There's nothing rational about this situation, Abbie. Do

you realize that this guy forever changed your life? That you will be tied to him permanently because you're keeping the baby? You don't get to just move on and put it behind you."

"I know. It's not an easy thing, but I believe there will come a point where I'm no longer angry and can live my life the way I always intended. Hating him forever is not part of my plan."

Ty arrives at the coffee shop and joins Christian and me. Christian congratulates him on our marriage. I explain to Ty that Christian has offered to help. This will be over soon. I bounce out of the café with an optimism that has eluded me for a long time.

CHAPTER 67

AFTER

W E PULL UP to the Wheeler mansion in Langley Forest, a posh neighborhood outside McLean, Virginia that afternoon. It's strange being back here after all this time. Large bouquets of poinsettias in the foyer and extravagant Christmas decorations give the place the warmth and glitter of the Christmas season.

Katherine Wheeler is still a dead ringer for actress Catherine Zeta-Jones with dark, shiny locks she still wears long, a dazzling smile, and smoky eyes. She escorts us into the Victorian-themed drawing room with a massive Christmas tree at its center. Christian is already siting on one of the antique sofas. He waves at us. Katherine then takes off to give the staff instructions, probably about lunch. I haven't had anything since breakfast in the coffee shop and I'm starving, but I need to mind my manners and not eat as if lunch will be my last meal.

The three of us make small talk about the weather, Christmas shopping, preparations for the New Year's Eve Ball, and Katherine's anxiety over every detail. My brain floods with memories of the ball when Christian and I attended together, and the sobering thought that my presence that night might have changed the trajectory of my life.

Katherine slips back into the room and we all sit. Ty and I on a short sofa, Katherine and Christian across from us in separate seats. I only told Katherine on the phone that I was attacked and I suspect that Spencer Rossdale might know more than he's saying. I explained to her that I did some digging and found out there was a connection between the Rossdale brothers and Mr. Wheeler. For some reason, it didn't shock her, and she agreed to share what she knew.

"I've never talked about this to anyone," she begins. She looks at Christian. "I don't want what I'm about to say to influence how you feel about your father. We have a complicated relationship and have not always been kind to each other."

That sounds ominous. Christian scowls at his mother, and then averts his gaze for a brief moment.

"Abbie, if what I'm about to say can help you find the man who attacked you, then it will be worth it. It's time the truth came out anyway. I'm tired of carrying the burden, of being his silent conspirator."

"Mom, just come out with it and save the drama," Christian says.

"Do you want to hear this or not?"

We remain quiet.

"All right then. For years, I ignored my husband's indiscretions. I told myself I knew what I signed up for, and that was the cost of being Mrs. Alan Wheeler. It's not right, but that's the decision I made, to stay with him. Anyway, I dealt with it. I didn't have to see the other women. I didn't want to know their names or anything about them. But one in particular got under my skin."

"Who?" I ask, even though I can guess the answer.

"Diana Rossdale."

"Why is that, Mrs. Wheeler?" Ty asks.

"She thought she was something special," Katherine says. "That little twit actually believed Alan would leave me for her."

"Oh," Ty says.

"She was his secretary for years. A tired cliché, I know," Katherine adds. "At first, I didn't take it seriously; there were others before her who fell by the wayside when Alan got bored and moved on. But then she pulled that stunt to trap Alan. I didn't think something like that would happen in my world."

"What stunt?" Christian asks.

"She got pregnant in the hope that Alan would divorce me and marry her. In the beginning, she claimed it was her husband's. Kurt Rossdale was an executive at Levitron-Blair. He left Diana soon after he discovered the truth, five or six years later. By then, they also had a daughter. Anyway, she had three young kids to raise on her own. Alan fired her. She threatened him over the years, said she would go public about the affair and announce to the world that her twin boys were really Alan's. For obvious reasons, that just couldn't happen."

"So she's been blackmailing Dad ever since," Christian finishes.

"I guess you could say that. I went along with it because

I had to protect you. You are the only legitimate heir to Levitron-Blair. Nothing and nobody is going to change that. I will fight for that until my dying breath no matter what that awful woman says or does."

It's beginning to make sense now. Alan was blackmailed into halting the investigation against Spencer and Zach. Diana Rossdale was protecting her sons from something awful they had done and used her secret to obtain Alan's cooperation.

"Mrs. Wheeler, was there ever a DNA test conducted to prove paternity?" Ty asks.

"There was no need. Alan admitted to me that he was the father of Diana's twins."

A wave of nausea works up from the pit of my stomach to my throat as the enormity of my situation crashes into me. "Katherine, do you know if Zach or Spencer has ever been in this house?"

"It's possible."

I know with an unshakable certainty that Spencer was here the night of the ball two years ago. The secret admirer who sent me those roses and notes, and Spencer are the same. He watched me that night. He knew me before he approached me at the frat party months ago. Justin was right. Our meeting was no accident.

If Spencer got angry because I rejected him as Dr. Shanahan proposed, would he have assaulted me? I begin to make retching sounds and then bolt from the drawing room. If I remember correctly, there are two bathrooms on this floor. I make a beeline for the nearest one, shut the door and throw up all over the vanity sink.

After I've cleaned up the mess, I splash water on my face and pull myself together.

"Cooper, are you okay in there?" Ty's panicked voice drifts through the closed door.

I open the door a crack. I'm fine. I'll be out in a minute."

He's not convinced I'm fine but waits anyway. When I come out of the bathroom, he takes me by the arm and leads me back to the drawing room. "Are you sure you're okay? We can go back to the hotel so you can rest if you're not up for this."

"I promise, I'm okay."

CHAPTER 68

AFTER

C HRISTIAN IS STARING out the window into the scenery when we enter the drawing room. Katherine is absent again. When he sees us, he wants to know if I'm okay. I tell him the same thing I told Ty only moments earlier.

"That was intense," he says. "I knew my dad fooled around, but this . . ."

He looks lost, a fragile soul whose world was just ripped apart, his entire existence turned on its head.

"Why don't I get you some water, Cooper? I'll be right back."

Ty is so perceptive sometimes it's scary. He knows Christian is in a state and may want to speak to me, so he made up the water excuse to give us some privacy. After Ty leaves, I go over to Christian who has returned to staring out the window.

"You feel like it's been all a lie. Your life, I mean."

He turns to look at me. "Exactly. Remember how you asked me if I wish I had an older brother to share the burden of inheriting and running Levitron-Blair one day?"

"Yes, I remember that conversation, at Joe's Pizzeria. It was our first date."

"My dad took care of that, didn't he? I have not one but two older brothers."

The anguish on his face is heartbreaking. I want to comfort him, but that would be weird and inappropriate. I give him a quick shoulder squeeze.

"Christian, this doesn't change who you are or how much your parents love you. Neither will it change your future with Levitron-Blair. Katherine will fight to the death to make sure you and you alone inherit the CEO chair. You heard her."

"I don't know if it matters anymore, Abbie. My father lied to me my whole life. I don't know if I can get past it."

"It's hard to see our parents as anything other than heroes. What your father did is inexcusable, but it doesn't have to be the end of your family. My parents had their issues. They were both unfaithful in the marriage. But they managed to work through it."

He raises a brow. "Your dad, too?"

"Yes. It was a long time ago, and Mom actually filed for divorce."

"How did they get through it?"

"My dad wouldn't give up. He fought dirty until he wore her down."

He musters a half grin. "The sad thing is, I don't think my mother would even go that far. I don't understand their relationship, to be honest. I don't know why she stays. It's not like your parents where they each made mistakes and fessed up. My dad has been doing this for years but she won't leave him. It's not as if she needs him."

"Maybe she does. Love is complicated."

"At this rate, I don't know if I want to get married, knowing what I know now."

"You're not your father."

"I don't know that for sure."

"If you turn out to be like him, don't forget I will hunt you down and beat sense into you."

He smiles. "I know you will."

"You will get through this, and no matter how it plays out, you will be okay."

"You've always been an optimist. Don't ever lose that."

Ty enters the drawing room, and Christian and I break up our discussion. I rejoin Ty on the sofa we occupied earlier and thank him for the bottled water he places in my hand. He said Katherine had an important call she needed to take and would rejoin us later.

"Now that we know the connection between Mr. Wheeler and the twins, how do we prove that one or both of them know what happened to Cooper?" Ty asks.

"The invitations," I blurt out.

Both men look at me like I've gone mad.

"What invitations?" Christian asks.

"The New Year's Eve Ball. I know why Spencer wanted an invitation so badly."

"What are you thinking?" Ty asks

"He was planning to expose the truth at the ball in front of everyone—friends, business associates, important people. He wanted a huge crowd."

"*What?*" Christian and Ty exclaim in unison.

I quickly explain the background for Christian's benefit, how Spencer targeted me at a party, his reaction to the news that Christian and I dated, how he Googled us, and such.

"What would he have to gain by publicly humiliating Dad?" Christian asks.

"An empire," I respond.

"You're not making any sense," a bewildered Christian says.

"I think what Cooper is saying is this," Ty says. "Zach and Spencer's paternity was kept a secret all these years. We have to assume their mother told them that Mr. Wheeler is their biological father. By publicly outing Mr. Wheeler at the ball, he would have no choice but to admit the truth. Once the truth is out, Mr. Wheeler would be forced to accept them into his life. As the sons of Alan Wheeler, Zach and Spencer would have it all: incredible wealth, privilege, connections, and a piece of Levitron-Blair."

"What Ty said," I confirm.

At that moment, Katherine barges in and looks from one person to the next. Our sour expressions leave no doubt that something serious just occurred. After Christian fills her in, I share with the group the idea that sails into my head like some big reward for finally connecting the dots.

"That's dangerous, Cooper," Ty warns. "I can't let you do that."

"I agree with Ty," Christian says. "Especially in your condition."

"What condition?" Katherine asks. Her suspicious gaze darts from one person to the next.

After a long exhale, Christian announces, "Abbie is pregnant."

Katherine opens her mouth to say something and then closes it. Then she says, "Wait a minute. Are you saying that—"

"Abbie is carrying my niece or nephew. Your Step-Grandchild," Christian bluntly interrupts her.

Ty and I look at each other. We've never heard it spoken out loudly before, so direct and unfiltered. As far as we're concerned, it's still *our baby*. Period.

"Oh my goodness," Katherine exclaims, her hands flying to her chest. "This is unbelievable."

"That's one way to phrase it," I say. "It's about to get even more so."

"What do you mean?" she asks.

I'm tempted to bite my fingernails but squelch the urge. I suck in a breath and expel it. Then I plunge in. "I need irrefutable proof that Zach and Spencer were involved in my assault. Once I have that proof, they're going down. I can't let them get away with it, no matter what information about their paternity has recently come to light."

Silence envelops the room like a large dust cloud. There is no mistaking my meaning. I don't care if Spencer and Zach are Wheelers, although that fact will take some time to digest. I sense that neither Katherine nor Christian is in a hurry to embrace the twins.

"We understand, Abbie," Katherine says. "Now, about getting this proof that you need. How can I help?"

CHAPTER 69

AFTER

I SIT ON the living room sofa with an anxious Ty hovering over me. I compose the following text message:

Me: I got the invitation.

Spencer: Are you kidding? That's fantastic news!

Me: I need to see you.

He doesn't respond right away. My stomach clenches. Beads of sweat form on my forehead.

Me: Are you there?

Spencer: I'm here. How did you manage that?

I attach a photo of a sleek, black invitation emblazoned with gold lettering on the front, and a second photo with the interior text to my response.

Me: I convinced Katherine. Some DC socialite is out. You're in.

Spencer: Thank you, Abbie. This means so much to me. Would it be possible to mail it overnight?

Me: Why? I have it here.

Spencer: It's my mother. She's been in an accident. I have to leave tonight to be with her.

Liar.

Me: Is your mother okay?

Spencer: She will be. Her friend took her home from the hospital, but I need to be there for her, just for a few days.

Me: I'm sorry about the accident and wish her a full recovery.

Spencer: Thanks. I'll text you the address.

Me: No. I need to see you and hand deliver the invitation. I insist.

Spencer: What's going on, Abbie?

Me: The truth. I know why you wanted that invitation so badly.

Spencer: What are you talking about? I told you why when I asked for your help.

I pull up a photo of Alan and me taken inside the mansion recently, and attach it to my reply.

Me: I know who he is to you.

GLEDÉ BROWNE KABONGO

Spencer doesn't respond right away so I plow ahead, not giving him time to think or run. Ty begins to pace, the tension in him adding to my anxiety.

Me: What he did was wrong Spencer. It was evil. Hiding the truth of your existence all these years. No wonder you wanted it all to come out at the ball. That's why you wanted to go, isn't it?

Spencer: Did you say anything to him about me?

Me: No, why would I? That's why I want to see you face to face. Maybe there's another way to get what you want.

Spencer: Why so eager to help me?

Me: What does that mean?

Me: Dude, I just convinced the matriarch of one of the most powerful families in the country to invite you to her high society soiree to further your ambition, and you're giving me grief?

Me: I don't need this. I have enough on my plate. You know what, forget it, all of it.

Instead of a response, my phone rings. I signal to Ty to come closer. I click the answer button on the third ring.

"What's with the attitude?" I snap.

"Sorry. It just sounds too good to be true."

"Why? You knew of my connection to the Wheelers. You Googled that, right?"

"Yes, but I didn't think you would actually come up with

356

the invitation. You told me not to get my hopes up."

"Look, I have to run. Do you want the invitation or not? And do you want to hear my plan on how you can get what you want from Alan Wheeler or not?"

"I do," he responds eagerly.

"Then meet me tomorrow morning at Annabelle's Restaurant at 6:30 a.m."

"Why so early?"

I sigh loudly into the phone. "Because it's before the joint gets too busy with the breakfast crowd. Because I have something I need to do as well. I'm heading home to Castleview right after. I want to get an early start to minimize driving in heavy traffic. Look, you're the one who wants to get back at the father who abandoned and ignored you all your life. If you don't want my help, I have no problem ripping up the invite and never—"

"No, don't do that!" he says, his desperation thick. "I'll meet you at the restaurant."

CHAPTER 70

AFTER

A MIDDLE-AGED COUPLE sits across from us, engrossed in each other. A restaurant worker removes the upside down chairs perched on top of the tables and sets up for the day's business. Otherwise, Spencer and I are the only other people at Annabelle's at this early hour.

"Are you okay?" I ask. "Your eyes are red and you're fidgeting."

"I'm fine." He pastes a smile on his face.

"He's not a monster, you know. Alan."

"You said he was evil."

"What he did was, abandoning you. But I don't think he's an evil person. What are you going to say to him?"

"What do you mean?"

"When you go to the ball."

Spencer shifts in his seat and rakes his hand through his hair. "I don't know. I guess I just wanted to ask him why. My mother didn't have it easy. She raised us on her own."

"Us?" I ask with a raised brow.

He's puzzled by the question. I explain, "You said your mother raised *us* on her own."

358

"Brynn and me."

"But Brynn isn't Alan's kid, is she? You never mentioned that."

"Um . . . well I just meant that my mom had it hard as a single mother. Maybe if Alan had lived up to his responsibility, it would have eased the burden."

I shake my head in agreement. "You make a good point."

He glances toward the side entrance of the restaurant. Then he turns to me and says, "So how about those invitations? Don't keep me in suspense."

"Those invitations?" I frown. "There's only one. What are you talking about? I only agreed to ask for an invite on your behalf."

"Of course. Sorry, I'm all over the place. I haven't had my coffee yet and I didn't sleep that much last night."

"Well, let's order coffee then."

"No, that's okay. I'll grab something from the dining hall."

I reach into my purse and pull out the invitation. I hold it up so he can see. He reaches for it. I pull back.

"There's something I want in exchange."

My request startles him. He glances at the side entrance again.

"Are you expecting someone? Why do you keep looking at the door?" I say loudly.

The middle-aged couple next to us peeps in our direction. I cover my face with the invitation, embarrassed by my outburst.

"It's nothing. I have to go."

"Without the invitation you went through so much trouble to get?"

"I don't know what you're talking about." He pushes back his chair and starts to get up.

"Sit! You wanted something from me and I delivered. Now it's your turn to reciprocate."

"Listen, Abbie, I really appreciate you getting that invitation, but as I told you, my mother was in an accident and I already postponed leaving by a day to meet with you. Whatever it is, can we discuss it when I get back?"

I clear my throat and sit up straight in my seat. My heart beats wildly in my chest.

"Spencer, I don't think your mother was in an accident. It was an excuse to avoid meeting with me. I feel used, if you want to know the truth. You got what you wanted and you didn't have the decency to meet and say thanks. You asked me to ship the invitation. Why is that?"

He looks at the door again. "Stop looking at the damn door," I shout. "I'm trying to have a conversation here."

Spencer jerks back in his seat, startled by my reaction. "Get a grip, Abbie. Stop flipping out."

"You know all about me flipping out, don't you? This isn't the first time you've seen me lose it. It happened on the shuttle bus the other day, for example."

"That was scary. I thought I was going to have to hit you hard to stop the hysteria. Glad I didn't have to resort to that."

Please don't blow this. If you don't stand up to him, it would have been all for nothing.

"Why the hesitation? You've hit me before. Isn't that what you did the night you kidnapped and assaulted me? You pack a mean punch. My face was swollen for days and hurt something awful."

He smiles but it doesn't quite reach his eyes. Something cold and menacing takes over his features. "You really should see a shrink, Abbie. I think your ordeal is causing you to hallucinate and make up things that didn't happen."

"I am already seeing a shrink. She's quite good. But what I can't figure out, Spencer, is why. You knew who I was before you approached me the night we officially met. You had seen me before, at the Wheelers' New Year's Eve Ball two years ago. Clearly, you had done your research although you pretended otherwise. So why did you kidnap me, drug me and assault me so viciously?"

He leans in, as if he wants to reveal a secret. "You're nuts. That shrink of yours can't be any good if you're losing your grip on reality. What happened to you was horrible, no doubt. But pinning the crime on me, that's just outrageous, and I won't sit here for another minute and listen to you make false accusations against me."

He stands up to exit and I say, "The rape kit came back from the police crime lab."

CHAPTER 71

AFTER

SPENCER ROSSDALE'S FACE is devoid of color. An ashen, pallid mask takes over. He plops down in the seat as if his legs can't support him.

He swallows several times. "What rape kit?"

"The one collected before I was released from the hospital. I was unconscious when I was admitted to the ER. Once they discovered I had been assaulted, they collected evidence. I gave my consent to have it processed when I came to."

"And what did this so-called evidence show?"

"You know what it revealed, Spencer."

"Liar!" A deep, arrogant voice slices through the air, startling us. I follow the sound to see who the voice belongs to.

My limbs begin to shake. I have the sudden urge to pee, but getting my heartbeat and shaking limbs under control takes precedence. He sports a gray hoodie under a black leather jacket and black jeans. He's as tall as Spencer, a little over six feet tall. There's no denying the resemblance. But there are some differences too. His hair is slightly darker and his blue eyes, ice cold. I shiver as he approaches the table.

"Hello, Zachary. Nice of you to join us," I say with an unnatural calm. "I was just telling Spencer that the jig is up."

"You don't know what you're talking about," he scoffs. "I told Spencer you couldn't be trusted. You're a lying, manipulative witch."

"This coming from a stone cold killer? Just because they didn't bust you for killing poor Jamie Reynolds doesn't mean you didn't do it. But don't worry, Zach, it's never too late for justice."

"Let's get out of here, Spencer," he says to his brother.

"Neither one of you is going anywhere," I say. "Do you think you're going to get away with what you did to me, Spencer? Your brother covered for you, which makes him an accessory."

They both start laughing and pointing at me as if I'm an idiot. Spencer slaps his palm against the table as if this scenario is quite literally the funniest thing he has ever heard.

"You're so stupid," Zach says. He hasn't taken a seat since he entered the restaurant.

"Why do you say I'm stupid?" I ask. Something about Zach's presence unnerves me. There's a dark, foreboding energy radiating from him. A flash of memory worms its way into my head. Spencer, handing me a cup of water the night I went missing. The same memory I experienced in Dr. Shanahan's office. Why is it popping up again? Is it because I never confronted Spencer about it?

"What did you put in the water, Spencer? That's how it all started. You went into the house to get me some water and after I drank it, everything went blank. You can't deny it. The toxicology tests confirm I was drugged."

Spencer blinks rapidly. Zach stares down at me and says, "Are you sure that's what happened, Abbie? Memory can be faulty sometimes."

"As I said, Zach, the rape kit results came back."

"And it proves nothing. This whole meeting was a trick designed to trap us. It was a nice try, Abbie, but your accusations amount to a big pile of nothing. You've wasted your time."

"And you know this how?" I ask Zach.

"That rape kit you keep mentioning, your ace in the hole proves nothing because there was nothing to be found."

"Is that so?"

"Yes, it is so," Zach says, confidently.

The shaking in my limbs returns. My head is pounding now. Zach's hoodie bothers me. The man in my nightmares wears a hoodie every time. The one who wants to strangle me with his bare hands. I look at Zach's hands. Massive. Strong. Long, with sturdy fingers. I look at Spencer's hands and see the same. One of those pairs of hands choked me. One of those pairs of hands punched me hard in the face. One of those pairs of hands drugged me, stripped me naked, and threw me out of a moving vehicle.

I screw my eyes shut and rewind to three months ago: *What did I miss? The party was crowded, wall-to-wall people. Did I see anyone in a hoodie? Not that I recall. Keep going. The backyard. Spencer. The kiss, he left afterward. He came back with the water. Next, I wake up in the hospital in excruciating pain. Rewind, what's missing? Fill in the blanks. That cold, fearful feeling returns. A presence. A room. A bed. I'm weak and can barely move my limbs. My head is swimming. I'm drowsy. Something heavy is on top of me. It hurts. I can't breathe. I want it gone. It's too heavy.*

Everything hurts. Hurts to breathe. I have to open my eyes. Open them. Too sleepy. Pain. Open them! I move my head to the side. It's hard to breathe. I try to open my eyes again. I'm so sleepy, so tired. Can't see. Blurry. Room. Dim. Bed. Shadow. Face. Can't move my arms. Look up. Eyes wide open. Hoodie. Stop. Please stop. Voice hoarse. Need strength. Stop it! Louder. I thrash around. I can't shake him off. Still heavy. Try harder. Look at him. Sweatshirt. Hood on. Face covered. I can move my hands a little. Look at him. Who is he? Get off. Get off. He freezes. Did he hear me? Get off. Stop it! He hears me. Hit him. Move your hands. Hit him! Hands up. I hit him in the face. Big hands come for me. Chokes me. Pain. More pain. Neck hurts. Can't speak. Lights out.

I cover my mouth to suppress a scream. Zach and Spencer stare at me with stunned looks on their faces. I look around the restaurant. A few more patrons have taken up seats. The middle-aged couple glances in my direction. Zach and Spencer do the same and then turn back to our table. My arms and legs tremble. I pull myself together. I can't fall apart in front of them. I won't.

I lift a finger and point to Zach. "It was you. You switched places with Spencer. You handed me the water, not Spencer. You sounded just like him. I couldn't tell the difference. You were even dressed exactly like him. It was you who drugged and assaulted me." My voice is almost a whisper as I try to absorb the enormity of the situation.

Spencer says, "You need a psych evaluation, Abbie. You're falling apart before our eyes."

That comment snaps me out of my daze. "I think you and your psychopath brother should be more worried about

365

how many years you'll each get in prison. Zach may have assaulted me, but you helped him plan it. The two of you plotted against me from the beginning. The roses, the notes, the gifts were all part of your scheme. I just want to know why. You owe me that."

"You want to take this one?" Spencer asks his brother. "Poor girl. She's in the middle of a mental breakdown. Her shrink isn't helping. Did you know she went nuts on the shuttle a couple of weeks back? She had to be restrained. Freaked out because I said hello to her."

"That's very sad," Zach says. "But that's what happens to girls like you. They get their comeuppance. You were not very nice to my brother, Abbie, and family is everything to Spencer and me. That's why we wanted to have a talk with dear old Dad, Alan Wheeler. Everything was going fine until I overheard you telling your fat friend how my brother was nothing but a distraction to you. I thought, well that's just mean. No matter how hard he tried, he couldn't get you to appreciate him. You tossed him aside like he was garbage, like his feelings didn't matter. What kind of brother would I be if I let it slide? Not a very good one."

"So the two of you planned the assault for revenge? After you conspired to use me to get to Alan Wheeler? Are you freaking kidding me?" I yell. All eyes in the restaurant turn in our direction. I don't care. These two psychos sit before me and dare to justify their heinous, cowardly act. It's more than I can bear.

"What's the big deal? It was as simple as a phone call for you," Zach says casually.

"It doesn't even matter. You're both going to prison."

"We don't think so," Zach says.

"Nope," Spencer says shaking his head. "It's like Zach said, that rape kit thing is a bluff."

"Because you were so careful, Zach? You used protection? Took all my clothes as a precaution? There's always something left behind."

"Let's go Spencer," Zach says.

"We'll have our answers once the results from the paternity test comes back," I say. "You may have used protection, Zach, but you couldn't even get that right. Your protection failed and here I am, my life ruined because I'm carrying the child of a murdering psychopath who's headed to prison. That's no fun, Zach. I had to lie to my parents about this pregnancy because I was too ashamed to tell them what really happened. You destroy everything you touch, but your reign of terror is over."

Zack looks at me, his gaze murderous and frightening.

Spencer says, "Don't be pathetic Abbie. Stop with the lies. You've lost. Move on."

"I can't do that. Luckily, science has come a long way. Paternity tests can be conducted while the baby is still inside the mother. A lab just needs my blood and yours, Zach."

There's a slight quiver of Zach's mouth. Both he and Spencer look down at my mid-section and then up at me— their eyes pleading with me to tell them the pregnancy is just a mean prank I concocted.

"You see that couple over there?" I point. "They've been here the whole time, right? They will make sure we get a court order to test your DNA, Zach. They will compare it to my blood. The baby's cells float around in my body. They will get a match. And off to jail you both go."

In a split second, the span of a breath, Zach grabs me around the throat with one hand, reaches into his waistband with the other, and pulls out a gun he aims directly at my head. The middle-aged couple, two police detectives, respond with speed, both with guns drawn and aimed at Zach.

"Drop it, Zach," the female officer says. Spencer puts up his hands. My throat aches from the pressure being applied. Zach yanks me up from the chair.

"If you shoot, I won't hesitate to kill her," he promises. "If you shoot at my brother, I will also kill her. All three of us are going to walk out of here nice and quiet."

Don't cry. Don't freak out. It will only make things worse.

The officers slowly advance toward Zach. He fires a warning shot into the ceiling and I quiver with fear. The handful of patrons in the restaurant run toward the exit door, screaming. It happens so fast that by the time I think of trying to wrestle free from Zach's grip, the gun is back at my head.

"We can't let you and your brother walk out of here, Zach," Detective Larkin says. He's the male officer dressed in plain clothes, with his partner Samantha Giles at his side.

Giles says, "It's over. Let go of Abbie, and we can take a nice ride down to headquarters and take it from there. It's best to give up now so no one gets hurt."

My heartbeat thrashes in my ears. The pressure on my neck is getting tighter as Zach's stress levels increase.

"I can't breathe," I stutter. "Ease up."

"Shut up." He tries to drag me toward the door. I put up as much resistance as I can. I plant my feet firmly on the floor to slow down the motion. The two detectives follow this with their eyes, guns still drawn.

Larkin says, "There's no point in making this worse, Zach. We know what you did to Justin Tate, how you arranged and carried out the hit and run. If he dies, you're looking at life in prison. That's not even counting what you did to Abbie and Jamie Reynolds back in Bethesda. That case has been reopened. It's not looking good, boys. And I don't think Alan Wheeler will come to your rescue this time."

"She's right," I say, hardly able to get the words out. "Alan is angry. I told him what you did. He won't help you. Katherine only gave me the invitations to help set the trap. It was all for nothing. You ruined my life for nothing."

A panicked Spencer looks at Detective Larkin and back at Zach. "I had nothing to do with Justin Tate getting run over or with Jamie Reynolds's death. I wasn't the one who attacked Abbie."

"Shut up," Zach says, pointing the gun at Spencer. "Not another word."

In his confusion and fear, Zach eases the grip around my neck. I use his distraction and confusion to my advantage. I crash my elbow into his stomach. He grabs his stomach, agony and shock on his face. I take refuge behind the two detectives. Zach still hasn't dropped the gun, though. The twins are exposed, cornered rabbits with nowhere to run. Zach points the weapon at the detectives. Sweat appears on his forehead.

"Talk some sense into your brother, Spencer," I say. "I'm wearing a wire. Everything we've said was recorded. Police officers surround the restaurant as we speak. There's no way out for either one of you."

"Put the gun down, Zach," Spencer says. Then he says to

the detectives, "I can tell you what you want to know, all the details. But I need immunity. I'm ready to make a deal."

Before anyone could think, before the detectives could respond to Spencer's offer to betray his twin to save his own skin, Zach shoots him three times in rapid succession, direct hits to the chest. In a split second, Detective Larkin fires off two shots, hitting Zach in the shoulder and knee. He goes down with a thud and lies next to his brother's lifeless body.

EPILOGUE

---◇---

Seven months later

L UCAS JASON RAMBALLY arrives in the world on a gorgeous summer afternoon in July, weighing in at eight pounds two ounces and screaming his head off. There are no less than seven people in the waiting area, anxious to meet him: My parents, Ty's parents, my brothers Lee and Miles, and Grandma Naomi Cooper.

After the tragedy of Zach and Spencer, I almost suffered a miscarriage. Zach got life in prison for murdering his twin in cold blood and is still awaiting trial for killing Jamie Reynolds, and assaulting and drugging me. All this on top of the attempted murder charge for causing the accident that put Justin Tate in a coma. Thank God Justin made it.

It was all too much to handle. I finally cracked and told my parents the truth, after which they convinced Ty I shouldn't return to school to finish out my sophomore year. So I stayed with my parents and worked for Mom part-time.

Ty commuted from New Haven to Castleview every weekend that semester. He graduated Summa Cum Laude this past May. I'm so proud of him I could burst.

"Here he is," the nurse says, smiling down at the bundle wrapped in a blue blanket. She places Lucas in my arms. Ty sits next to me. It's the first time we both get a good look at him. The nurse goes on and on about how adorable he is and how she's never seen a more beautiful baby in all her years on the maternity ward. Ty and I just stare at him.

Once the nurse leaves the room, we look at each other and then at Lucas and back again. I peel back the blanket slowly so I can see his entire body. I cover him up and then remove his hat. Then he opens his eyes for the first time and stares straight at us, as if he can see us. I could swear he winked at us and closed his eyes again.

"His eyes are so blue, and he has brown hair. He looks just like Zach and Spencer," Ty says.

"I know."

"How do you feel about that?"

"You mean if it will be a reminder of what happened?"

He nods.

I look down at Lucas, content in my arms. "He didn't ask for this any more than I did. He's depending on us to be his mom and dad. That's all that matters now."

"Can I hold him?" Ty asks.

"Sure, but don't drop him."

"Thanks for the vote of confidence, Cooper."

"I'm only kidding. Scouts honor." I hold up my right hand, grinning.

Once Lucas is securely in his father's arms, I snap a couple of photos with my phone and compose a text to Zahra, Christian, Katherine, Callie and Frances. It simply says:

Lucas is here.

I guess I should have included Alan, but I'm still mad at him. His irresponsible actions changed my life forever. At least, that's what I tell myself. No one but Zach and Spencer were responsible for their actions, but still . . .

After we arrive in the post-partum suite, Ty places Lucas in the bassinette next to the bed while I go to the bathroom to make myself presentable for the deluge of family members about to descend on us. I shed the hospital gown and replace it with a pretty, floral silk robe, and then brush my hair.

When I exit the bathroom, there's a knock on the door. Ty opens it and they all pile into the room.

"Did everybody remember to wash their hands?" I ask. "Nobody has a cold or any strange, communicable diseases, right?"

They all ignore me as if I shouldn't even have asked, and make a beeline for the bassinette. Dr. Rambally beats everyone to it and picks up Lucas first. They all gather around him, cooing and making baby noises. Ty is caught up in the mix, just taking it all in. Mom and Grandma Naomi come over and sit on either side of the small bed I now occupy.

"How are you, sweetheart?" Mom asks. "Are you in pain?"

"I can manage," I say. "But I did it, Mom. With no medication."

"I know, my fearless girl." She gives me a hug and a squeeze.

"Don't you worry about a thing," Grandma says. "You and Ty and my great-grandson are going to be just fine."

"You think so, Grandma? Even with the strange familial

relationships?"

"You and Ty are Lucas's parents, period," Mom says. "Now that Spencer is dead and Zach is in prison, Alan has no reason to publicly admit their paternity, and no one has to know the truth."

"But the Wheelers know."

"So what?" Grandma scoffs. "I don't think they will stake any claim to Lucas if that's what you're afraid of."

"Maybe not anything official. But I know them. They will want to be part of his life," I insist.

"We'll let the Grandpas fight that battle," Mom says. "Your dad has been itching to punch Alan in the face ever since this whole tragedy came to light. He swears he will never play golf with him again. He even accused Alan of cheating."

All three of us giggle, and then Grandma Naomi gets serious. "Lucas is a lucky little boy to have so many people who love and care for him. Focus on that. The rest will work itself out."

After Mom and Grandma Naomi leave to take their turn holding Lucas, Ty's mother approaches. Her steps are tentative, as if she's not sure I won't toss her out of the room. She's wearing a pale yellow sundress and strappy sandals. Her hair is pulled back in a ponytail, giving her the appearance of a woman ten years younger. I pat a spot next to the bed, and I can see the relief on her face.

"I owe you a huge apology," she begins. "It's not easy for me, but I think it's time I beg your forgiveness."

"What for?"

"The way I've behaved. Instead of getting to know you and understand why Tyler is crazy about you, I focused on judging you. I wasn't very nice to you on the few occasions we met. I'm happy to say that he got it right. But then again, he could always see what others couldn't, including his mother."

"Dr. Whistler, you don't owe me an apology. I know how hard it is for parents to let go of their children or accept the decisions they make. My mother almost had a heart attack when I announced I was pregnant. My dad, he wept. That was hard to watch. So I get where you're coming from."

For the first time since I've known her, Dr. Whistler smiles at me, a warm, genuine, sunny smile. I guess that's her way of welcoming me to the Rambally clan.

"When Tyler explained what happened, it broke my heart," she says. "The way you've handled yourself throughout all of this is admirable. You're a courageous girl, Abbie. I couldn't have asked for a better wife for my son. And you can call me Mom."

I look at her sideways and she must have caught the skepticism in my gaze. "Jenny is fine," she says quickly. "You can call me Jenny if that works for you."

I give her the thumbs up sign and she hurries off to fawn over Lucas with the other family members. Dad immediately replaces her.

He gathers me in his arms and hugs me like he never wants to let go. When he eventually does, he says, "My precious girl, you were made to do hard things. I know that now. You make me proud to be your dad. I've told you that before, but it's especially true now. We could all take a lesson in courage from you."

"You handled this situation way better than I thought you would."

"What, you thought your old man was going to blow a gasket?"

"A big one."

"That's how much you know. I didn't blow a gasket. I simply called Alan Wheeler and politely told him what a prick he is and that I regret that my first grandchild carries his genes."

I look at Dad like he's lost his mind. "You're joking, right?"

"No. Ask your mother. She was there."

All I can do is shake my head. He drops a kiss on top of my head and takes off to chat with Ty's dad.

"Abbie, did your mother tell you about the wedding?" Jenny asks.

"What wedding?"

Grandma Naomi begins to detail the huge, blowout wedding in the works. Ty and I have no say in the matter. I guess it's our punishment for getting married last year without telling anybody. They've even decided on the proper wedding present in their mind. In fact, they've already made the purchase and we can't give it back. A beautiful house in Lexington, less than twenty minutes from Cambridge, so Ty can commute to Harvard. But the most incredible news? Grandma Naomi will be moving in with us to help take care of Lucas.

Ty plops down next to me and drapes his arm around my shoulder. We hold hands just trying to take it all in. We had everything planned, how we were going to manage with a baby and his medical school, but our parents put their heads together and turned our plans upside down in the best way possible. I feel humbled and blessed to be surrounded by so much love. Though he came into the world under difficult circumstances, Grandma Naomi is right. Lucas is a lucky boy, and so are his parents.

"Abbie, a friend of mine is a dean at Boston University. If you want to consider BU to complete your degree, just say the word and I'll talk to Eddie to make sure they take all your credits from Yale," Dr. Rambally offers.

"That's a great idea, Dad," Ty says.

"Thank you. Maybe I could start going part-time when I'm ready. We'll see how things go."

I glance at the clock on the wall. It's after 2:00 a.m. My sleep has been restless. I need to get some rest before Lucas wakes up for his feeding. I change positions a few times. Ty is sound asleep on the pullout bed. I peek in the bassinette to make sure Lucas is still there. He is. Satisfied, I give sleep another go.

I don't know how long I've been asleep, but something awakens me, a strange noise. I sit up in the semi darkness. "Is anyone there?"

The room is quiet. I peek into the bassinette. Lucas is gone. Panic builds inside my chest. I look across the room. Zach Rossdale is holding Lucas.

"I came for my son, Abbie," he says. "You can't keep him from me. He's mine, not Rambally's."

"Ty *is* his father. He doesn't need you. Now give him back, Zach."

Ty pops up from his slumber. "Cooper, what's going on?" he asks, sleepily.

"Zach wants to take Lucas," I say forcefully. "We can't let

him get away with it."

Someone is shaking my shoulders. The voice sounds far away.

"Cooper, wake up. You're having a nightmare. Wake up, it's just a bad dream."

It sounds like Ty. He's right here. Now Zach won't get away with it. I open my eyes, which takes a few seconds to adjust to the semi dark room. Zach is gone, and Ty is leaning over me.

"Where's Lucas?" My gaze darts around the room like a crazed creature.

"He's fine," Ty says. "He's fast asleep."

I get up to see for myself. I breathe a heavy sigh of relief when I see our son swaddled in a blanket, asleep on his back. Ty stands behind me.

"It wasn't real." He rubs my shoulders. "Just your imagination playing tricks on you."

"It felt real. I thought Zach somehow escaped prison and came to steal our baby."

"That will never happen," Ty assures me.

"Promise, me," I insist. "Promise me that Zach will never get his hands on Lucas."

"I promise."

###

AUTUMN
A FEARLESS NOVEL
OF FEAR

GLEDÉ BROWNE KABONGO

1. In the opening chapters of the book, we learn that Abbie was violently assaulted and had no memory of the attack. When it was revealed that she had attended a party prior, what scenarios did you think played out before she was discovered near the ER?

2. Ty immediately stepped up and took on the responsibility of caring for Abbie. What were your initial impressions of him just based on his actions while at the hospital?

3. When Spencer Rossdale arrived on the scene, were you suspicious of him? Why or why not?

4. Abbie searched Ty's apartment without his consent or knowledge in an attempt to uncover the identity of the Humble Admirer. Is betraying the trust of a close friend ever justified, no matter the circumstances?

5. Abbie made it clear that she didn't want a romantic relationship with Spencer yet she continued to spend time with him. Was it fair to Spencer who wanted to take things further? Did Abbie lead him on in spite of the ground rules they established?

6. Who did you think was the stranger in the hoodie?

7. Abbie kept the truth of the assault from her family for fear it could cause her father to relapse. Was that brave and selfless on her part or no? Would you have done the same in a similar situation?

8. How do you think Abbie handled the aftermath of the assault?

9. Abbie faced a gut-wrenching decision and returned to the clinic multiple times with Zahra. Do you think she

made the right decision in the end? Did that decision ruin her life? Would you have handled it differently?

10. Ty and Abbie decided to form a family. What are your thoughts on what it means to be a family? Were they too young to take on that responsibility?

11. Were Diana and Spencer Rossdale sympathetic characters? Were they victims of circumstance or opportunists?

12. Do you think that Justin Tate informed on Spencer because he was hoping for a chance with Abbie or because he was concerned that she could be in danger?

13. When Abbie announced her pregnancy to her parents, what did you think of their reaction? Would you have reacted the same way under similar circumstances?

14. Both Katherine and Alan Wheeler kept their connection to Spencer and his brother a secret for years. Do you think they bare any of the responsibility for the tragedy that unfolded?

15. Kristina Hayward was bitter when she discovered Ty and Abbie were engaged. Was her reaction justified? Was Ty unfair when he ended their relationship because of Abbie?

16. Did the final scene shock you? Did Abbie's deception cause Spencer's death or did he sign his death warrant when he volunteered to tell the police what he knew? How would you have ended the story if you were advising the author?

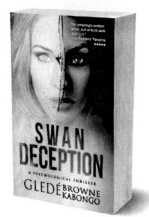
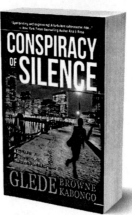

ABOUT THE AUTHOR

Gledé Browne Kabongo writes intense psychological thrillers—unflinching tales of deception, secrecy, danger and family. She is the author of the *Fearless* Series, *Swan Deception*, *Conspiracy of Silence*, and *Mark of Deceit*. Her love affair with books began as a young girl growing up in the Caribbean, where her town library overlooked the Atlantic Ocean. She was trading books and discussing them with neighbors before Book Clubs became popular.

Gledé holds both an M.S. and B.A. in communications. She was a featured speaker at the Boston Book Festival and has led workshops on publishing and the craft of writing. She hopes to win an Oscar for screenwriting one day. Gledé lives outside Boston with her husband and two sons.

Visit Gledé at **www.gledekabongo.com** to learn more.

CPSIA information can be obtained
at www.ICGtesting.com
Printed in the USA
FFOW02n2112200318
45903945-46785FF